DEVIL IN THE DETAILS

VEGAS SLAYERS - BOOK 2

CHRISTINE POPE

DEVIL IN THE DETAILS

Copyright © 2025 by Christine Pope

ISBN: 978-1-946435-84-2

Published by Dark Valentine Press

Cover design by Indie Author Services

Ebook formatting by Indie Author Services

Chapter One

—·‹‹‹·☾·›››·—

CALEB LOCKWOOD HAD BEEN EXPECTING her, so he wasn't surprised to see his friend Delia Dunne's white Hyundai Kona pull up to the curb in front of the house and stop. No room in the driveway; it was occupied by a truck that had arrived about fifteen minutes earlier to deliver the new furniture. When he'd first ordered all those pieces, his intent had been to stage the newly renovated house and then keep what he wanted and sell the rest, but the closer the Pueblo Street property got to completion, the more he knew he wanted this to be his home, rather than the flip he'd purchased almost three months ago, not long after he arrived in Las Vegas once he'd clawed his way out of Hell. The first house had given him a place to land, but he knew it had never felt like home. Not really.

1

Exactly how Delia—the woman who'd helped him find the Pueblo Street house but had become far more than merely his real estate agent—was going to react to his about-face regarding the sprawling mid-century home, he wasn't sure. Of course, he owned the house and could do whatever he wanted with it, but he knew it wouldn't have possessed the same polished perfection and understated style without her thoughtful input. That was part of the reason why he wanted to wait a little while to reveal his actual plans for the property and pretend as though he was just showing off the final result rather than claiming the house as his own.

He watched as she got out of the little SUV and locked the vehicle. Because it was a Saturday, she wore jeans and a pretty elbow-sleeve top with pale green embroidery rather than her usual skirt, dress blouse, and high heels. Caleb liked her both ways, but he thought he liked casual Delia best, with her coppery hair hanging loose on her shoulders and toes painted with soft peach polish revealed by a pair of flat sandals.

And now that they'd reached late March, the weather was the sort of perfection an Indiana native like himself could only have dreamed of. Sure, it would get blisteringly hot soon enough, but for the moment, he was just going to enjoy these wonderful stretches of days in the seventies.

"I still can't believe you got the place done so quickly," she said as she met him on the front stoop. The house was a little over three thousand square feet in size, but it didn't have much of a porch.

"You saw it happening," he replied with a grin.

"Some of it." She glanced over his shoulder, clearly trying to get a peek at the interior through the partially open door. "But placing flooring orders and choosing lighting isn't quite the same as having boots on the ground during the entire process."

Caleb thought she'd done a little more than that, but if she wanted to downplay her part in the remodel, so be it.

"They're still setting up the furniture," he said. "So I thought we'd check out the backyard first."

He inclined his head toward the side gate, and her brows drew together for just a moment. It seemed obvious to him that she thought he was taking the whole "surprise reveal" schtick to unnecessary levels, but she only nodded in response and followed him back to the driveway and then over to the gate that led into the side yard.

Even that part of the grounds hadn't been neglected—he'd had pavers installed and a small arbor built that would one day be covered in climbing flowers.

"Nice," Delia observed, taking in every detail

with keen gray eyes. "This part of the yard probably won't get used as much, but buyers like to see that every bit of a flip has been attended to."

About all Caleb could do was make a small sound of affirmation. Yes, of course he was going to tell her that he had no intention of selling the house...and yet, he didn't think this was the right moment.

Not yet.

The side yard led into the section of the backyard where the pool was located. When he'd first viewed the house, he wasn't sure he liked that positioning, since it wasn't directly behind the living room and the massive wall of glass he'd already imagined in that space and therefore wasn't as easy to see when you were hanging out in that part of the house, but the secluded nature of the pool's original location did make it feel more private.

Too bad he knew there was no way in the world Delia would ever go skinny dipping with him, no matter how cloistered the pool might seem.

"Wow, this turned out nice," she said as she moved closer to the edge, which had been redone in flagstone pavers. "This thing was definitely a wreck when you bought the place."

"Wreck" might have been something of an overstatement. True, the plaster had been cracked and he'd known there was no way he was keeping that border of electric blue tile—he guessed it wasn't original to the house and probably had been installed sometime in the eighties—but it wasn't as if the entire pool had needed to be removed and a new one put in.

But now, with the plaster refreshed and an understated border of tile in shades of gray and beige and soft blue replacing that neon '80s tile—and with new pavers installed all around the border—the thing had a new lease on life.

Besides...even though he knew better than to bring it up now...he had a feeling Delia also had a negative view of the pool in its original state simply because the home's resident ghost had tried to push her in the deep end with the hope that she'd break her neck when she dropped ten feet to the hard, cracked plaster below.

Good thing Caleb had sent that vengeful ghost straight to Hell where it belonged. The previous owner of the house had been a serial killer, with the bodies of five women buried in the ground beneath the rumpus room on the lower level next to the garage.

But quarter demons didn't have much to fear from ghosts, and Caleb knew with the owner of the house dispatched and the remains of those poor women discreetly zapped into the Las Vegas medical examiner's office, there wasn't anything here that could possibly bother him.

Except maybe a few more minion demons like the ones the demon Calach had sent after him to keep him away from the local casinos, but everything had been utterly quiet these past couple of months. True, Caleb—with a massive assist from Delia—had also banished Calach to Hell, and there was no chance of him coming back any time soon, so the odds of that particular demon causing any further havoc were probably pretty low.

Then again, Caleb had spent an endless two years there before he was able to escape, and therefore he knew that if there was one thing Hell had plenty of, it was demons.

He'd worry about that later, though.

A glance through the huge bifold doors that opened onto the living room told him the movers and the stagers he'd hired were still busy putting everything in place, so he'd need to stall for time for just a little while longer.

Which meant he might as well let Delia know what he intended to do with the house.

"The whole thing came out awesome," he told her. "And you'll get to see inside in just a couple of minutes. Once I give you the tour, you'll understand why I made this decision."

"'Decision'?" she echoed, one russet eyebrow lifting slightly.

"About the house." He paused there, gaze taking

in the drought-tolerant lawn planted to one side of the yard and the water feature built into the corner there, the tall palms that had now been neatly trimmed and looked much more reputable than they had when he'd first bought the place. "I've decided to keep this one and sell my other house."

Not even a flicker of surprise in her expression, which told him she must have suspected for a while that he might change his mind about giving up the Pueblo Street house.

In fact, her full lips quirked just a little. "It's that amazing, huh?"

"I think so," he said. "And I like that the property backs up to the golf course, and I don't have any rear neighbors. It feels more...private."

Delia didn't bother to ask why he felt privacy was so important. Early on, he'd told her exactly what he was, a little shocked at himself for confiding in her...even as he'd somehow known in his gut that she wouldn't betray his trust.

And she hadn't.

But because she knew he was part demon and doing his best to build an entirely new life for himself here in Las Vegas, she understood at once why he'd want a house where it didn't feel as if the neighbors were peeping in from all sides.

That same quirk showed at the corner of her mouth again. "You're reducing my commission, you know," she said in mock-severe tones, and he grinned.

"I could have just handled the sale myself," he countered, and now she chuckled.

It was only the truth. While working on the house, he'd taken a bunch of online courses so he could get his Nevada real estate license—not because he had any intention of becoming a full-time realtor, but because he figured it could only help if he decided to buy more investment properties and Delia wasn't available to handle those transactions, for whatever reason.

"You could have," she replied before adding, "But I don't know whether you would have gotten top dollar."

Caleb didn't, either. Sure, he was good at getting himself out of sticky situations, and yet he'd never handled a real estate negotiation and didn't know whether he'd be at the top of his game during the process...especially since he was very new to all this.

He was just considering what sort of reply he should give her when Maggie Nicholson, the woman who had been coordinating the house staging, pushed open the bifold doors and stuck her head outside.

"It's ready," she announced. "The movers are taking out all the packing material now."

Perfect. "Thanks, Maggie," he said. "We'll be inside in just a minute."

She tilted her head in acknowledgment and then closed the door, taking the hint that he wanted to be able to explore the house with only Delia as his company.

"Excited?" she asked.

Caleb had to think about that one for a second or two. "I suppose so," he replied. "Or maybe it's more that I'm just glad it's done and I can let myself enjoy the place."

A nod, but then Delia's expression turned thoughtful. "And you're really not worried about the history of the house?"

A valid question, he supposed, but he knew there was nothing to worry about here. "That ghost has been banished for months," he said. "And I know the spirits of those women never lingered here. So I think the house is about as psychically neutral as it can be."

Delia pursed her lips. No doubt she was thinking she'd be the judge of that, which he supposed was fair. He might be a quarter demon and have some unique psychic abilities, but she was the one who was able to sense whether houses were haunted...the one with a singular talent that allowed her to help any lingering spirits make their way to the next world.

"Come on," he said. "I want to show you around."

Delia was definitely appreciative of everything she saw, from the shining white oak floors that had been installed throughout the house to the bold black kitchen, which she'd been dubious about but now seemed to agree was perfect for the space. They explored the downstairs and then the bedrooms on the upper level. He had to admit it felt a little strange to have her in the master bedroom when he'd entertained a few fantasies about what it would be like to share the king-size bed with her, but she was all business, praising the millwork on the feature wall behind the bed and the sleek black standalone tub in the bath. Yes, he'd had to pay a lot extra to get one that wasn't white, and yet he was so pleased with the effect that he knew he probably wouldn't have blinked at the cost even if it had been double.

After they were done with the tour, they headed back down to the kitchen, where she sat down on one of the barstools at the enormous nine-foot island of black soapstone, and he poured a cup of coffee for her. Sure, it was late morning and she'd probably already had her coffee, but a little extra caffeine never hurt anyone.

"I can see why you would want to sell the other house," she said. "This one is magnificent. And it's very you."

Caleb wondered if that remark meant he was magnificent as well, then decided it would probably be better not to ask. Anyway, even though Delia had offered a lot of sound advice and had helped guide him to the best suppliers and contractors, he was the one who'd had the final word on the design decisions.

Maybe that was why he felt so invested in the house. His current residence was also a flip, but one that had been designed by other people, and the whole time he'd lived there, he'd sort of felt as if he was camped out in someone else's home or a fancy vacation rental rather than a place he actually owned.

Whereas this house?

He'd felt as if he'd come home the second he stepped into the living room. In fact, he felt much more at home here than he had in the house where he'd grown up. That grand edifice in Greencastle, Indiana, had been his mother's pride and joy, and being there had been kind of like living in a museum.

"Also," Delia went on, then sipped some more coffee, "the market's a little better now than it was a few months ago, thanks to that recent drop in interest rates. I think we should be able to get a good price for your current home." A pause, and her blue-gray eyes glinted at him. "How soon do you want to put it on the market?"

"As soon as I'm fully moved in here," Caleb replied. "The house is furnished, obviously, but I still have to get my stuff out of the other place. The movers are coming tomorrow."

She shook her head. "Sounds like you didn't want to waste a moment."

"I don't."

And there really wasn't much that needed to be moved—his wardrobe, which hadn't expanded that much since he first got here, since clothes had never been his thing—a few odds and ends, the big TV that was currently hanging in the living room at the other house but would go in the rumpus room downstairs. He hoped to sell that house fully furnished. If not, though, he'd either put everything in storage or hire someone to sell it all off for him.

Either way, it would get handled, and he would have tied off one more loose end.

"I want to get situated as quickly as I can," he went on, doing his best to sound nonchalant even though he wasn't sure how successful he was. "I don't want anything to interfere with the Desert Paradise poker tournament. It starts on Thursday."

Delia stared at him as if he'd sprouted horns. Not that implausible for someone who was a quarter demon, he supposed, even though he knew he didn't have enough demon blood in his veins for him to ever display that kind of outward show of his demonic heritage.

"'Poker tournament'?" she repeated, as if she wasn't quite sure she'd heard him correctly. Before he could reply, she added, "What happened to keeping a low profile?"

He only grinned back at her before swallowing some of his coffee. "I wouldn't say that flipping a house like this is very low profile."

"You're not flipping it, though," she pointed out. "You fixed it up so you could move in."

"Still," he said, "having dumpsters in the driveway and contractors coming and going for the last eight weeks kind of made me visible, you know? Anyway," he went on before she could offer any further arguments, "this isn't one of those big televised tournaments. It's just a smallish local competition. I'm not stupid enough to get involved in something that would attract a lot of attention."

Those words seemed to relieve her somewhat, since she shifted on the barstool so she was finally leaning against the backrest. "But why a poker tournament? Wouldn't it make more sense to take up golf, considering where this house is located?"

Caleb supposed it probably would. Hell, he could probably throw a bag of golf clubs over the back wall of his property and have at it if he wanted to.

Well, except for the part where it was a private course and the greenspeople might have a few words to say about that kind of trespassing.

He actually had considered getting a membership, but something inside had made him balk. If he'd really wanted to analyze his reaction to taking up golf, he probably would have realized that his antipathy to the game was mostly because of the way his father and the other half demons back in Greencastle had played on the weekends whenever the weather allowed that kind of activity. Not because they actually enjoyed the game, but because as the pillars of the community they were pretending to be—bank presidents, high school principals, lawyers—it was the sort of pastime they were expected to indulge in.

"I thought about it," he said vaguely, then went on, "but I like the idea of poker more."

Delia tapped her fingers on the black counter in front of her. As always, her nails had a coating of clear polish and were kept fairly short, a contrast to some of the talons he'd seen women around town sporting. "But won't you have an unfair advantage? I mean, with your powers...."

The words trailed off, but she'd already made her point. When he'd first arrived in Vegas last November and for the several months that followed, he'd accumulated the cash required to buy property and a car and any other necessities of life by using his demonic gifts to influence the cards at the poker tables or the ball on the roulette wheel...or the dice at the craps table. Poker wasn't necessarily a game of skill for him.

But he wanted it to be. He wanted to prove to himself—and to Delia, to be perfectly honest—that he could win a bunch of money using only his brains and his instincts, and nothing more.

"I want to do it the old-fashioned way," he said, a comment that made her brows lift again. "I've been practicing, and I've won a decent chunk without using any of my powers. So I thought it would be a good idea to join a low-stakes tournament to test my skills."

"How 'low stakes'?" she asked, that hint of a smile playing around her mouth again.

"The purse is only fifty grand," he replied.

Now she grinned outright. "Oh, is that all?"

"Well, you know I won a lot more back when I was using my powers."

Millions, to be accurate. Only about three or four million, just enough to get him started, but it had been sufficient to make the casino owners suspicious...and for casino executive Robert Hendricks to set his demon minions after Caleb. Of course, back then neither he nor Delia—whom Hendricks had hired to see if she could track down the person involved in winning such riches—had realized the man was a little more than he seemed.

And they still had no real idea as to precisely when Calach had taken over Robert Hendricks' body, or why the demon had made the man his target. There seemed to be some ties to an outfit in California called the Styx Group, but even Delia's private detective friend Prudence Nelson hadn't been able to dig up very much about the company.

Maybe it was all a red herring. Then again, Caleb couldn't deny that he'd been attacked by minion-level demons multiple times, which meant that someone had clearly thought he was a threat.

"So, you want to play in this tournament to prove that you can be a winner even without using your powers," Delia said, and he nodded.

"That's kind of a bald way of putting it, but sure. If I fold early on, then I'll know I can't hang up my demon powers just yet."

"I think that might be a good thing," she said, giving him a meaningful look.

She might be right. If it hadn't been for his ability to shapeshift and teleport, a few of the confrontations he'd had with Hendricks' demons might have turned out very differently.

All the same, he didn't like to use those powers any more than he had to. Sure, Calach had been banished, and Caleb didn't think he'd picked up on any signs of other demons lurking around the greater Las Vegas area since then, but still, there was always the chance that he might be giving away more than he intended every time he needed to make a demonic flex.

"But I promise I'll do everything I can to not stand out," he said. "Well, except not try to win. There's a big chance I'll wash out in the first round, though."

"Don't sell yourself short," she replied, then set down her coffee cup. It was black, too, although with a glaze that had certain washes of beige, the perfect complement to the black soapstone counters with their veining of pale tan.

"I'm not sure I'm capable of that," he said with a grin. "Anyway, are you available to walk the other house today? I know it's Saturday, but—"

"It's fine," she broke in, her smile mirroring his. "I didn't have any big plans today anyway. And I understand you wanting to get the place on the market as quickly as possible."

The words ended on a slight upward inflection, almost as if she was trying to figure out whether the cost of the remodel had turned out to be more than he'd planned. As with any other project of that scope, it had gone over budget, but not by too much, only around $20K or so.

And that hadn't been enough to put even a dent in the money he had stashed in various banks and credit unions around town, especially now that he had a financial advisor who handled his stock portfolio and had already earned him more than double that, thanks to some very wise investments.

"I do like to keep as much liquid as possible," he said, and her eyes danced, telling him she'd noted the evasion but wasn't about to call him on it.

Instead, she asked, "Do you have a spare set of keys to the other house?"

At once, Caleb pulled out the little envelope with the keys he'd had made at Lowe's just two days earlier, when he'd finally admitted to himself that he wanted to keep the Pueblo Street house and dispose of the other one. "It's ready and waiting for you," he said. "The house cleaners were there yesterday, and it's in great shape. I'll disable the security system from my phone so you won't have any trouble getting in."

"Perfect," Delia replied. "I've got my camera in the car, so I'll just go ahead and shoot the photos while I'm walking the place. That'll speed up the process."

Because Delia, unlike quite a few other real estate agents, didn't rely on her iPhone to take pictures of her listings. No, she had a big professional Nikon and made sure to massage everything in Photoshop before she posted it, so Caleb knew the other house would get the best possible presentation.

They chatted a little bit about the current real estate market, but then she excused herself, telling him that if she went and took the photos now, she should be able to get the listing up by the end of the day.

"And with any luck, someone will snatch it right up," she said as he walked her to the door. "With interest rates down, most properties are moving pretty fast, and there isn't a lot of inventory. And I know the house having been featured on a cable show back in the day will probably help, too, if only because people will probably look up some of the video clips online. That'll make my job a little easier."

"I'm sure your excellent photos would be enough," he said, and she only shrugged.

"Maybe. But it never hurts to have a secret weapon." A pause as she shifted her purse strap on her shoulder. "Anyway, once I have the listing put together, I'll email you the password so you can take a look at it before it goes live. That way, you can fix any mistakes."

"I doubt there'll be any," he said with a smile, and she only shrugged again.

"Oh, you'd be surprised. Little things tend to slip through even when you've read something over a dozen times."

He supposed that was true, or else he wouldn't have caught the typos that had popped up in some of the books he'd read in college, books he assumed had been vetted by multiple editors.

"Sounds like a plan," he said.

Delia gave him a wave and then headed down the front path to her car. As she went, her bright hair blazed in the sun, bouncing against her back.

Damn, she was beautiful.

Too bad he'd probably never have the guts to tell her.

Chapter Two

—‹‹‹‹•◎•›››·—

On this bright, sunny day—not that Las Vegas had much of anything else—Caleb's current home looked more like something out of the Brady Bunch than ever. Like the house on Pueblo Street, this one was mid-century in design but more modest in size, not quite 2,300 square feet. Certainly big enough for a family, if not nearly as showy.

Delia parked at the curb, then went around to the rear passenger side of her SUV so she could open up her camera case and extract her beloved Nikon D850, which almost always rode back there. While she supposed she could have pulled up in the driveway, she wanted to get an unobstructed view of the garage and the house as a whole so it would look as appealing as possible.

Ten snaps from different angles—she always

shot at least twice as much as she thought she would need—and then she slung the camera strap over her shoulder and headed for the front door. After getting out the little envelope with the spare keys, she unlocked the door and went inside.

The foyer's floor was covered in slate that she guessed was original to the house, although the rest of the flooring was luxury vinyl plank that she assumed the flippers had installed when they completely remodeled the home a few years earlier. Delia took photos of everything, from close-ups of the flooring to a panoramic view of the great room with its floor-to-ceiling fireplace and the overhauled kitchen beyond. When the house was built, it probably had many more walls, since home layouts were a lot more compartmentalized back then, but now it was mostly wide open spaces.

As Caleb had said, everything looked neat and clean, almost like no one lived there at all. One mug sat on the kitchen counter, as if he'd had his coffee and then hurried off to the other house without taking the time to rinse out the cup and put it in the dishwasher.

Figuring he wouldn't mind if she took care of that one small detail, she went ahead and splashed some water in the mug and then set it in the top rack of the machine. With that handled, she took more pictures, getting close-ups of the appliances and the fancy brass faucet that accompanied the farmhouse-style sink.

The flippers had done a good job, so Delia didn't think it would be too hard to move this place quickly, especially since, while they'd included a few fun, gimmicky choices, most of the design was classic enough in style that it wouldn't be out of date in a couple of years.

More snaps of the downstairs powder room and the family room at the back of the house, and then she made her way up to the second level. All the bedrooms appeared to be located here, three smaller ones arranged along the upstairs hallway, with the main suite located at the end of the hall.

Even though Caleb had told her it was fine to roam wherever she needed to get her photos, Delia still felt a little strange about going into his bedroom. Like the rest of the house, it was very neat, the bed made, and no random socks on the floor or anything else to show that a man lived here by himself.

Well, maybe quarter demons were neatniks…or maybe Caleb had known she'd want to come over here immediately to get pictures after he told her he intended to put the place on the market, so he'd made a special effort to be tidy.

Either way, he'd made her job a lot easier. She took dozens of photos, trying to get things set up from exactly the right angle so they'd translate well on a computer or phone screen. Doing so took her the greater part of an hour, but she wasn't too concerned about that.

After all, she'd only been telling Caleb the truth when she'd said she didn't have much planned for today. While she tried to get together with her friend Prudence a couple of times a month, they'd just gone out for drinks on Thursday night and hadn't made any follow-up plans yet.

Besides, Pru hated venturing out on the weekends and always planned their girls' nights during the week when they would have a better chance of getting a decent table somewhere and didn't have to compete with quite so many tourists.

And it was okay with her. Although Delia hadn't been called to cleanse any homes of their ghostly occupants for more than a month now, she'd still been busy with plenty of regular listings, especially since her mother, the other half of the Dunne & Dunne real estate team, had gone to Hawaii with Delia's father for a belated anniversary trip and Delia was covering her mom's clients as best she could. Doing double duty at the office didn't leave her a lot of free time.

Even so, she couldn't help thinking that it would have been nice if Caleb had invited her to go out to lunch or something. They'd done that quite a few times while working on the Pueblo Street house, and she'd halfway expected he would do the same today.

However, it seemed he was more interested in getting his current home listed than spending any additional time with her.

Which was fine. While she wouldn't lie to herself and pretend she didn't think Caleb was attractive, she also knew that getting involved with a guy who just happened to be a quarter demon probably wasn't the smartest thing in the world. No, much better that their relationship remained strictly professional.

A quick scan through the pictures she'd taken told her she had more than enough for the home's interior. Time to snap some photos of the back-yard, especially the pool. Looking out through the French doors that opened onto the patio, Delia estimated that the one here wasn't as big as the one at the Pueblo Street house, but then, the yard wasn't nearly as large, either.

Still, having a pool, especially one that looked new and sparkly like the one in Caleb's backyard here, was just another excellent selling point.

She headed over to the French doors, camera slung over one shoulder. Her hand went automati-cally to the deadbolt.

It wasn't locked.

In fact, the door itself wasn't shut all the way,

had barely caught enough to keep it from blowing open in the wind.

Delia frowned. She supposed Caleb might have gone out for a morning swim and been careless about shutting the door on his way back into the house, but she didn't think that was terribly likely. Although they hadn't spent a lot of time in this particular house, she still knew he was careful about security—hence the panel for the alarm system that she'd noted in her interior photos, now safely shut off, thanks to Caleb's phone app.

Well, everyone had a brain fart now and then, even quarter demons. She'd just make sure to lock the back door once she was done taking photos of the yard and the pool.

That took her another twenty minutes or so. Just as with the interior of the house, the backyard here was immaculate, everything swept, with no weeds in the beds of drought-tolerant plants and the pool sparkling clean. Clearly, Caleb didn't have a problem parting with his gambling winnings to keep his property in good shape.

As she was approaching the back door, she noticed a couple of smudges on the glass that hadn't been detectable from inside. Here, though, with the midday sun beaming straight down on that side of the house, those cloudy spots seemed very obvious.

In fact....

Were those fingerprints?

So what if they are? she asked herself. *Caleb told me the cleaners came yesterday. If he went out for a swim this morning, it wouldn't be too surprising if he got some prints on the door when he let himself in.*

That sounded logical enough. Delia squinted at the smudges and held up her hand against them to see how they compared in size. They were a little bigger, enough so they certainly looked as if they could have been Caleb's.

But what had she been expecting? Something monstrous, something that could have been made by a demon?

A few months ago, she would have laughed herself silly at the thought of even entertaining such a notion. Now, though....

Now she knew demons were real. Not just because of Caleb Lockwood's part-demon heritage, but because she'd faced down the real thing in the executive suite at the Dunes casino and resort. Maybe once upon a time, Robert Hendricks had been a man, but he'd long since been taken over by the demon named Calach.

Or at least, that's what Caleb had told her, and Delia was inclined to believe him. Quarter demon or not, he hadn't steered her wrong so far.

That didn't seem to be what she was dealing with here, though. No, as far as she could tell, her original suspicions had been correct, and he'd just been careless about closing the door on his way into the house.

Except....

He'd said he was going to turn off the security system using the app on his phone. The back door hadn't caught all the way, which meant it should have given him an error message when he engaged the thing as he was leaving the house.

Probably. But maybe it had an override or something. Although she'd worked with plenty of alarm systems during the seven years she'd been a real estate agent, she wouldn't pretend that she knew the inner workings of all of them.

As she was mulling that conundrum, her phone buzzed from inside her purse, which she'd left sitting on the kitchen island. She hurried over to dig out the iPhone, then looked down at the screen.

Caleb.

"Hey," she said as she lifted the phone to her ear. "I'm just finishing up over here."

"Great," he replied, sounding cheerful as usual. She still hadn't quite figured out whether that was his real disposition or whether he was so relieved to be out of Hell and creating a new life for himself that he wouldn't allow too many things to get him down. Either way, it was a nice change from some of the decidedly cranky clients she'd had to deal with over the years.

Not that she really viewed Caleb as a client anymore. Business partner, she supposed.

Or, she thought with a mental grin, partner-in-crime, the way he'd described their relationship to Calach the demon.

"I was so preoccupied with the house stuff that I totally forgot to ask if you wanted to grab lunch," he went on. "I mean, if you haven't already eaten."

Delia wondered when he thought she would have had the time to grab something, considering she'd come straight over here from the Pueblo Street house and gotten to work. Her phone told her it was not quite one, certainly still a good time to eat.

"No, I was probably going to make something when I got home," she said, which wasn't too much of a lie. Yes, she'd planned to eat, although her meal would have been nuked leftovers or maybe a frozen dinner if nothing in the containers in the fridge looked appealing, neither of which was exactly something you had to "make."

"Then I'll come pick you up at the house."

It seemed to her that it would have been more time effective for them to decide on a restaurant somewhere in between the two properties and meet there, but Delia decided to roll with it. Besides, when he got to the house, she could ask him about the unlocked French door off the family room and whether it had been simply an oversight...or something a little less innocent.

"Okay," she said. "See you in a few."

More like fifteen minutes if the traffic cooperated, but in the meantime, she could go back and look at all the photos she'd taken and delete any obvious duds. That way, when she got home and started working on editing everything and putting the listing together, she wouldn't have to wade through so much chaff.

They ended the call there, and Delia picked up her camera. Everything here seemed utterly quiet—the soundproofing on the house must have been excellent, because a bunch of kids had been hanging out in the yard of the property next door, lounging on their bikes and talking loudly about where they wanted to go after this, but she couldn't hear a thing inside—and she wondered if she was being extra hinky about the situation with the back door. After all, everything had been mellow the past couple of months, with not a single hint of any demon activity.

Well, she'd wait and see what Caleb had to say about it.

He stared at the back door and frowned. Delia had already closed and locked it, so there wasn't any real evidence that it had been almost ajar when she got here, but Caleb had no reason to believe she was misrepresenting the situation.

"I'll see if I can lift those prints off the door," he told her, and she raised an amused eyebrow.

"What, you're a forensics expert now?"

He found himself smiling a little.

A very little.

"No," he replied. "But I read about how you can lift prints with just some talcum powder and a piece of tape. Let me go get the powder from the bathroom upstairs. I think there's some Scotch tape in my office, too."

If she thought it odd that a grown man had baby powder on hand, she didn't say anything about it. To be fair, he hadn't even cracked open the container; it had been among a bunch of things he'd picked up at Target right after he bought this house, figuring he should have some basic supplies like hydrogen peroxide and rubbing alcohol and a first aid kit. All that stuff still sat untouched in the vanity of the second bathroom upstairs, but at least it seemed as though he finally had a reason to use some of it.

While Delia waited in the kitchen, he headed upstairs and got the necessary supplies, then returned to the ground floor so he could take a closer look at the fingerprints she'd spotted. Although he knew better than to touch them, he still lifted a hand and spread his fingers apart so he could hold them up against the smudges on the glass and see if they matched his hands at all.

They sort of did—well, at least they looked as if they'd been made by someone of the same approximate size—but his fingers were a little longer.

"I know I didn't leave these here," he said, and Delia's mouth compressed.

"But why break in if they weren't going to take anything?" She paused, then added, looking even more worried, "I mean...have you noticed anything missing?"

"No," he said at once. When he'd first moved in, he'd kept his valuables in a safe in the main bedroom, but all the cash had been moved to various accounts around town. And although he'd spent an indulgent chunk of change on his watch, he wore it all the time and didn't leave it lying around for anyone to simply take. "Or at least," he added, "nothing obvious. It's not like there's anything super-valuable here except the TV."

Which still hung on the living room wall above the low, modern television stand that held his Blu-Ray player and collection of discs.

"What, you don't have a stash of gold chains somewhere to go with your new gambler personality?" Delia inquired with a twinkle in her eyes.

Even though she was being snarky, Caleb didn't mind too much. He liked it when she looked a little bit devilish...and it made him wonder what she would be like if she ever decided to take a walk on the wild side.

He'd need to leave those speculations for later, though. Right now, he had more pressing matters taking up his brain space.

"Could be neighborhood kids," he said. "Whoever left this, their hand looks a little smaller than mine. Maybe the door really was unlocked and they tried it and then got freaked out and left when they realized they actually could get inside."

Delia didn't immediately dispute this theory, although the way her lips pressed together again told him she didn't think too much of it.

That was all right.

Neither did he.

But he knew he was trying to come up with harmless explanations because he didn't want to face the possibility that something dark and demonic might be meddling in his life again. They'd had a blessedly uneventful couple of months, and he wanted things to stay that way. Nothing much going on meant that Hell's imps had more important things to do than mess around with Caleb Lockwood.

The only interesting element he wanted in his life was maybe getting Delia to unbend a little bit so they could be something more than just casual friends and business partners.

"Let's see if I can get any prints," he said, then lifted the bottle of baby powder he was still carrying so he could sprinkle some on the door. It mostly wanted to slide right down and then get carried away by the wind, but enough remained that he thought he might be able to lift a print.

If he was really, really lucky.

He set the baby powder down on the patio's stamped concrete floor and then extracted the Scotch tape from his jacket pocket. The day was probably getting too warm for the jacket to even be necessary, but he'd slid it on early in the morning while it was still cool out and had sort of forgotten about it.

Gingerly, he pressed the tape against one of the prints and then just as carefully lifted it off. When he looked down to see what it had caught, though, he only found himself frowning.

"What is it?" Delia asked. She'd maintained a respectful distance while he was working, but he could tell she itched to come closer so she could see what he'd discovered.

"No prints," he said, even as he did his best to ignore the uneasy sensation in his gut.

Demons didn't have fingerprints.

"You mean, like whoever did this burned them off?" Delia said, now sounding uncertain, as though she knew what she'd just suggested was something you might encounter in a movie but rarely in real life.

He wished it were that easy. Or at least, while he thought maybe he could consider the remote possibility that someone had decided to case the house, a career criminal who'd removed their fingerprints so they could commit breaking and entering with impunity, he thought it far more likely that his first impression had been the correct one.

"Doubtful," he replied. "No, I think a demon did this."

Delia had the naturally fair skin of most redheads, so when she paled, she looked almost stark white. "A demon?" she repeated. "But I thought...."

Caleb knew what she'd been thinking, since the same hopeful thoughts had occupied his brain as well these past few months. Calach was gone, and everything seemed quiet, so Caleb had assumed they'd scored a major victory by banishing the demon and that they could just go on with their nice, tidy lives.

"Demons don't have fingerprints," he said. "And sure, there are people who've removed theirs, but the kind of person who does that doesn't generally gain entrance to a house and then leave without taking anything."

"Still...." she said, then stopped, as though

she'd just realized that any argument she'd been about to offer wouldn't hold up for very long.

"It's probably nothing," he told her, and she sent him an unbelieving look.

"How can you say it's 'nothing' if a demon was breaking into your house for some reason?"

"Because demons love to stir the pot," he said. "And because this happened here, I have a feeling they don't know anything about the house on Pueblo Street. Even if they've been watching me, they probably think I'm just working on a project and have no idea I was planning to move in there. In fact...."

Caleb stopped himself, his mind working furiously. He had planned to have movers with a small truck take over the few items he didn't plan to leave here, but if demonic forces had decided to keep an eye on him, then having a panel truck pull up in front of the house would be pretty much the same as sending up a flare that announced, "I'm moving!"

Most of what he wanted to take could fit in the back of his Range Rover, even the big hundred-inch TV. And if he could get Delia to help out with some of the smaller items, then they could move him over there with no one the wiser.

After all, as he'd already told her, demons knew a lot more than humans, but they weren't omniscient, not by a long shot. He hadn't gotten a hint of any demonic presences around the property, so whoever had left that smudge was long gone. Most likely, the demon responsible had come by while he was asleep.

Come to think of it, he'd had a couple of nasty dreams last night. Maybe his subconscious had picked up on the intruder's inherent nastiness, even though the disruption hadn't been enough to wake him up all the way.

"Change of plans," he said.

"No lunch?" Delia asked, looking resigned.

"Oh, we'll get lunch," Caleb promised. "It's just going to be a late one."

Delia understood why he wanted to move things out quietly and avoid tipping his hand. If she'd learned that demons had been creeping around her property while she was asleep, she probably would have wanted to bail as soon as possible, too.

Caleb opened the garage so she could back in, and then they proceeded to load their two vehicles with everything he appeared to deem valuable—his TV and Blu-Ray player and discs, clothing and toiletries, a few pieces of art. In a way, it was interesting to see what he wanted to save and what he was okay with leaving behind, just because it gave her a little extra insight into his character. The art surprised her, since she hadn't thought he was the type to care about that sort of thing.

Or maybe it was just that he'd invested a lot in those modern, semi-abstract paintings and wasn't about to leave them to the wolves.

She left first, and he followed about five minutes later. They'd already agreed to take a circuitous route to the house on Pueblo Street, even though Caleb had told her this wasn't exactly like trying to avoid the CIA and that there was a good chance no one was watching at all.

"Better safe than sorry, though," he'd said as he closed the Range Rover's hatch, and she was inclined to believe him on that.

The entire drive over here, though, she hadn't noticed any vehicles following her. Everyone had been busy running their Saturday errands, whether to Costco or soccer practice or the local garden center, and no one seemed to be paying any particular attention to her.

Then again, would demons even be driving?

She reminded herself that a demon had pretended to be an Uber driver and had done its best to kill off Caleb in an intentional car accident back in January, but she had a feeling that had been a special circumstance. After all, if you had the power to teleport, why would you waste time getting stuck in traffic?

But a demon still had to know where it was

going, and if they didn't have any idea that he planned to move into the newly remodeled house, then his disappearance from his current residence might stump them, at least for a little while.

Hopefully.

And there was Caleb, pulling up to the three-car garage of the new house and backing in. He rolled down one window and waved a hand in her general direction, which seemed to be the signal that he wanted her to do the same. That made sense. It would have been kind of stupid to drag all the stuff from the back of her little Hyundai SUV—mostly clothing and a few other odds and ends—into the house from her spot at the curb rather than simply going through the garage.

Once they were both situated and he'd closed the garage doors, they spent another half hour or so unloading everything. "Now we can have lunch," he said as he leaned one of the paintings up against the side of the leather sofa in the living room. The wall above was conspicuously bare, telling Delia that he'd obviously intended that piece of art for that space all along.

By then it was past two, and she was famished. "Sounds good."

They headed back to the garage, and he pulled out into the driveway, pausing for just a moment to press the button for the remote.

"In the mood for anything in particular?" he asked as they drove away.

"A cheeseburger as big as my head," she replied. Most of the time, she tried to be careful about what she ate, but she figured all the manual labor she'd just performed had used up a decent amount of calories.

He grinned. "I think I can manage that."

They went to a sports bar kind of place, not too crowded since the lunch hour was now long past. Sure, there were guys glued to the various TVs mounted all around, watching several different basketball and soccer games, but they weren't so noisy that she and Caleb couldn't hear each other speak.

All the same, they were careful to talk about neutral topics...at least until they were done with their meal and back out in their Range Rover.

"No sign of any demons," he said cheerfully. "I think we gave them the slip."

From your mouth to God's ears, Delia thought. But she only said, "You don't think they'll be able to find your new house?"

"Oh, eventually," he replied, still sounding way too peppy for the circumstances as he pulled out of the restaurant's parking lot. "But now I know—or at least, now that I think I know—they're surveilling me again, it'll be easy to keep them out. A few squirts of holy water on the doors and windows will make them want to stay far, far away."

Although on the surface that sounded much too easy, Delia knew Caleb wasn't being overconfident. She'd seen how Calach's face had begun to melt after getting hit with a couple of blasts of the blessed water, and she also knew that the demons who'd been harassing him had pretty much disappeared from the scene once she and Caleb had spritzed holy water all over his house.

Speaking of which....

"Do you think they came back because the holy water we sprayed everywhere finally wore off?"

His shoulders lifted. "Hard to say. To tell the truth, I'm not really sure how long the effects last. I suppose I just thought I was safe because there hadn't been any disturbances since then. Getting sloppy, I guess."

Was he being too hard on himself? Delia didn't know for sure, so she only made a noncommittal sound.

"Anyway," Caleb continued, "now that I'm safely out of there, it's even more important to get the house listed as soon as we can. Once they realize it's for sale and there's no sign of me, their pointy little heads are going to explode."

That comment created a mental image that Delia wasn't sure she'd be able to get rid of any time soon. Pushing it away as best she could, she said,

"Well, I already went through the photos and dumped the ones I knew weren't any good, so putting the listing together should go fairly quickly. What do you want to ask for the place?"

"Seven-fifty," he replied promptly.

A decent price. Maybe a little high—she'd need to run some comps to be sure—but the house was in a very good area and had been completely remodeled within the last couple of years, so it would already be at a level above many of the other homes in the neighborhood.

"That should probably work," she said, knowing her tone sounded too carefully neutral.

Caleb didn't take offense, though, and only said, "I'm open to adjusting the price if you think it's too out of whack. But I've been paying attention to what other homes in the area are going for, and I think it's pretty inline."

Then he'd done more research than she had. Her focus had been on the neighborhood where the Pueblo Street house was located, since she'd thought he'd be selling that one instead.

"In fact," he went on, "I think you should go over there and stick a big ol' 'For Sale' sign in the front yard even before you go home and post the listing. If anyone's watching the place, it's going to really stick in their craw."

She supposed she could see that. "You're the client," she said with a smile.

No real lingering at Caleb's new house—he pulled into the garage, she thanked him for lunch, and then she got in her Kona and headed over to the old place. Lucky for him, she almost always had at least one or two Dunne & Dunne Realty signs floating around the back of her SUV, so it wasn't that big a deal to put up the sign before the house was even officially for sale.

The street was quiet enough when she got there, the group of middle-schoolers on their bikes long gone. She got out of the car and went around to the back to retrieve one of the signs, along with the mallet she always kept there as well.

Unlike newer homes in Las Vegas, which either had artificial turf or drought-tolerant native plants, the house had a lawn with real grass, grandfathered in after laws had been passed to protect the area's water supply. While Delia understood those restrictions, she was always sort of glad when she could put up one of her signs in actual grass. Even with a mallet, pounding those things into gravel or turf was a massive pain in the ass.

But this sign went in easily, telling her the lawn had probably been watered the night before, or maybe even this morning. A pause to adjust it ever so slightly so it sat perfectly straight, and she figured her job was done...or at least, mostly done. She still had to go home and put together the actual listing.

As she was getting back into her SUV, though, a flicker of movement caught the corner of her eye. She quickly turned in that direction, and could have sworn she saw someone disappearing behind a large clump of Mexican honeysuckle planted on the side of a house two doors down.

Probably one of those kids, she told herself. *Now they're playing hide and seek, or whatever.*

Did kids that age even play hide and seek?

Whoever it was, though, they were long gone, and standing here and staring at the luxuriant plant with its cheery sprays of yellow and orange-red flowers wasn't going to make them come back.

No, she needed to get back to her house and put that listing together.

All the same, she kept looking over her shoulder the entire drive home.

Chapter Three

·──·‹‹❁···❁›››··──·

THE LISTING LOOKED GREAT. LOTS OF
pictures, all of them crisp and clear and shot from
angles to maximize the feeling of spaciousness in
the open first floor, with close-ups of the materials
used and images of the pool that were so stunning,
they looked as if they'd come from a brochure
advertising some sort of resort rather than a listing
for a single-family home in suburban Las Vegas.

Well, Caleb had already known that Delia was
very good at her job.

She'd texted him to let him know the sign was
up at the house and included a link to a private
page on the Dunne & Dunne website so he could
look everything over. While he appreciated her
conscientiousness, it was clear that he hadn't
needed to vet the listing, not when everything
appeared perfect to him.

Still, he carefully read it three times, doing his best to keep an eye out for any pesky typos that might have slipped through. He didn't see anything, however, so he sent her a reply letting her know it was good to go. She answered a moment later with a brief, *It's live,* and that seemed to be that.

Well, except for the part where he wished he could have thought of a good way to invite her over for drinks by the pool. Temperatures outside were just kissing eighty, and it would have been perfect.

But she'd done enough back and forth on his behalf today, not to mention helping him haul his stuff over here. No complaints, no annoying questions, just an understanding that they needed to get it done and, with any luck, give the demons who'd been surveilling his house the slip.

If it even was demons at all. Caleb knew he couldn't entirely discount the theory that a regular human with burned-off fingerprints had been the one to leave the back door ajar, but that scenario still didn't feel right to him. A regular burglar would at least have stolen the TV and some of the art, even if there wasn't a stash of jewelry or cash at the place.

Thanks to her work helping ghosts move on, Delia had a handy supply of holy water at her house, and she'd loaned him a half-dozen bottles of the stuff, just to be safe. He hadn't used any of them—and he was kicking himself for that now, because splashing some on the doors and windows of his old house might have kept the interlopers at bay—but better late than never.

Or rather, he wasn't going to make the same mistake twice.

He carefully traced lines of holy water around the glass doors that opened onto the patio at the new place, then did the same thing for the front door and the one that led into the garage. From there, he drew more lines of the blessed liquid on the fireplace and all the windows on the ground floor, as well as his bedroom window and those of the secondary bedrooms upstairs.

Not for the first time, he reflected that it was a good thing his mostly human blood protected him from suffering any ill effects from the holy water. It was anathema to demons, but he might as well have been shielding his house with Evian water for all the damage it did to him.

Although sometimes his mixed blood could be a real pain in the ass—such as allowing him to be banished if the person doing the banishing had the right tricks up their sleeve—during instances such as this, he could only look on it as a blessing.

Once that task was handled, he headed back downstairs, figuring he'd maybe watch the last bit of the Golden State Warriors game that had just started as he and Delia were leaving the restaurant.

Although he wouldn't have done anything so rude as to ignore her to pay attention to basketball, he was still kind of glad that he would be able to catch the final quarter.

He grabbed an IPA from the fridge and headed down to the rumpus room—well, it was more of a man cave now, with dark green paint on the walls and leather couches. The big TV he'd brought from the old house still sat upstairs, waiting to be moved down here, but a slightly smaller one was already in place in the man cave, which made this the logical spot for basketball watching.

Some people might have been bothered by the admittedly gruesome history of the room, how the serial killer who once had resided here had hidden the corpses of five women beneath this very floor. But Caleb knew the killer's victims had never haunted the house, and with their remains now safely interred—he'd seen a small piece online about how two of the women still hadn't been identified, but all of them had been given proper burials—he figured he didn't have anything to worry about.

Well, not from ghosts, anyway.

At the moment, he was more annoyed than worried that demons might have been meddling with his former house. Here he'd thought he'd settled into a new normal...or at least, as normal as his life could ever be, considering who he was and where he'd come from...and now it seemed as if Hell wasn't quite done with him yet.

So far, though, there didn't seem to be any sign that they knew he'd moved here, and he knew he'd do everything in his power to keep it that way.

Maybe he should get a different car?

He liked the Range Rover, but he supposed it was possible that it would be harder to track his movements if he had a couple of vehicles he could switch between when necessary. Something completely different from the big black SUV, possibly a Porsche convertible or another similar car. Las Vegas had plenty of high-end vehicles on the streets, so a Porsche most likely wouldn't even merit a second look.

Well, he'd figure that out eventually.

He picked up the remote and turned on the TV. Commercials, of course, one for a Chevy SUV, with the one that followed a pitch for Budweiser. His nose wrinkled. That stuff might have been okay when he was drinking under the bleachers with friends at his old high school's football field, but he liked to believe that his palate had improved since then.

And then there was a fast flash of an ad for the poker tournament at the Desert Paradise casino, a quickie with some splashy graphics and a reminder that qualifying rounds started on Thursday and ran through Saturday, with the quarterfinals, semifinals, and finals following the next week.

Since Caleb had already read up on the competition, this was all old news to him. Still, he was a little impressed that the tournament organizers had gone to the trouble of paying for an ad, even a short fifteen-second spot that probably hadn't cost too much.

Were they trying to get more participants, or simply doing their best to get the word out whichever way they could?

The people running the tournament hadn't sent an email blast detailing the number of people who'd actually be playing, so he didn't have any real idea as to their motivations. Now, though, as he sipped some more of his IPA, he began to wonder if maybe Delia had the right idea and it wasn't very smart to participate in anything quite so visible.

Another swallow of pale ale reassured him, however. This wasn't one of those huge tournaments that would be televised on ESPN or whatever. No, this was just an attempt by a second-tier casino to draw more spectators in to watch the game play—people who would be inspired by the professionals or semi-professionals playing in the competition and head to the gambling tables to try their luck...and lose, of course, because otherwise, the casino wouldn't see any real profit.

And profit was king, whether you were the

biggest casino on the Strip or some tired old relic from the 1960s that was just trying to get by.

Most likely, if Delia were here now, she'd try once again to persuade him that playing in the tournament wasn't the smartest idea in the world, especially now that it seemed as if the demon faction had poked up their ugly heads again. However, he'd only argue that he had just as much chance of being spotted by one of them at the local Safeway as he did at the casino, since the tournament was the sort of thing that would probably fly under most people's radars, even with those short blips of strategically placed TV ads.

Besides, he had no intention of using his powers at the tournament. This was all about honing his actual poker skills, not using magical shortcuts. Without any flashy displays of demonically fueled luck, there was far less chance of any demons noticing him.

Or anyone else taking a second look at his playing, for that matter.

And while winning might be nice—the $50K minimum payout could only help to plump his coffers—it wasn't as if he needed the money. He would get much, much more from the sale of his former house, especially since the comps seemed to show that it would probably go for at least fifty grand above what he'd paid, thanks to the recent improvements in the market and even the time of year. People liked to buy houses in March. Late November?

Not so much.

The game came back on, and the Golden State Warriors were ten points ahead. He settled against the back of the couch, taking in his surroundings, reminding himself that this was his new home and everything was going to be fine.

Of course it was.

———

Real estate agents were on call pretty much seven days a week, so Delia couldn't let herself get too annoyed that her phone started ringing at around five-thirty that afternoon, the home screen showing a number she didn't recognize. Over the years, she'd trained herself to let calls go to voicemail when she wanted to be left alone, but it wasn't as if she was busy doing anything important today, not when the listing for Caleb's house was finished and already live, and she should have been sitting on the couch with her feet up, watching something mindless.

That was exactly what she'd been doing when the phone rang, but she wasn't so engaged that she couldn't hit the mute button on the remote and then reach for her iPhone, which she almost always kept within arm's reach unless she was in the shower or something.

"Delia Dunne," she said, making sure she sounded crisp and professional even though she was on her sofa with bare feet curled under her and a muted *House Hunters* on the TV a few yards away.

"Hello, Ms. Dunne." A man's voice, also smooth and businesslike. No trace of an accent, so she thought he was probably from the West Coast somewhere.

Or was he just good at hiding his origins?

"My name is Evan Matthews. I was calling about the property you just listed on Piñon Drive."

Well, that was fast. Then again, she knew plenty of people practically camped on Zillow and Redfin and the other real estate sites, just waiting to pounce if an especially juicy property popped up.

"What did you need to know?" she asked as she unbent her legs and set her feet on the floor. The rug was a friendly blend of soft with just the slightest bit of scratchiness, proof that it was real wool and not that polypropylene stuff.

"I represent a firm called the Aegis Group," Ethan Matthews replied. "We invest in properties in California, Nevada, Oregon, and Washington State. Is that neighborhood zoned for vacation rentals?"

Like Las Vegas didn't already have enough hotels, Airbnbs, timeshares, and everything else. Still, a lot of those tended to be smaller places, condos or townhouses with only one or two bedrooms, and she could see how bigger families traveling together might want a rental that allowed them to spread out a little.

And because she'd checked on the zoning in the area and knew there was no HOA, she was able to answer the man's question easily enough.

"Yes, it is," she said. Whatever her personal feelings about big investors coming in and snapping up houses for rentals when they might have gone to couples and families just starting out, she knew she was representing Caleb here and couldn't let her opinions get in the way.

Which meant she needed to get him the best price for the house in the fastest timeframe.

"Excellent," Evan replied. "Everything looked good online, but I'd still like to view the property in person. Can we set something up for Monday morning?"

Good thing she carried her calendar in her head, which meant she knew her earliest appointment wasn't until three that day. "Absolutely," she said. "What time works best for you?"

"Ten o'clock?"

"Sounds good," she said. "Do you want to meet at my office or at the property?"

She assumed he'd rather meet at the house,

since it sounded as though he was only interested in that one. If she had a bunch of homes to show a client, then it made more sense for her to play chauffeur rather than have them try to caravan from place to place, but that didn't seem to be the case here.

Ethan confirmed that notion by saying, "At the house is fine. I'll see you there on Monday."

"Looking forward to it," she replied.

They ended the call after that exchange, and she paused to put the appointment in the calendar on her phone before she returned it to the coffee table. For a moment, she wondered if she should tell Caleb she already had a showing scheduled, and then she decided it was probably better to wait and see if her Monday morning appointment bore any fruit. Yes, Evan Matthews had sounded motivated on the phone, but he might get to the house and decide the layout wasn't right for an Airbnb, or there weren't enough bedrooms, or the fireplace was too much of a liability for a property that would be rented by a succession of vacationers.

Or maybe something else she hadn't even thought of yet. Over the years, she'd seen a bewildering variety of reasons as to why a certain buyer decided in the end that a house just wasn't for them.

If all went well, though, then Ethan Matthews would decide the Piñon Drive property was the perfect investment for his company, and they could go from there. The nice thing about transactions like this was that they were almost always cash offers, meaning Caleb could have that money in his hands in as little as two weeks.

She'd keep all this to herself for now, though. He trusted her to handle the transaction, and that meant she didn't need to go to him until she had a firm offer on the table.

In the meantime, she figured she might as well do what she could to enjoy the rest of her weekend.

With that thought in mind, she picked up her remote and turned the TV's sound back on.

Although Caleb had discussed the poker tournament at the Desert Paradise casino with Delia, he still hadn't officially signed up. He'd told himself that was because he wanted to keep his options open until the last minute, but he knew deep down it was also because he'd thought it might be a good idea to get her opinion on the subject.

She'd been decidedly lukewarm, but because she hadn't come right out and told him it was a horrible idea and that he was an idiot for even entertaining the notion, he figured that was enough of a green light for him to proceed.

Which was why he drove over to the casino early on Sunday afternoon, since sign-ups closed at five and he couldn't put it off much longer without missing out entirely. Maybe he could have come in the morning, but because temperatures had inched up to the mid-eighties, he'd wanted a late morning swim in the pool.

His new pool, with its gleaming tile and the palm trees off to one side providing just enough shade that the sun felt comfortable rather than hot. It was a good swim, and when he got out, he'd been gladder than ever that he'd decided to pull up stakes and make this place his home. Sure, the house where he'd grown up in Greencastle, Indiana, had a pool, but they couldn't use it for more than five or six months out of the year.

Come to think of it, he was the only one who'd ever even swam in the damn thing. His father probably would have thought it too undignified to be seen outdoors in swim trunks— even if the property had been surrounded by hedges and tall trees, and it was almost impossible to even get a glimpse of the pool—and his mother had been far too concerned about preserving her skin and her hair to risk exposing them to the sun's cruel rays.

Not for the first time, he found himself very, very happy that he hadn't tried to pick up his life in Greencastle and instead had come to Las Vegas. His miraculous return could have been explained away, he supposed, but much better to be very far away from Indiana winters and his equally icy mother.

The Desert Paradise—like his new home—had a definite mid-century vibe, one that had been freshened somewhat with new landscaping and paint, even though he guessed the actual contours of the place hadn't changed much since it was built in the early 1960s.

He pulled into a space near the lobby entrance, noting that the parking lot only looked about half full. On a Sunday afternoon like this, he would have expected to see more cars, and he guessed that the casino was holding the tournament to draw more gamblers in...as well as enough spectators to fill up the place.

A small placard had been placed just inside the lobby. *Tournament sign-ups this way,* it said, and had an arrow pointing toward a hallway off to the right.

Well, at least it looked as if they were organized.

Another sign was posted on the wall next to a meeting room near the end of the corridor. *Sign-ups here!*

People weren't lined up out the door or anything close to it, but there was still a small queue waiting to fill out their paperwork. Caleb had wondered why the casino didn't simply allow online sign-ups, since it seemed as if that would have been a lot simpler. As he watched, though, he saw the woman who was processing the paperwork take a man's driver's license over to a copy machine nearby and scan it, telling him they wanted to make sure they were properly vetting everyone who entered.

There were three people ahead of him, so it took about five minutes for him to get to the table. "Signing up for the tournament?" the woman asked politely. She looked as if she was in her early forties, slim and attractive. Maybe she'd worked as a cocktail waitress or a dealer here before she moved up into management.

Caleb couldn't think of any other reason why someone would be standing in line in this obscure meeting room unless they wanted to register for the competition, but he only smiled back at the woman. "Yes," he said.

"Just a couple of things," she replied, and pushed a piece of paper toward him. "We need your name, address, and phone number, and a copy of your driver's license or other ID."

He'd already been anticipating all that, so he pulled out his wallet and handed over his license so she could take a scan of it while he was filling out the rest of the paperwork. She headed back to the copy machine, and they synced up well enough that he was just finishing scrawling out his signature as she approached to return his license.

"I don't think I've seen you at one of these

before," she said, gaze almost appraising as she looked him up and down. "New in town?"

Although he was plenty used to women looking at him like that, he didn't get many who had to be at least ten years older than he was, maybe more.

"New to poker tournaments," he said easily. "But I'm a fast learner."

Her dark eyes glinted at him. "I'm sure you are."

Luckily, Caleb couldn't really linger, not with more people queued up behind him, so he gave her a casual nod and walked back into the hallway. A tall, heavyset man with thinning light brown hair who also looked as if he was in his forties— although closer to fifty than otherwise—stood there, apparently absorbed in whatever he was reading on his phone's screen. As Caleb approached, though, the man put the phone in his pocket and sent him a friendly smile.

"First time, huh?" he said, and Caleb paused.

"You heard that?"

"I have sharp ears," the man said, then extended a hand. "Hank Bowers. I've been doing this for a while, and I thought I knew most of the people who play in the Desert Paradise tournaments."

"Caleb Lowe," he responded, glad that after three months of giving people that fake name, he was mostly used to saying it rather than the one he'd been born with. "And yeah, I'm a newbie. But my friends kept telling me I should try a tournament one of these days, and then I saw the ad on TV for this one and thought, why not?"

"You picked a good tournament," Hank replied. "Lots of great players here, but the overall atmosphere is a lot more low-key than some of the big-money competitions." He paused there, still wearing the easy smile of a man completely at home in his surroundings. In his polo shirt and khaki slacks, he could have come straight off the golf course, and a tan that was probably in place all year 'round only reinforced that impression. "Did you get a brochure from Lauren?"

Caleb shook his head. "Is she the gal who's registering the players?"

"The very one," Hank said. "We've been pretty slammed today—a lot of people like to wait until the last minute to sign up—so it probably slipped her mind. I'll go grab you one."

Before Caleb was able to say that he could fetch the brochure, Hank had already headed over to the meeting room they were using as a registration station and come back with a nicely printed four-color leaflet.

"Here you go," he said. "Most of it is pretty straightforward stuff, but if you've never played in a tournament before or have watched too many of them on TV, then it would probably be helpful for you to read it over before the first elimination round starts on Thursday."

Considering that was four days from now, Caleb didn't think he'd have too hard a time reading and absorbing the information the brochure contained. It wasn't as if Hank had handed him a copy of *War and Peace* or something. "Thanks," he replied. "How many players have signed up?"

"I think we're around eighty or so," he said. "We don't have anyone feeding in from satellites, though, because the buy-in for this tournament isn't high."

Caleb had read enough about how poker tournaments worked that he knew "satellites" were simply smaller competitions with lower buy-ins that would feed people into the larger, higher-stakes tournaments. "Does this competition feed into bigger ones?"

"Nope," Hank said cheerfully. "It's more of a standalone, just-for-fun kind of event. That's what makes it more approachable to people who're getting started, like you."

Well, at least the older man hadn't called him a rank amateur. True, Caleb had never formally competed, but those months he'd spent gathering funds for his new life here in Las Vegas had given him plenty of intel on how to get by at a poker table.

Except for the part where he'd used his demonic powers to ensure that he always came out ahead.

Even so, he knew a lot about poker and the rules of the various games than he had three months ago. He'd do fine.

"Good to know," he said. "Anyway, I need to get going—I still have some errands I need to run. See you on Thursday."

"See you then," Hank replied, then turned and headed back into the room where people were signing up.

Maybe he was affiliated with the tournament in some way, or maybe he was just the event's unofficial greeter. He did seem pretty at home here.

Caleb headed for the exit. No, he didn't have any errands to run—that had been a complete fabrication—but he hadn't seen the need to hang around and keep chatting. People who seemed friendly with no real motivation for being that way always put him on his guard. Hank Bowers might simply have been a genial sort of guy...or maybe he liked to engage with the people who'd come in to register for the competition so he could size them up beforehand and see if they had any weaknesses he could exploit.

Possibly that was a pretty jaded way to look at

the situation. On the other hand, Caleb hadn't run into too many purely good people in this world. Rosemary McGuire, the woman he'd thought he loved back in L.A., the one who turned out to have an angel for a father?

Sure.

Delia Dunne? Probably. She was much more smoothly efficient than Rosemary could have ever hoped to be—and Caleb guessed that Rosemary hadn't been a punk rock chick in high school like Delia—but his new friend still seemed to be motivated by a sense of justice, of making sure things were right in the world, even if her mechanism for doing so was simply finding a family the perfect house where they could be happy.

Which sort of begged the question as to why she was all right hanging around with a quarter demon like him. He didn't think it was purely business, not when they could have parted ways just as soon as the purchase of the Pueblo Street house was complete. Instead, she'd stuck around and provided design advice...had even helped him move his most valuable possessions into the new place without a single complaint.

Then again, maybe all that was just part of her bid for sainthood.

Smiling to himself, he headed outside, pulling his sunglasses from where they'd been hanging from the neck of his T-shirt so he could plant them on his nose to protect his eyes from the fierce sun overhead. It wasn't nearly as hot as it would get in the next couple of months, but even though the temperature outside was comfortable enough, the light was extremely bright.

So bright that it was easy enough to see the smudges on the driver's-side door of his Range Rover near the handle once he got close enough. Eyes narrowing, he bent down to take a closer look.

Those smudges looked suspiciously like the ones Delia had first noticed on the patio door at the old house.

Straightening, he glanced around the parking lot, but no one was nearby. That didn't mean much, though. If they were really dealing with a demon here, it could have blinked itself away less than a second after it had touched the Range Rover's door.

A scowl pulled at his brow as he clicked the remote to unlock the vehicle. His T-shirt was untucked anyway, so he wrapped the hem around his fingers as he opened the door and got in. Even doing that much might have wrecked the prints— or whatever those smudges were—but it wasn't like he could just stand here in the parking lot forever.

No, he wanted to go home and check to see if those blurry smudges were also suspiciously missing their prints.

He had a feeling he knew the answer already.

Chapter Four

—·《《·☾·》》·—

EVAN MATTHEWS PULLED UP TO THE HOUSE on Piñon Drive at precisely ten o'clock on Monday morning. He was driving a shiny white BMW 7-Series, and when he emerged from the car, he looked almost exactly the way Delia had imagined him—expertly cut brown hair with a few touches of gray at the temples, expensive shirt and dress slacks but no tie, shoes she guessed had probably cost four figures.

At times like this, she wondered if she might have been doing this for too long. Things were getting way too predictable.

No wonder she liked hanging out with Caleb Lockwood. He was sort of the monkey in the wrench...but in a good way.

"Hi, Evan," she said as she came down the

front walkway to meet him. "Any trouble finding the house?"

"None at all," he replied, then reached out so he could shake her hand. "This is an easily accessible neighborhood, which makes the house even better suited for a vacation rental."

"Then let me show you the interior and the backyard," she said. "I think you'll be pleasantly surprised."

"I'm sure I will."

They went into the house, where Delia described all the recent renovations and how the home had been featured on an episode of *Flip or Flop Las Vegas,* which she thought would be an additional selling point. Evan Matthews appeared to be of a similar mind, because he nodded and looked pleased after hearing that bit of information.

"People do like to stay in places that have a bit of notoriety," he said. "It's something our marketing people can play up in the listing—if we decide that the house suits, of course. Let's take a look at the upstairs."

Dutifully, Delia led him to the second level, where he seemed to be happy with the size of the bedrooms and the number of bathrooms. True, it wasn't like a lot of newer houses, where each bedroom had its own *en suite* bath, but there was the powder room downstairs and then the bathroom in the main suite and one in the hall for the remaining bedrooms, so that would probably be enough to accommodate everyone.

Well, unless they were like her college friend Madison, who could easily spend an hour and a half blow-drying and then straightening her hair. Delia had never been sure whether the task truly required that much effort, but Madison wouldn't step foot outside unless she was absolutely sure she'd vanquished the last of the frizzies.

And Evan seemed equally happy with the backyard, which, in addition to the pool, had an outdoor kitchen built into the covered patio. It probably wasn't quite as over-the-top as the one Caleb had put in at his new house, since that kitchen also had an Ooni pizza oven and a Big Green Egg in addition to the built-in barbecue, but still, this should be more than enough to satisfy any vacationers who chose to stay here.

"I think it could work," Evan told her after they'd gone back inside and she'd closed and locked the French door that opened onto the patio—and double-checked it, since she didn't want a repeat of whatever might have happened here a few days earlier. "I'll need to present the property to the board before we can make an offer, of course. But I should know something by the end of the week."

In her mind, she'd had fantasies of him whipping out a checkbook and writing a huge check right then and there, but that wasn't really how these things worked.

For one thing, no way in the world would she accept a personal check that big. Cashier's check or wire transfer for this sort of thing, thank you very much.

"Of course," she said. "I'm having a broker's open house on Thursday, though, and I expect the property to generate a lot of interest."

"I expect it would," Evan replied smoothly, not much put off by the subtle threat that someone might come along and scoop up the property before the board of directors at Aegis Holdings had a chance to decide whether the Piñon Drive house was suitable for their purposes. "But we have our way of doing things, and I need to stick with that. However, please let me know if you get any serious offers so we can direct our search elsewhere."

"Not a problem," Delia replied. She'd done what she could, so at this point, the outcome was mostly up to fate. "Let me walk you to your car."

She went with him down to the curb, where he thanked her for her time before climbing into the BMW and driving away. For some reason, she lingered there for a moment, wondering if her impression that there had been something off about the whole exchange was valid, or whether she was seeing things that weren't there because of hers and Caleb's discovery that demons appeared to be active in Las Vegas once again.

But Evan Matthews wasn't a demon...or was he?

Now you're thinking everyone's a goddamn demon, she scolded herself. *Okay, you had a bad experience with Robert Hendricks, but that doesn't make every successful man on the planet some kind of hellspawn in disguise.*

This all seemed to make an inordinate amount of sense. Even so, she had to hold back a shiver as she made a minute adjustment to the "For Sale" sign in the front yard before she headed up to the house to make sure everything was locked.

Maybe one day she'd stop jumping at shadows.

Caleb got a text from Delia saying she'd shown the house to a potential buyer but that she wasn't sure whether anything was going to come of it. Those words made a stab of disappointment go through him, but after she sent another text explaining that she would be doing a broker open house on Thursday, it seemed clear that she was working hard to make sure the property sold as quickly as possible.

In the meantime, he had other things to keep him occupied.

"It's a very good choice, sir," the salesman told

him as he circled the vehicle, taking in the sleek lines and the unusual pale green color, a shade Caleb wasn't sure he'd liked at first but was now growing on him by the minute. Sure, something white or gray would probably be less distinctive, but on the other hand, the metallic sage was about as different from his black Range Rover as you could get. "Only one in Nevada in this color."

Maybe that was true, maybe it wasn't. What mattered was that the car was on the lot now, which meant he could buy the thing and drive off in a vehicle the demons who'd been surveilling him wouldn't recognize. His sleep the night before had been utterly undisturbed, so either the holy water was working or there was another perfectly logical explanation for those print-less smudges on the French door at his old house, and all this worry about demons had been in his head and nothing more.

He'd taken a taxi to the Porsche dealership, figuring that if he did end up buying something, he wouldn't want to be stuck with two cars there at the lot. Ever since that scare with the demon Uber driver who'd deliberately attempted to get him killed, he'd been wary of the ride-share service and had opted to call a cab on those rare occasions when he didn't want to drive, for whatever reason.

Luckily, Vegas still had plenty of taxis.

"She's a beauty," he agreed. "Let's go inside and take care of the paperwork, shall we?"

———

Delia hadn't heard anything from Evan Matthews yet, but it was only Tuesday afternoon. Even an individual buyer would probably take at least that long before they decided to jump into something as life-changing as buying a house, and that was without having to run the purchase past a board of directors.

Still, that didn't mean she couldn't do a little research while she was waiting.

Things had been busy enough at the office so far this week that she'd barely had a chance to catch her breath, what with covering for her mother and taking on three new clients. That felt like a lot, but she knew a good number of people tried to set the house-buying wheels in motion around this time of year so they could get moved before the real heat of summer set in.

But her next client wasn't coming to the office until four-thirty, which meant she had a bit of free time.

Not that she'd been able to find much so far. Aegis Holdings was based in Santa Monica and appeared to have been in business for around ten years. The company specialized in residential property management and acquisitions, and seemed to have branched into vacation rentals about five years ago. The members of the board of directors were listed on the company's website, although there weren't any photos attached to their names.

The regular staff members each had their own page, though, and there was Evan Matthews, listed as vice president of acquisitions. It seemed a little odd to Delia that a VP would deign to tour houses in person, but maybe he was a more hands-on kind of executive.

At any rate, the operation seemed on the up-and-up, as far as she could tell. It didn't surprise her too much that a corporation based in California would be scouting Las Vegas for properties, not when houses were cheaper here and the gambling mecca was the sort of place that attracted visitors from all over the world at all times of the year.

In a way, she was a little disappointed. It would have been nice to find some kind of smoking gun, something to show the company was nothing more than a front for a bunch of demons, just as she and Caleb still suspected The Styx Group was, despite their lack of any real evidence on that front.

But, just as Sigmund Freud had once famously —and perhaps apocryphally—said, sometimes a cigar was just a cigar.

At least she had a showing of the house sched-uled tomorrow, and then there would be the broker's open house on Thursday. Delia hadn't yet decided when to have another open house, one that was intended for the public and not other real estate agents, but she figured she'd wait and see how it went on Thursday. While it was always optimal to be both the listing and the selling agent so she wouldn't have to split her commission, she was just fine with another realtor bringing in a buyer. Whatever it took to get the house sold.

Well, the market was pretty hot now, and it wasn't as if Caleb was carrying an expensive mortgage he needed to get out from under. A speedy sale was always the best scenario, of course, but if it took a couple of weeks to sell the place, it wouldn't be the end of the world.

In the meantime, she needed to remember that he wasn't her only client...even if he did somehow manage to occupy her thoughts a lot more than she would have preferred.

An escape of breath, and she closed the tab with the Aegis Holdings website and pulled up the MLS listings once again, just in case something new had come on the market since the last time she'd checked. Her four-thirty client had a fairly long list of wants, and she would prefer to have more than just three houses to show him.

It was as good a way as any to push demons... and Caleb Lockwood...out of her mind.

When Thursday afternoon rolled around, Caleb realized he was actually nervous. It had been so long since he'd experienced such a feeling that he had to let himself sit with the emotion for a moment, analyzing the anxious flutters in his stomach and their probable cause.

Well, he supposed it wasn't so strange to be a bit on edge, considering he'd never played in a poker tournament before. A small, friendly one, according to Hank Bowers, but still, a few butterflies should be considered perfectly normal.

Especially since Caleb had vowed to himself that he wouldn't use any of his demonic gifts to win. Either he would do this with his own brain power, or he'd fail miserably and realize he wasn't the world-class card shark that he thought he was. If someone had asked him to articulate precisely why this was so important to him, he wasn't sure whether he would have been able to answer accurately. He just knew that, while having powers that arose from possessing demon blood could come in handy, he didn't want them to define him.

Anyway, ever since he'd decided to play in the competition, he'd been watching poker tournaments on ESPN, finding older replays on YouTube, whatever he could track down to help him analyze the moves the players were making...

and, with any luck, decipher the why of what they were doing as much as the how.

But nothing beat real-life experience, which was why he was determined to do this, no matter how many butterflies might have been flapping around in his gut right now.

The drive over to the casino helped, the top down on the Porsche Cabriolet, warm wind ruffling his hair. No sign of anyone following him, although the convertible got a few head turns as he rolled down Fremont Street. It seemed like even in a town that had its fair share of luxury vehicles, his latest acquisition was flashy enough to attract attention.

Maybe he should have bought the graphite gray model, rather than the metallic sage.

Too late now, though. As far as he could tell, people were looking at the car and not at him, which he supposed was a decent enough form of diversion, sort of like a magician distracting his audience with some sort of showy move with one hand while he performed the real trick with the other.

The parking lot was much more crowded today than it had been when he came here on Sunday to register for the tournament. He supposed that made sense; while Hank had made it sound as if there weren't a huge number of competitors, Caleb guessed that a lot of those vehicles belonged to people who'd come to watch.

No problem there. It had been a while since his quarterback days, but he still didn't have a problem with being the center of attention...as long as those watching had no idea that he was anything more than a regular guy.

Just like on Sunday, there were signs just inside the doors instructing players where they needed to go to check in. Dutifully, he stood in line and then handed over his ID so the woman working at the check-in table—not Lauren, the dark-haired woman who'd been there on the weekend, but an older blonde so deeply tanned that her skin looked like it could be used for a pair of saddlebags or maybe the saddle itself—could get him logged in.

The process went smoothly enough, though, and in less than five minutes, he had a lanyard around his neck with a badge that identified him as a participant in the competition and was walking down the corridor to the casino floor. Rather than being shunted off to a ballroom, the players would be gathered in a roped-off area on one side of the casino, allowing them to be part of the regular hustle and bustle.

He hadn't been playing much lately, since most of his energy had been directed toward finishing the remodel—and with his investments performing nicely, it wasn't as if he needed the money—and his pulse quickened a little at the familiar sights and sounds and smells around him, the clinking of the slot machines, the murmur of voices, the faint acrid haze of cigarette smoke. All casinos had designated areas where smoking was allowed, but it wasn't as if he had to walk through a cloud of the stuff to get where he was going, and it didn't look as if anyone was smoking in the roped-off area.

Good. While his time in Hell had gotten him somewhat used to bad smells, he still didn't want to be inhaling that crap while he was trying to concentrate.

Another woman, this one dark and pretty, maybe Native American, waved him into the players' area and guided him to a table set up with four chairs.

"You'll play the first round here," she told him. "As the rounds go on, we'll take out tables as players are eliminated. The final four in your group will play over there."

She pointed to a table set somewhat apart from the others. It had its chairs tipped in against it, telling him the tournament organizers didn't intend to use it for the preliminary rounds and were saving it for the time when the four survivors of his subgroup would play against one another.

Caleb had read about most of this in the brochure Hank Bowers had given him, but still, it was entirely different to see the setup in person.

Once again, his stomach tightened, although he told it to get its act together, or he'd never get past the first round.

"Thanks," he told the woman with a smile, and she smiled back, her expression showing a certain warmth that told him she wouldn't mind if he slipped her his phone number at some point during the day.

The Caleb he'd been up until a few months ago probably would have done that very thing. Now, though...now that Delia Dunne was a part of his life, even if not in exactly the way he would have liked...he found himself singularly uninterested.

Which he thought was all kinds of messed up. Just because he was friends with the woman didn't mean he had to turn into a monk.

But something in his expression must have been off-putting enough that the gal who'd shown him to the table where he'd be playing got the message, since now her face turned almost cool.

"There's a complimentary water and tea and coffee station over there," she said crisply, pointing to a rectangular table set off to one side that was furnished with multiple pitchers and lots of glasses in neat stacks. "No booze during the competition."

That made sense, although Caleb thought the alcohol prohibition was in place just as much for cost reasons as it was to ensure the players remained sharp during the tournament.

"Got it," he replied.

She seemed to understand that he didn't need any more guidance, because she gave him a brisk nod and headed off toward the next player who'd wandered into the roped-off area, a nervous-looking guy with a prematurely bald head and a Hawaiian shirt that wasn't doing him any favors.

Caleb couldn't help being glad he wasn't the only rank amateur here. Good thing he knew he didn't look anywhere that uncomfortable.

It turned out that the bald guy in the Hawaiian shirt was one of the four designated for his table.

"Jeff Kosky," the man said as he extended a hand before taking a seat. "First tournament?"

"Caleb Lowe," he returned, even as he wondered whether it would be better to admit that he was a complete noob and then surprise everyone with his acumen, or to try intimidating them from the start with hints of tons of experience.

Well, he'd been trying to turn over a new leaf here in Las Vegas, to be a new and improved version of himself, and that meant not spreading around lies unless it was absolutely necessary.

"Yep, my first," he said cheerfully. "I only moved to Las Vegas a few months ago, and I heard about this one and thought it would be a good place to get started."

"My feelings, too," Jeff Kosky replied. "And my wife thought it sounded like fun, what with the way I've been cleaning up at our neighborhood poker nights for the past couple of years."

He tilted his head slightly toward the area where spectators could gather to watch. In answer, a petite woman with light brown hair in a choppy bob smiled back at him. Caleb wouldn't have said she was exactly pretty when in repose, but she did have a megawatt smile.

"Something in it for her?" he asked, and Jeff grinned.

"I told her if I won, we could go to Paris for our anniversary. So I've got a lot riding on this."

Whereas Caleb was only here to prove something to himself.

Would it be mean to win and deprive Jeff and his wife of their anniversary trip?

That wasn't the sort of thought which would normally go through a demon's head...even a quarter demon's. But Caleb didn't want to be that guy anymore. He couldn't model his behavior on what he'd seen from his mother, either, because she was almost as bad as the half demons that made up his father's generation, even if she happened to be wholly human.

By birth, anyway.

On the other hand, anyone competing in one of these tournaments knew there could be only one winner. The odds of Jeff Kosky making it all the way to even the final round, let alone winning, probably weren't all that great.

The other two players arrived then, an older, dignified Black women, Nita Strcct, whose air of brisk confidence told Caleb she might be the one to look out for, and another man in his thirties, with dark hair pulled back into a ponytail and the kind of easygoing, almost Zen manner that made him seem an unlikely candidate to be playing in a poker competition.

Or maybe the guy—who introduced himself as Ty Carter—had only adapted that kind of attitude to lull the other players into a false sense of security.

After they'd all greeted each other, they lapsed into an awkward silence...one that didn't last very long, as a middle-aged man Caleb didn't recognize approached a podium placed near the table where the final round would be held and spoke into the microphone.

"Welcome to the sixth annual Desert Paradise poker tournament," he said. "I'm Lew Phipps, the general manager here at the casino. I just wanted to welcome all our participants, whether they're new or coming back for another chance this year. Today we'll be playing three rounds, with the winner from each table moving on to play against the other winners until we've narrowed things down to thirty-two. Those winners will advance to the quarterfinals next Thursday."

This was all information Caleb already knew, since it was in the brochure he'd been given, but hearing the details spoken out loud just made him that much more determined to get past this round. The last thing he wanted was to tell Delia he'd been forced to slink home in ignominy after not even being able to make it to the quarterfinals.

If that happened, then he'd know for sure that his demon powers had been the only thing propping him up, and he might as well stay far away from any casinos unless he was going there to see a show or maybe stuff himself at a buffet. He couldn't exactly be the new Caleb Lockwood if he kept trotting out the same old tricks.

Men and women wearing white shirts, black bow ties, and black pants began fanning out to the various tables. Obviously, they were the dealers, here to play a double role of dealing out cards and keeping an eye on everything to make sure there weren't any shenanigans. No doubt, closed-circuit cameras were also monitoring the tournament, but Caleb couldn't let himself worry about that too much. Everywhere you went in Las Vegas, you were being recorded. It was fine...as long as none of that footage was being broadcast.

Everyone at his table wished the other players good luck, and he murmured the empty words as well. Or maybe they weren't that empty. Nothing wrong with everyone having good luck...just as long as it wasn't better than his.

Their dealer—a Latino woman who looked around Caleb's age, maybe a little older—broke the seal on her deck of cards and began expertly shuffling them, fingers almost a blur. She wasn't wearing any rings except a gold band with a thin line of diamonds set into the center, a ring that he guessed was deliberately low profile so it wouldn't get in the way as she worked.

He already knew the preferred game for the tournament was Texas Hold 'Em, so he had his chips ready since he was seated immediately to the left of the dealer and therefore would be the first to put in his "blind," or the small bet necessary to get the pot going.

Except the tournament had already begun, and the blinds were set at twenty-five and fifty dollars for this first level.

The dealer button was positioned so that Caleb found himself in the small blind, which meant he had to put in twenty-five dollars before seeing his cards. Nita, sitting to his left in the big blind position, posted fifty dollars. The tournament structure was beyond his control now—no more choosing his own stakes like he could in cash games.

"Hole cards," the dealer said briefly, and dealt everyone their designated two.

Caleb looked down at his hand and schooled himself not to respond.

A four and an eight. Both spades, true, but there wasn't much he could do with that unless he got really lucky.

Naturally lucky, not the kind of luck influenced by his demon powers.

The action started with Jeff, who was sitting to Nita's left in the under-the-gun position. He had the choice of folding, calling the fifty-dollar big blind, or raising to at least one hundred dollars.

"Call," Jeff said, matching the big blind.

Ty was next. "Raise to one-fifty," he said smoothly, pushing his chips forward.

When it came around to Caleb in the small blind, he had to decide whether to fold, call the one-fifty, or raise to at least three hundred. With a four and an eight of spades, he had next to nothing —but then again, that was exactly the kind of hand where his demonic abilities would have come in handy in the past.

But no. He'd made a promise to himself, and he was going to keep those powers out of this even if he crashed and burned.

"Call," he said, adding another $125 to match Ty's raise. Nita called as well, and Jeff folded rather than put in an additional hundred.

The dealer's fingers flew as she laid out the flop: king of hearts, seven of spades, two of diamonds.

Now Caleb was first to act, since the small blind acted first on all betting rounds after the initial one. For a fraction of a second, he could have sworn he saw Ty's cards shimmer, like heat waves rising off hot asphalt. He blinked hard. When he looked again, everything seemed normal, but there was something about the way Ty's mouth quirked at one corner that made him uneasy.

"Check," Caleb said, tapping the table.

Nita checked as well, but Ty didn't hesitate. "Bet two hundred," he said, that same knowing smile playing at the edges of his mouth.

Caleb had nothing but a flush draw, and he knew the smart play would be to fold. But there was something about the way the cards seemed to dance at the edges of his vision, something that made his quarter-demon blood sing with recognition. He called. Nita folded with a shake of her head.

The turn brought the jack of spades.

Three spades. One card away from a flush. Caleb's heart quickened—not because of supernatural intervention this time, but from genuine excitement. This was what he'd wanted: the pure thrill of the game.

"Check," Caleb said.

Ty's cards flickered again, and this time Caleb

was sure he wasn't imagining that odd shimmer. There was some kind of magic at work here, subtle but present nonetheless.

The kind of magic that wouldn't show up on security cameras...but which any supernatural creature worth their salt would recognize.

"Bet five hundred," Ty said.

Caleb studied the other man carefully. If Ty was using magic, he wasn't doing it the way Caleb would have in the past—no blunt force making the right cards appear at the right time, just a slight edge, a whisper of insight into his opponents' hands. The kind of thing that would be nearly impossible to prove.

The responsible thing would be to report it. But then Caleb would have to explain how he knew the other man's playing wasn't on the up and up, and that would lead to questions he couldn't answer. Besides, wasn't this exactly the kind of challenge he'd been looking for? Beating someone who was cheating by doing it fair and square?

"Call," Caleb said. He had position on Ty—if the river brought another spade, he could make his move then. If not, well, he still had enough chips to recover.

The dealer burned a card and turned over the river: the queen of spades.

The flush was complete.

"Check," Caleb said, wanting to see what Ty would do.

Ty's cards shimmered one final time, and Caleb caught the briefest glimpse of what looked like two pair—kings and jacks. Good, but not good enough.

"All in," Ty said smoothly, pushing his remaining chips forward—about six hundred dollars.

It was decision time. Caleb had the flush, but there was still a chance Ty might have a higher spade hand. The old him would have known for certain. The new him had to trust his instincts—his human instincts.

"Call," he said as he pushed his chips forward.

Ty revealed his cards first: king-jack off-suit for two pair. He looked expectantly at Caleb.

With deliberate slowness, Caleb turned over his four and eight of spades. "Flush," he said quietly.

The dealer gave a single nod. "Flush wins."

As Caleb raked in the chips, he caught Ty's eye. The other man's easy smile had faltered slightly, replaced by something sharper, more calculating. It was a look that said he knew Caleb had seen something he shouldn't have, even though he wasn't quite sure what to do about it.

Ty pushed his chair back from the table with a sigh. "Well played," he said, though there was an edge to his voice.

"Still plenty of tournament left," Caleb said, trying to sound reassuring, but his attention remained on Ty, who was now gathering his things. Their eyes met again, and this time there was a silent understanding between them.

They both had secrets...and they both knew it.

The dealer began shuffling for the next hand. Caleb's stomach butterflies had transformed into something else entirely—the pure, clean excitement of competition. No powers, no shortcuts, just his wits against the other players...even if some of them weren't playing entirely fair.

He could win this thing. More importantly, he could win it *right*.

Chapter Five

—·《《·☾·》》·—

DELIA'S PHONE RANG, AND SHE LIFTED IT
from where she'd set it on the counter at Caleb's
old house. The broker's open house was due to
start in ten minutes, and she hoped no one was
calling to cancel. The more people here to look over
the place, the better the chance that one of them
would have a client who thought it was absolutely
perfect.

But she recognized the number on the screen
right away.

Caleb.

"How's it going?" she asked, since she knew he
was at the tournament.

"Great," he said. "We just played the first three
hands, and now we're taking a break. There'll be
two more after this, and then that's it for the day."
A pause, and he added, "I won my first two hands."

"You did?" she responded, then hoped she didn't sound too surprised.

"I did," he said, and now his voice was clearly amused. "Straight-up regular playing, no hanky-panky."

By "hanky-panky," she assumed he meant he'd accomplished those wins through pure skill and none of the same powers he'd used to amass his current fortune.

"That's great," she told him. "I knew you had it in you."

"Did you?" he returned, his voice now teasing. "You were sounding pretty doubtful a couple of days ago."

"Just doubtful about you doing something so public," she said at once. "It had nothing to do with your skill as a poker player."

"Good to know." He paused there for a second, then asked, "What time are you going to be done with your open house?"

"Around six, probably."

At least, that was her best guess after holding dozens of these over the years. Sure, there was always that one agent who turned out to be a real chatty Cathy and wanted to stay behind, but mostly, brokers came to these things to get the information they needed and then headed right back out again.

"Serendipity," Caleb said. "I should be done

around the same time. Want to meet for dinner somewhere?"

Probably smart of him not to come by the house. Although she hadn't noticed anything odd today when she'd come by to set up and make sure everything looked picture perfect, she still couldn't shake the feeling that someone was watching the property. If that turned out to be the actual case and not just her nerves getting to her, then much better for him to stay far away.

Before she could respond, he added, "I noticed something weird this afternoon during the game, and I wanted to talk to you about it."

"Weird" was a general word that could have meant almost anything, but in this context, she had to believe Caleb was talking about some kind of demonic activity.

"Oh?" she managed.

"I'm not totally sure," he said. "Still, I thought it would be better to get together and discuss it."

"Where would you like to meet?"

"At Battista's," he replied, naming a restaurant that wasn't too far away, one they'd already gone to once before.

Well, she'd never been one to turn down some carbonara.

"Okay," she said. "Let's aim for six-thirty, just in case someone decides to hang around after the open house is officially over. I could kick them out, but—"

"But you don't want to offend someone who might bring you a client," he finished for her. "It's cool. Then I'll meet you at Battista's at six-thirty."

"Sounds like a plan."

They ended the call there—good thing, because the first of the brokers were just starting to show up. Delia recognized them, of course; while there were plenty of real estate agents in the greater Las Vegas area, the pool wasn't so big that she hadn't gotten to know most of them over the past seven years.

And Marcy Talbott always came early because she wanted to get her pick of the treats Delia made sure to lay out for all her open houses, whether they were intended for brokers, like this one, or for the general buying public.

"Ooh, snickerdoodles," the other agent said, making a beeline for the platter Delia had set out on the kitchen island. "My favorite."

She scooped up two cookies and put them on a napkin. Immediately behind her was Thomas Littleton, a slim, elegant man somewhere in his late forties or early fifties, the kind of guy Delia was pretty sure had never eaten a cookie in his life.

"Mid-century, tasteful remodel," he said as he looked around with some approval. "When were the renovations done?"

"A little over three years ago," she replied. "But the people who did the flip were careful to choose elements that were timeless."

Well, timeless for Las Vegas, anyway. She had a feeling the neon sign in the family room and the cobalt blue cabinets might not have flown in a more conservative part of the country.

Thomas only nodded, though, then commenced moving from room to room, making notes on the yellow pad he carried with him. A lot of brokers just took a record of everything with their phones or their iPads, but clearly, Thomas Littleton wasn't about to let modern technology take the place of good old-fashioned pen and paper.

Marcy somehow managed to devour both cookies in record time, then wiped her fingers on her napkin and pulled a phone out of her oversized purse and typed something into the Notes app. "Built in 1963, right?"

"Yes," Delia said. "But all the plumbing and the electrical were updated at the time of the remodel. The roof is only three years old as well."

The other broker looked pleased by that information and entered it into her phone, then headed off to wander and take more notes.

By that point, more real estate agents had arrived. Delia gave the same spiel to all of them, encouraging them to pick up one of the flyers she'd left out on the island near the refreshments and to please come to her with any questions the flyer didn't cover.

She doubted there would be many; everyone here was a professional, and they'd done this same song and dance many times before. Mostly, it was about following the ritual so everyone would know exactly what they were dealing with.

And grabbing some free cookies, since Marcy wasn't the only one to indulge. In fact, Delia wasn't sure whether the platter of treats would last through the open house.

Probably a good thing. Otherwise, any leftovers would have to come home with her, and she knew she'd feel guilty if she let a single cookie go to waste.

People filtered in and out, taking notes, getting photos, although Delia thought the original listing, with its fifty-plus images, should have been enough to satisfy even the pickiest buyer. But if it helped move the property faster, then she certainly wasn't going to argue.

A little after five, an agent she vaguely recognized came in, a man named Aaron Sanchez. He was fairly new on the Las Vegas real estate scene, but he'd attended one of her broker open houses in February and had toured clients through a couple of her properties, although nothing had come of those visits. After catching her eye, he came over to the spot where she stood by the kitchen island.

"Good turnout," he said as one of the realtors

who'd been inspecting the second floor came down the stairs and gave her a brief wave before heading out the door.

"Yes," Delia replied. She'd gotten the impression in the past that Aaron's friendliness had a bit more to it than simple professional courtesy, so she tried to be neutral around him without being utterly off-putting. It wasn't that he was unattractive—he was in his mid-thirties, so five or six years older than she was, with thick dark hair, warm brown eyes, and the kind of build that suggested he spent some time at the gym when he wasn't showing houses—but long ago she'd told herself that she wouldn't get involved with someone else in the real estate business. Her work consumed enough of her life on its own that she didn't want to be with a man who had the same crazy schedule.

And all right, Caleb Lockwood had gotten his real estate license, and they'd definitely worked on a project together, but that was different. There was nothing going on between them.

Well, except the unspoken agreement that they'd fight whatever demons that decided to rear their ugly heads in her hometown.

But Aaron didn't seem too put off by her casual tone. "I can see why you have so many brokers interested. Great neighborhood, good-sized house, newly updated—it's a dream for a lot of buyers."

Delia had thought so, too. "Yes, it's the whole package. I doubt it will last long. Do you have any clients in mind for the property?"

"A few," he said. "In fact, I have one who was jonesing to come over and look at it right away, but I told her that since the broker's open house was happening today, I might as well drop by and make sure it looks as good in person."

"And does it?"

The glance he gave her didn't seem to have much to do with the house. Nothing lewd or lascivious, but Delia got the feeling he was much more interested in her than in the quartz countertops or the luxury vinyl plank floors.

"Definitely," he replied, then paused. "What can you tell me about the owner?"

She wanted to narrow her eyes at that question but then told herself she needed to relax. Some brokers wanted to know exactly who they were dealing with, while others didn't.

"He bought the house last November," she said, and Aaron's eyebrows lifted slightly.

"That wasn't very long ago. Why would he want to sell the property so soon after buying it?"

On the surface, it did look a little odd, especially since this was a house that had been remodeled before Caleb even moved in and didn't need any updating.

But even though Aaron's questions seemed

innocent enough, Delia knew she shouldn't say anything that might point toward Caleb's new home.

Well, a little creative obfuscation never hurt anyone.

"Oh, he decided the place was too big for him, and he didn't want to deal with all the yard upkeep and that kind of stuff," she said, hoping she sounded completely reasonable and not like a woman who was lying through her teeth. "So I just sold him a condo in Lido Isle."

Which was a gorgeous neighborhood down in Summerlin with lakes and canals, just far enough away that she doubted Aaron would head over there to investigate.

He seemed to accept the story, and gave a nod as he said, "I can see why this house might be a lot for one person. It practically screams 'family home.'"

"That it does," Delia replied, since her first impression of the place was that it was pure Brady Bunch—updated for the twenty-first century, of course.

"Well, I'll take a look around," Aaron told her next. "There are just a few things I'd like to get some extra photographs of."

"Take your time," she responded at once, although she hoped he wouldn't dawdle too much. Officially, the open house was supposed to end at five-thirty, but she knew some people liked to linger, which was why she'd told Caleb she'd meet him for dinner at half past six rather than right on the hour.

Aaron sent her a friendly smile and then headed into the backyard, phone already out so he could get whatever supplemental photographs his client might need. While he was outside, several more brokers left, and she wondered if she was going to get stuck alone here with him.

A little chill went down her spine, and she told herself not to be such a baby. It wasn't as if she'd never met the guy before, and besides, she couldn't spend the rest of her life jumping at shadows.

Especially since neither she nor Caleb knew for sure whether the smudges he'd spotted on the back door had even belonged to a demon.

She supposed that was another annoying thing about the hellish creatures. Once you'd admitted the truth of their existence, it was almost impossible not to start seeing them everywhere.

Sort of like cockroaches.

But there was Marcy, coming by to snag the penultimate snickerdoodle.

"I probably shouldn't," she said, even as she placed the cookie on a napkin and broke off a piece. "But I didn't have any lunch today, and I'm just famished!" After consuming the bite-sized morsel, she added, "Did you make them?"

"Oh, no," Delia replied at once. "I'm not much of a baker. There's a great bakery just a few blocks from my office—Short and Sweet. That's where I get all of my goodies."

"And you always have the tastiest treats," Marcy said. "I'll have to check that out. I've been trying to make my own things for my open houses, but it's just so much work that I think I'd be better off grabbing something from a bakery instead." Another bite, and she went on, "I have a buyer who I think will be perfect for this house. Is it all right if I bring them by tomorrow?"

For all her outward flightiness, Marcy was an excellent real estate agent and very good at matching houses to clients. If she had someone she thought was a good fit for Caleb's former home, then it might be a done deal. And thank God for that. Delia had the feeling that the sooner they unloaded the place, the better. "Whenever you like. I'll be putting the lockbox on after the open house today."

"Then I'll look up the code on the MLS some-time tomorrow. Thanks again for the cookies!"

And Marcy headed out, breaking off another piece of her snickerdoodle as she went.

Only one left—both in terms of the cookies and the agents who'd been looking at the house. Delia was sorely tempted to wrap up that final cookie and put it in the bag from the bakery so she could take it home, but professional courtesy told her she needed to leave it on the platter while Aaron was still here. If he didn't scoop it up, then she could safely consider it hers.

He came back downstairs as she was straightening the flyers on the kitchen island, more out of a desire to look as if she was doing something than because they'd actually gotten shifted out of place.

"The upstairs bedrooms are really nice-sized," he said as he approached her. "That was something I wanted to check on, since it's one of the hardest things to tell when you're just looking at a picture."

"Your client has children?" Delia asked, knowing she needed to remain polite and professional, even though now it was almost a quarter to six and she just wanted to get the hell out of there.

Aaron nodded. "Two. And she works from home half the time, so being able to use the extra bedroom as an office is a real selling point." His gaze moved from her to the one remaining cookie on the platter. "Mind if I take that?"

Delia repressed an inner sigh. "Not at all," she replied, even as she told herself she didn't need the calories, especially since she was meeting Caleb at Battista's. "Saves me having to pack it up."

It wasn't as if she couldn't order a cannoli after dinner if she needed to satisfy her sweet tooth.

"Thanks," Aaron said, then picked up the cookie and a napkin. "Anyway," he went on after he'd taken a large bite, "I have a feeling my client will probably want to see the house sometime tomorrow."

"It'll be ready," Delia said. "Like I just told Marcy, I'm going to put on the lockbox as I'm leaving tonight, so the house will be available to be shown whenever you like."

His eyes narrowed slightly. "Marcy, huh."

His tone wasn't too thrilled, and Delia could see why. Marcy Talbott had been selling houses in Las Vegas for a long time, and he had every reason to be concerned that she was going to beat him to the punch on this one.

Which was just the way it worked. Real estate was all about timing.

And location, and money, and a whole lot of other things, but if someone got ahead of you in the queue, there wasn't a whole lot you could do about it.

"But I don't know when she's going to show the place," Delia said, doing her best to sound cheerful and upbeat, and to give Aaron some hope that he hadn't been outmaneuvered yet. "So maybe you'll want to see if your client is available to come look at it during their lunch break."

His expression brightened at once. "That's a good idea," he replied. "I'll text her and see what she thinks." Another two bites, and the cookie was gone. He wiped his hands on the napkin, then tossed it into the stainless steel trash can discreetly placed under the island's overhang. Now looking almost diffident, he said, "Any dinner plans?"

One of the more oblique ways of asking a person out, Delia supposed, but she still couldn't view the question as anything other than an invitation to a date.

Luckily, she had the perfect excuse ready—and it wasn't even a lie.

"Actually, yes," she said. "I'm meeting a friend for dinner." A glance at her watch, and she added, "And I need to start closing things up if I don't want to be late."

At least Aaron was perceptive enough to recognize her comment for what it was. "Of course," he said quickly. "Then I'll get out of your way. And I'll let you know if I'm going to come by with my client tomorrow."

"Sounds great."

He headed out, and she emptied the crumbs off the wooden platter she'd used to serve the cookies before slipping it into the tote bag she'd brought it in. With that taken care of—and after using a damp paper towel to wipe away the few crumbs that had escaped—she went upstairs to make sure nothing had been disturbed and no one had left anything behind.

However, everything looked just as neat and tidy as it had been when she opened up the house a few hours earlier, so she descended the stairs, performed the same visual survey of the lower floor, and had the place closed up and the lockbox installed about ten minutes after six o'clock. That would give her barely enough time to get to the restaurant, but she wasn't too worried. If Caleb arrived before she did, she knew she could trust him to get a table—or put their name on the hostess list if it turned out there was a wait.

Hopefully not, though. It was still a little early for people to be going out to dinner, and even on weeknights, people tended to eat later unless they were seniors who wanted to get their buffet discounts and head home before *Celebrity Jeopardy* was on.

Traffic had probably died down a little from its peak right after five, but enough cars packed the roads that Delia guessed she'd be at least a couple of minutes late. Not much she could do about it now; Caleb knew she was coming straight to the restaurant from her open house, and obviously, she couldn't have left until everyone was gone.

Luckily, there were plenty of open spots in the parking lot, confirming her suspicion that most people wouldn't be venturing out to dine until a little later. When she came into the restaurant, she spied Caleb's shaggy, dark blond head at one of the booths, so she murmured to the hostess that she was meeting someone and hurried over there.

"Sorry I'm late," she said, knowing she sounded breathless as she slid into the booth. "Traffic was worse than I thought it would be."

"It's fine," he replied. "I just got here a couple of minutes ago."

He looked cheerful and relaxed, wearing his usual black leather jacket over a dark green button-up shirt. Most of the time, he wore tees or henleys, so she guessed the dress shirt was a nod to the poker tournament.

"How'd it go?" she asked, although the expression he wore was a pretty good indication that his luck had held.

"I'm going on to the next round of eliminations tomorrow," he said and paused, since a waitress had just approached them and asked if they wanted any appetizers.

They both declined and then picked up their menus after she'd departed, promising them the glass of chianti that came with all the meals here.

"Still no hanky-panky?" Delia asked, not quite suppressing a smile.

She'd expected him to grin back at her. Instead, his expression sobered abruptly.

"You didn't," she said, her tone flat, and at once he shook his head.

"I absolutely did not," he returned. "But I'm kind of worried someone else did."

For a moment, she only stared at him. "What?"

His mouth opened as if he intended to reply, but the waitress came back then with their glasses of wine and asked what they wanted to order. Delia stepped in, since she figured she knew the menu better than he did, and ordering first would give him a chance to quickly scan it and decide what he wanted to eat.

"Pasta carbonara, please, and a side salad with balsamic vinaigrette," she said as she handed over her menu.

The waitress made a notation on her notepad. "And you, sir?"

"The same," he replied, a bit of that devilish glint back in his dark eyes.

Another note, and the waitress took Caleb's menu and headed back to the kitchen.

Once she was safely gone, Delia said, "So... someone else at the tournament is a demon?"

He might have winced a little at the "also," and she realized that had been kind of tactless. Yes, Caleb had demon blood running through his veins, but far more of him was as human as she was.

"I'm not sure," he said. "I could have sworn one of the guys playing at my table was using some kind of magic to influence his cards, but he didn't win, so maybe I was imagining the whole thing."

Delia had scolded herself today for seeing things that most likely weren't even there, so she could relate. On the other hand, Caleb wasn't the sort of person who manufactured that kind of stuff out of thin air. If he thought he'd seen something, then he probably had.

"Did you sense anything off about the guy?" she asked as she reached for her glass of chianti, and immediately, Caleb shook his head.

"Not a damn thing. That's part of the reason why I was so startled to see that weird shimmer around his cards."

No, that probably wasn't normal behavior for a pack of playing cards. "Did anyone else notice?"

At once, he said, "Not that I could tell. And usually, I can get at least a whiff of sulfur from a demon—metaphorically speaking, anyway—when I'm close enough to one. This guy seemed utterly human."

"Could he be a part demon like you?"

It seemed Caleb didn't much like that idea, because his brows drew together and he picked up his glass of chianti and took a sip. "Doubtful. As far as I know, our community in Greencastle was the only one like it in the world."

"But you don't know for sure," she pressed, and his shoulders lifted.

"No, I don't. It doesn't seem very likely, though. Ours was...a special case."

Delia supposed that was one way of looking at it. From what Caleb had told her, the demon lord Belial had been summoned to this plane and then took over the body and spirit of the very person who'd summoned him, a man named Jeffrey Whitcomb. During his time on earth, Belial had brought his lieutenants here and had them pass themselves off as human, marrying mortal women and having half-demon sons who in turn went on to have a generation of quarter demons, Caleb's group. The original demons had returned to Hell at some point, and the half demons had all been banished during a confrontation with a group of demon hunters back in California, with only Caleb managing to escape after several years of captivity on that other plane.

Knowing all that, Delia could see why he didn't believe there were any other colonies of demons or part demons in the world. Yes, they came here to wreak havoc or go slumming or however you wanted to look at it, but they never stayed long.

However....

"Just because it doesn't seem likely doesn't mean it might not be true," she pointed out, and now Caleb looked almost pained.

"I suppose. I mean, sure, the possibility has crossed my mind from time to time. But it could also be that this is just a regular demon masquerading as human, one that has some way to hide its nature from someone like me."

"Is that a thing?" Delia asked, and again he shrugged.

"I don't know for sure. My father didn't explain very much about the demon world. He told me about my powers and how to use them, but the rest of it he sort of pushed aside, as if he thought I was going to be living here and not in Hell, so there wasn't any reason for me to know about most of that stuff."

Kind of short-sighted of him, but she'd been able to read between the lines and guess that Caleb's father hadn't exactly been a candidate for one of those "World's Best Dad" mugs. All the same, you'd think he would have passed along at least a few tidbits of useful information to his son, just in case some contingencies became a reality.

"Any way to find out if it *is* a 'thing'?" she asked.

Caleb let out a breath and swallowed some more chianti. At the rate he was going, he'd definitely need to order another glass.

Not that she could really blame him.

"As far as I know, not really," he replied. "It's not as if there's a hotline I can call to get the skinny on all things demon. But at least now I know to be on my guard."

Both of them already had been, thanks to the mysterious smudges they'd found at his former house. However, this felt different.

"You still beat him, though, right?" she said.

Caleb's chin lifted, and he didn't look quite as

deflated as he had a moment earlier. "I sure did," he responded. "So even if he was a demon in disguise, he's out of the tournament. I suppose he can still hang around and cause trouble as a spectator if he really wanted to, but he won't be playing."

Well, that was something. She had to wait to reply because the waitress returned with their food and a basket of garlic bread. Most of the time, Delia tried to watch her carbs, but she wasn't about to do something so foolish while having dinner at an Italian restaurant.

They murmured their thanks to their server, and once they'd both helped themselves to some bread and eaten a few bites of their pasta carbonara, Caleb added, "I didn't see or feel anything else out of the ordinary, though, so with Ty sidelined, maybe this will turn out to be nothing."

"'Ty'?" Delia repeated. "That's the guy's name?"

"Yeah, Ty Carter." Caleb bit off some garlic bread, chewed, and then said in musing tones, "Maybe what I saw wasn't demonic at all. Maybe it was some other kind of magic."

She lifted an eyebrow. Since she'd already been forced to acknowledge that demons were real, it would be a little disingenuous to claim that magic wasn't real. "How many kinds are there?"

"I'm not sure." He swallowed the rest of his

wine and looked regretful that he hadn't asked the waitress to bring him another glass. However, she must have had eagle eyes, because almost immediately she returned to their table and inquired if he would like a second round.

He said he would, and their server looked over at Delia. However, since she'd been nursing her glass and had no intention of having another one, not when she had to go into the office early tomorrow morning to accommodate a client of her mother's who couldn't go see a house at any other time, she only said, "I'm fine. Thank you."

Once the waitress had departed, Caleb went on, "I knew a woman in California whose family could use magic. Mostly psychic kind of stuff, but they all were capable of much more, thanks to how their father was an angel."

By that point, Delia honestly didn't think she could be surprised by much of anything, but she felt her eyes widening all the same. "An angel?"

Caleb grinned, looking much more like his old self. "Does that shock you? I mean, why not? Is the concept that different from demons interbreeding with humans?"

At its core, maybe not. But demons seemed like pretty down-and-dirty creatures, and she could much more easily imagine them getting it on with human women than she could see an angel doing the same thing.

She gave a helpless lift of her shoulders, and he smiled again.

"It's probably less common," he said. "But it's not impossible. So I suppose I could see that if someone had angelic blood that had been passed down, they might have their own particular brand of magic in their bag of tricks. If nothing else, it would explain why Ty was using magic even though I couldn't sense anything demonic about him."

Even if that were true, it sort of begged the question as to why someone who was descended from angels would be playing in an off-brand poker tournament in one of Las Vegas's third-tier casinos.

That was a question she would leave for another day, though. Right now, she supposed the most important thing was that whatever kind of mischief the other player had been up to, it still hadn't been sufficient to keep Caleb from triumphing...or from moving on to the next round.

Thinking it was time to change the subject, she told him about the open house and how at least two of the brokers who'd attended had clients who would probably want to look at the house tomorrow. He seemed pleased by that, and if he'd noticed how she'd pivoted from their discussion of part angels and part demons, he clearly didn't want to mention it.

He paid the check, which she'd guessed he

would do. In the beginning, she would have tried to argue with him and say that she should at least pick up part of the tab, but now she knew to just roll with it. While she did perfectly fine for herself, she wasn't swimming in money like he was, and if he wanted to be all magnanimous, she might as well let him.

They went outside, and he pulled a fob out of his pocket. Immediately, a flashy Porsche cabriolet in an unusual shade of pale metallic green flashed its lights, and she sent him an amused glance.

"New toy?"

"Yep," he said. "Just picked her up yesterday. I thought maybe the demons knew what I drove, so it just made sense to get a set of alternate wheels."

True, the Porsche was almost the polar opposite of his Range Rover...except for the price tag, she supposed.

"I'm not sure that's the most inconspicuous car in the world," she observed, and he only chuckled.

"I know. But I've already discovered that when I'm driving it, everyone's looking at the car and not me."

Delia hadn't considered the situation from that angle. Deep down, she might have admitted to herself that if she saw Caleb driving down the street in that Porsche, she still would have paid more attention to him than the vehicle, but no way in the world would she ever say something like that to his face.

His ego didn't need the boost.

No, she only said, "I suppose I can see that."

Voice a little too casual, he asked, "So...do you have a lot of appointments tomorrow? It might be fun to have you come watch the tournament if you're not too busy."

"I'm pretty much booked all day," she replied. Disappointment flickered across his face, and she hastened to add, "But Saturday's looking pretty clear right now. What time are you playing?"

"The final round of eliminations starts at three," he said. A corner of his mouth lifted. "So does this mean you think I'm going to make it through tomorrow's round?"

"Absolutely."

"Then I'll take that vote of confidence with me —and I'll text you to let you know how it all went."

She offered him a smile, and they said their goodbyes and headed to their respective vehicles. He was the first to pull out of his parking space, the sage green Porsche zooming away down Fremont Street with an aggressive rumble.

About all Delia could do was shake her head. Whatever she might have wanted to say on the subject of Caleb Lockwood, she had to admit he never did anything by half measures.

And she kind of had to respect him for that.

Chapter Six

—·‹‹‹·✧·›››·—

LUCKILY, CALEB KNEW HE DIDN'T HAVE TO go straight home from Battista's. No, after that day's play, Hank Bowers had approached him and said a group of the players would be getting together for drinks at one of the lounges at the Desert Paradise, and while Caleb had been noncommittal because he wasn't sure how late dinner with Delia was going to be, he realized now he had plenty of time to get over there. Sure, he'd already had two glasses of wine with dinner, but he'd eaten plenty, and besides, the demon blood running through his veins guaranteed that he could drink enough to knock out a moose and not suffer too many ill effects.

Not that he planned to get anywhere close to that drunk. Although this sounded like a friendly gathering, he couldn't forget that the other people attending were his fellow competitors. The last thing in the world he wanted to do was give them any kind of an advantage, even if it was something as minor as seeing what he was like when he'd had a few too many. The competition didn't allow drinking at the gaming tables, but there wasn't any reason why someone couldn't still get boozed up beforehand.

When he pulled into the parking lot at the Desert Paradise, it looked about as full as it had been when the tournament was going on. Made some sense—while everyone watching the players compete might have left, they would have been replaced by the regular crowds who liked gambling on a weeknight rather than sitting at home and watching TV.

This was a casual get-together, so no signs had been posted. However, Hank had already told him the gathering was being held in the Oasis Lounge, and it wasn't too hard to take a quick look at the directory just inside the lobby and weave his way through the slot machines and back to the bar in question.

It was a kitschy kind of space, with lots of fake palm trees and a palm-leaf motif woven into the close-pile carpet underfoot. About twenty or so people were gathered there, including a few who Caleb knew hadn't advanced to play again tomorrow. It appeared that Hank had invited all the competitors, not just those who'd survived the first round.

A brief scan told Caleb that Ty Carter was nowhere in evidence, though. Sour grapes, or was he just worried that being close to that many people in a social gathering might give something away about his true nature?

Hard to say. Or it could be something else entirely. After all, the group hanging out in the lounge was nowhere near the number of those who'd played in the opening round of the tournament, so it seemed as if quite a few others weren't up to socializing tonight, either.

He didn't have time for any further speculation, since Hank approached, a pint glass in one hand, even as he extended the other. "Good job, Caleb," he said with a smile. "Not bad for the first day of your first tournament."

"I think I was just lucky," Caleb replied, but Hank just shook his head.

"We all know there's more to poker than mere luck."

True. He'd gotten some decent cards, but if he hadn't known what to do with them, he wouldn't be playing in the next round tomorrow.

And he'd done it under his own power, too. For some reason, that was the element of his victory that mattered the most to him. While he'd definitely use his demonic talents to get himself out of a sticky situation if necessary, it still felt good to know he could be successful being just a regular human being.

"Go ahead and get a drink," Hank said. "It's not an open bar, unfortunately, but the casino's giving us all ten percent off anything we drink tonight."

Such a deal, Caleb thought wryly, especially since the Oasis Lounge probably wouldn't have seen this much business on a Thursday night if the group from the poker tournament hadn't gathered here.

But he only thanked Hank for the information and headed over to the bar, where he ordered a glass of merlot. While beer or mixed drinks seemed more appropriate for this gathering, he'd started the evening by drinking wine and figured it probably wasn't a good idea to switch now.

Glass of wine in hand, he wandered the room, meeting the other competitors—none of whom pinged his demonic radar at all, which seemed to tell him that Ty had been a one-off—taking their measure. Put together, they seemed like a pretty ordinary group of people, although with more men present than women. Caleb didn't find that too surprising; while women players were becoming more common on the professional poker circuit, they were still far outnumbered by the male half of the population.

Not that there was anything about this group which indicated they were anywhere close to professional poker players. No, they were skilled amateurs who were looking to hopefully win the purse and put it toward a new car or a vacation or maybe improvements on their house, accountants and public relations executives, doctors and lawyers and small businesspeople.

Still, he found it valuable to chat with each of them and take their measure, even as he knew they were doing exactly the same thing with him. Caleb wasn't too bothered by that, especially since he knew he was very good at hiding his tells. Whatever they were looking for, they weren't going to find it.

He was glad he had come, though, if only because stopping by Hank's little get-together meant he hadn't been forced to go home to an empty house right after his dinner with Delia. Although he understood that it was a work night—and it sounded as if she had an early client and a full day tomorrow—he still thought it might have been nice to go back to his place and have a nightcap and chat.

Well, except for the part where he didn't have any booze suitable for post-dinner drinking, thanks to the way he'd been forced to leave his old house.

Maybe that was being a little disingenuous. He could have grabbed his bottles of brandy and whisky, but he'd deemed other items more important, since the liquor he had on hand wasn't anything special, just stuff he'd picked up on one of his trips to Total Wine.

He'd need to remedy that lack, though. If nothing else, it would be good to have a bit of the stronger stuff on hand just in case he crashed and burned in the next round tomorrow.

And while he learned that a player named Eli Whitaker had a left eye that twitched a little when he got excited about something and another one—Colin Jackson—reached up to smooth his hair if he was embellishing a story, Caleb was just fine with going home about an hour later, thinking he'd put in enough face time and realizing it had been kind of a long day.

Guess that happens when you pass thirty, he thought wryly as he walked out to his car. That momentous birthday had come and gone while he was trapped in Hell, but another birthday was heading his way again this summer.

Maybe by then he would know enough people in this town whom he could count as acquaintances that he could have some kind of party. His new house was practically built for entertaining, and it would be fun to fill it with friends.

Well, probably not friend, friends, except for Delia Dunne.

When Caleb got to his car, he looked all around for anything suspicious, but this part of the parking lot was empty, brightly illuminated by the light poles installed at strategic intervals across the stretch of asphalt. No sight or smell of demons lurking nearby, no one at all, not even someone weaving toward their vehicle after too much blackjack and booze.

Maybe, as Delia had once said, he really was jumping at shadows.

There definitely didn't seem to be anything here.

A lift of his shoulders, and then he climbed inside the Porsche and touched the ignition button. He'd already put up the roof before he went inside the casino, figuring he didn't want to leave his new car wide open and unattended like that. Yes, he'd seen a lone security guard slowly making the rounds of the parking lot in a golf cart as he headed inside an hour earlier, but he didn't know how much good the guy would have done in an actual emergency.

But there hadn't been an incident. All the same, Caleb wasn't about to let down his guard. If he'd learned anything over the past couple of years —ever since the *Project Demon Hunters* crew had entered his life—it was to take nothing for granted.

Delia knew she should have put her feet up when she got home and just watched some TV. It had been a long day, and, with any luck, her broker's open house would end up producing at least one interested buyer and a quick sale.

But after she'd taken off her heels and slipped into some yoga pants, flip-flops, and a beloved baggy T-shirt, she found herself too restless to sit down on the couch and find something that wouldn't engage her brain too much, whether another of an endless lineup of home improvement shows on HGTV or maybe a sitcom...preferably one she'd already seen before so she wouldn't have to pay too much attention.

Instead, she wandered into her office and woke her big iMac out of its sleep. A few months ago, when she and Caleb had first stumbled across The Styx Group, she'd done her own investigating...and later on, had asked her friend Prudence to look into the company as well.

But even Pru's vastly superior sleuthing skills hadn't unearthed anything out of the ordinary, so Delia had let it slide. She'd been busy with work and helping Caleb with the renovation, and because everything had seemed peaceful again, there hadn't seemed to be much reason to keep digging.

Maybe they'd have better luck investigating Aegis Holdings. She hadn't heard anything from

Evan Matthews, and it sure sounded as if one of the buyers represented by Marcy Talbott or Aaron Sanchez had a better chance of stepping in and scooping up the place, but she figured it couldn't hurt to do a little looking around just in case Aegis came out the winner in a bidding war or something.

Rather than waste time with her own fumbling efforts, though, she just opened the Messenger app on her computer. It was a weeknight, so Delia supposed there was a chance Pru might be out, but since she didn't seem to be seeing anyone at the moment, much more likely that she was at home.

Sure enough, she responded almost immediately to Delia's, *You there?*

Yeah, I'm here. What's up?

Not much. Or maybe something. I had a guy from a company called Aegis Holdings tour one of my properties this week. Sounds like he wants to turn it into a vacation rental. Can you try looking them up and letting me know if you find anything?

Sure. Just give me a couple of minutes.

Thanks.

In Pru-speak, "a couple of minutes" could mean anything from just one or two all the way up to a half hour, depending on how elusive the information she was seeking turned out to be. To amuse herself, Delia bopped around on a couple of different websites, adding a cute pair of sandals to her wish list over on Zappos, dipping into the MLS to see if anything interesting had popped up since the last time she'd checked.

About fifteen minutes later, Pru came back online.

I couldn't find much. It looks like the company was incorporated about ten years ago. Based in California.

Of course, Delia already knew that because Evan Matthews had come right out and told her the company was located in Santa Monica.

Anything else?

It looks like they run targeted ads on Facebook and other places aimed at people who are upside down in their homes and need to get out. I guess then they go in and scoop them up and turn them into vacation rentals.

A distasteful practice, taking advantage of people who were already feeling desperate, but there wasn't anything technically illegal about it.

Do they manage the properties themselves?

Delia couldn't see her friend—although their last get-together had revealed that Prudence had tired of her turquoise blue hair and had switched it over to a gorgeous ombre of deep purple to pale lavender on the ends, which just brushed her collarbones—but she had a feeling Pru's dark eyes had lit up with excitement right then.

That's the interesting thing. I dug around and

found out that they hire people to manage all their vacation homes—maybe one person handling three here, and another taking care of four in a different location. All of them are superhosts on Airbnb, and the listings are written carefully to make it sound as if they're the owners, and not some big property acquisition and management company.

Again, nothing illegal about that. Misleading, sure, because she knew that most of the people who rented those properties wanted to believe they were working directly with the owners.

But adding a layer of obfuscation made it much less likely that Aegis would have to deal with any direct complaints from their temporary tenants while at the same time raking in money hand over fist.

Any idea what they pay their rental managers?

Not really. They don't have an employment page on their website or anything like that. But I can look into it if you want.

Delia had asked the question mostly because she was curious and nothing more. On the other hand, it couldn't hurt to get a little more insight into Aegis's business model, if only because she could present that information to Caleb in case he got multiple offers. Most people who didn't know him would have probably said that he'd just go for the best one without caring who had made it, but she knew he didn't operate that way. Yes, he wanted to make some money from the deal, but she had a feeling he would much rather sell to someone who wanted to move into the house with their family, rather than some faceless corporation that would turn it into a vacation rental, a company that quite possibly exploited its workers.

Of course, she didn't know that for sure. However, Evan Matthews certainly looked as if he was doing quite well for himself, and if his chunky salary came at the expense of the people who did the actual work for Aegis?

She got the feeling he wouldn't lose much sleep over it.

Sure. And anything else you can find out about them. I suppose they're just another company operating in a morally gray area, but it can't hurt to know as much as possible.

Just in case Evan got the winning bid on Caleb's house after all.

She found herself wondering why Aegis was even interested in the property. True, it was a very nice house, one that didn't need any work at all and was move-in ready, but still, if they sponsored a bunch of ads aimed at underwater homeowners, it seemed as if they must do a lot of their business with bargain-basement kind of stuff, which Caleb's former home definitely was not. Maybe it wasn't priced at the top of the market, and yet it still represented a place that would need to pull in a decent chunk of rental income every month to justify paying so much.

Well, Delia had to admit that she didn't know a huge amount about the short-term rental market. She'd had a couple of buyers who'd purchased a house through her for that express purpose, but it wasn't as if they'd gone into any great detail about what they planned to charge or what all their operating costs might be.

Pru's response came back after a moment.

Working on it...around all my cheating husbands and the other fun stuff.

Because unfortunately, a lot of Pru's business tended to involve surveilling spouses to get the dirt on their extracurricular activities. Nevada was a no-fault divorce state, and no one needed to prove their partner had been cheating to get a divorce, but evidence of adultery could affect alimony, so it was still often valuable to gather evidence that someone in the marriage had been straying.

It's not urgent. Just whenever you have time.

That is, Delia hoped their investigation of Aegis's holdings wasn't too urgent. If Marcy and Aaron's supposedly motivated buyers fell through, then maybe she'd end up having to sell the house to Evan Matthews after all.

She supposed it was kind of funny how completely unthrilled she was about the whole situation.

On that Friday afternoon, the parking lot at the Desert Paradise casino was much more crowded than it had been the day before. People getting a jump on the weekend, Caleb supposed, although his usual luck kicked in and he was able to snag a prime parking spot right up front, thanks to someone backing out just as he approached.

He could only hope that kind of luck would continue to hold once he was inside. Sure, he'd made it through the first round relatively unscathed, but now he'd be playing against people who'd won at their tables and therefore, he assumed, would be that much more skilled.

Or just damn lucky, in which case he still needed to be at the top of his game.

Today he didn't need to look at the signs guiding players in, but went immediately to the roped-off area of the gaming floor. Thanks to the lanyard he wore around his neck, he was let in at once and guided to a table where the three other players were waiting. He recognized two of them from the mixer the night before—a middle-aged man named Brad Norton and a guy younger than Caleb, maybe not even twenty-five, whose name was Lonnie Briggs.

The fourth at their table was a coolly attractive brunette with no-nonsense dark eyes and the kind of brisk manner that told him he'd better not try even the most harmless flirting. Not that he'd had any real intention of doing so, not when he couldn't seem to get Delia Dunne out of his mind no matter how hard he tried, but something about the woman—who introduced herself as Sherene Kruger—indicated he would have been shot down immediately even if he'd been so inclined.

Today, the crowds beyond the velvet rope were proportionally larger than they'd been the day before, but Caleb wouldn't let all those watching eyes get to him. No, he had to keep his eyes on the prize...not to win, necessarily, but to get as far as he could in the tournament without using any of his powers.

Not for the first time, he wished Delia could be here, even though he knew she had plenty to keep her busy this afternoon. He'd just have to comfort himself with the knowledge that she'd promised to come watch the tournament tomorrow, when she would finally be free of all her responsibilities at the office.

Everyone had taken their seats, so the dealers fanned out to the various tables, somewhat reduced from the day before, thanks to all those players who'd already been eliminated. Caleb allowed himself an inner breath, hoping it would help steady him for the upcoming play. No way to know for sure whether there would be any more possible magical intervention today, or whether—now that Ty Carter had been knocked out—everything would run smoothly.

Today's dealer was a silver-haired man who handled the cards with practiced efficiency, although without quite the same flair that yesterday's dealer had shown. Caleb found himself in the middle position, with Brad Norton on his left and Sherene to his right. That positioning could work to his advantage...provided he played it smart.

Then again, that was exactly what he'd come here to do.

The first few hands were cautious affairs, with everyone feeling each other out, trying to get a sense of their various strengths and weaknesses. Sherene won a small amount of chips with a pair of queens, while Lonnie managed to take the minimum bets twice with aggressive early betting before anyone saw the community cards. Standard tournament poker behavior, but something about Brad Norton's steady gaze made Caleb's demon senses tingle.

He looked down at his pocket jacks—not aces or kings, sure, but still strong enough to play. Deciding to go for it, he called Lonnie's initial raise, watching carefully as Brad Norton's eyes seemed to gleam with an unnatural amber glow for just a fraction of a second.

It could have been a trick of the lighting... or not.

Sherene folded, muttering something under her breath about garbage cards.

Then the flop came out: jack of diamonds, seven of clubs, seven of hearts.

Now Caleb had a full house. A strong hand, nearly unbeatable. Lonnie bet half the pot—a move that could have meant he was maybe sitting on pocket aces...or complete air and was just trying to bluff his way through this thing. Brad Norton called almost immediately, that strange gleam flickering in his eyes again.

Caleb's demon blood stirred, recognizing that some kind of magic was at work, even as he fought to ignore the sensation. This was exactly the kind of situation where he would have used his powers in the past—just a little peek at his opponents' hands, just enough to know whether to push all in or make a strategic retreat.

But no. He'd promised himself. He had to trust his reading of the situation, his instincts, his understanding of the game.

He called.

The turn brought the ace of spades. Lonnie checked this time, showing the first crack in his aggressive façade...and letting Caleb know that he probably wasn't sitting on as many aces as he'd feared. Brad Norton bet big, nearly half his remaining chips. The move screamed strength, but at the same time, there was something almost artificial about it, something off that again made Caleb's supernatural radar ping.

From the rail, someone coughed, and Caleb caught a glimpse of an older man with iron-gray hair watching Brad with particular intensity. A handler, maybe? Someone helping to channel or focus whatever power Brad was using?

The pot was massive now, and Caleb had to make a decision. His full house was strong, but if Brad had hit that ace....

No. The magic he was sensing wasn't about the cards themselves, the kind of manipulation he would have employed if he were using his demon powers to win. No, this was subtler than that— some kind of influence over people's emotions, maybe? Something that would make other players more likely to fold when Brad wanted them to?

Well, two could play at that game. Or rather, one wouldn't play at that game at all.

Caleb pushed his chips forward, doing his best to fight back the grin that wanted to spread across his mouth. "All in."

Lonnie folded immediately, but Brad's face twisted into something that, for just a moment, looked barely human. Then the mask slipped back in place, and he called with an almost mechanical precision.

"Jack-ten of diamonds," he announced, turning over his cards. A strong hand with a flush draw, but not strong enough.

Caleb showed his two face-down cards, which were both jacks, and watched as the final community card dealt was a two of clubs, which didn't help anyone's hand. He'd won the hand straight up, no powers needed—even as he couldn't help wondering if Brad's supernatural assistance had actually worked against him this time, making him overconfident when he should have folded to Caleb's all-in move.

As Brad got up from the table, the older man Caleb had noticed earlier slipped away from the velvet rope, disappearing into the crowd. Brad's gaze followed him, and Caleb caught a glimpse of something like relief in the other man's expression —as if a weight had been lifted...or a connection severed.

"Nice hand," Sherene said crisply, already focused on the next deal.

"Thanks," Caleb replied as he stacked his newly won chips. He was one step closer to the finals now, and he'd gotten there entirely on his own merits.

Well, his own merits...plus a little help from someone else's overconfidence in their supernatural edge.

Lonnie was eyeing him with new respect, but

Caleb kept his expression neutral. There would be time to celebrate later. Right now, he had to focus on maintaining this momentum—and keeping an eye out for any other supernatural players who might be lurking in the tournament.

After all, if two of his opponents so far had been using magic, who knew what he might face tomorrow?

The idea sent a stir of unease through him, but he knew he had to stay cool, no matter what.

With Brad gone, the rest of that evening's play went smoothly. Something of an air of unreality descended as he realized he'd survived today's round and would be going on to the final round of eliminations tomorrow.

Which meant Delia would be there to watch him play.

After accepting congratulations from the players he'd bested—and the others who would be playing tomorrow—he sauntered out to the parking lot, whistling as he went. Because he'd been able to park so close, he didn't have to walk very far, and soon was inside his Porsche and heading for home.

Just as there had been many more people attending the tournament tonight, a lot more cars choked the roads as well. Under different circumstances, he might have cursed under his breath at all the clueless drivers with out-of-state plates, but now he just wanted to get home so he could call Delia and tell her the good news. True, he could have called while he was driving, but the traffic was just gnarly enough that he thought it better to keep his eyes on the road.

Good thing, because just as he was approaching an intersection, the light turned yellow, and his foot instinctively went to the brake pedal.

Except nothing happened.

Correction—something happened, just not the outcome he'd expected.

The pedal went straight to the floor, but his Porsche kept barreling toward the intersection without the slightest hesitation.

Shit.

The cars that had been waiting for their light to turn green were already beginning to move forward. Luckily, no one seemed to have floored it, which meant he had a small opening.

A *very* small opening.

He'd already lifted his foot off the gas, so the Cabriolet had begun to slow ever so slightly. Maybe that would be enough.

Even with its brakes malfunctioning, the Porsche had been designed to hug the road on curves and turns, and Caleb took advantage of its low-slung proportions to whip the vehicle to the left to avoid someone in a Prius who'd jumped the gun on his right, and then mirror that maneuver to prevent himself from slamming into a minivan that shouldn't have been nearly so gung ho. Tires squealed and smoke billowed everywhere, but he didn't hit anything.

No, somehow he managed to make it to the other side of the intersection, the Porsche slowing with every foot until he managed to drift it over to the curb, where he promptly put it in park and then sat there for a moment, adrenaline screaming along every nerve ending and his heartbeat a rapid, frightened pounding in his chest.

Some part of him wondered if the car would start up again, if it was truly possessed, but that didn't seem to be the case. No, it just sat there, one hundred and fifty thousand bucks' worth of heart-attack-inducing steel.

Caleb swallowed, then pulled out his phone and looked up the number for Triple-A. He didn't know what the hell had just happened, but he knew he wasn't getting behind the wheel of the Cabriolet again until he'd had it inspected from top to bottom.

That had been *way* too close.

Chapter Seven

—·‹‹(·☾·)››·—

SOMEONE RANG THE DOORBELL A LITTLE after six, and Delia frowned. She knew she wasn't expecting anyone, and since her neighborhood had "No Soliciting" signs posted everywhere, she didn't get many random callers.

Heels clicking, she went to the front door. She'd had a late showing at five and had just gotten home, and hadn't had time to change out of her work clothes.

Let it be a couple of Girl Scouts and not some Seventh-Day Adventists, she thought. Although she tried not to keep too many sweets in the house, she made an exception for Thin Mints and Samoas.

But it wasn't girls trying to sell cookies or missionaries attempting to pass out religious tracts. No, that was Caleb Lockwood standing on the doorstep, looking wrung out.

"What happened?" she asked, even as she stepped out of the way to let him inside.

Even though his face was much paler than normal, he still flashed her his usual insouciant grin. "I look that bad, huh?"

Delia couldn't help smiling in return. "Well, let's just say that I've seen you look better."

He ran a hand through his shaggy, dark blond hair, mussing it that much more. However, it just made him look rakish rather than rumpled, which she guessed had been the desired effect.

"The brakes on my new Porsche just failed."

That was about the last thing she'd been expecting him to say. "*What?*"

His smile didn't fade. "Pretty much my reaction. Somehow, I managed to get through the intersection without smashing into anyone. I suppose if the whole house-flipping thing doesn't work out, I can always try for a career in NASCAR racing or something."

Somehow, she doubted the Porsche's brakes had given out spontaneously...and, if the suddenly sober look Caleb now wore was any indication, he didn't believe that for a second, either.

"Go ahead and sit down," she said. "Want a drink?"

"I'd kill for one."

Now she couldn't help smiling. "I'm pretty sure murder won't be necessary."

While he took a seat on the living room couch, she headed into the kitchen and got down two wine glasses, then pulled the cork out of a bottle of red she'd had open for a day or so and poured the remaining wine into the glasses.

One of them was a little fuller than the other, so she gave that glass to Caleb before she took a seat in the accent chair to his right. "I'm glad you're okay."

"Oh, I'm fine," he said at once, then swallowed some of his wine. "I called a tow truck and had the Porsche towed to the dealership. The service department had already closed for the day, but the guy who sold me the car was still there, and he assured me they'd look at it first thing in the morning."

Delia drank some wine as well. "Do you really think they're going to find anything?"

Dark eyes glinted at her. "Are you implying there's some kind of demonic intervention going on?"

"It was my first thought, yes," she said.

Caleb eased himself backward on the couch, then pulled in a breath. "Maybe. Probably. I don't know. I mean, the car was sitting in the casino parking lot unattended the whole time I was inside playing, so I suppose it wouldn't have been too hard for someone to come along and mess with the brake lines."

Delia couldn't think of too many people who'd be bold enough to tamper with a car as conspicuous as his Porsche in broad daylight like that, especially in such a public place. Voice dubious, she said, "Doesn't the casino have any security out in the parking lot?"

"Oh, sure," Caleb replied, and then gave a derisive chuckle. "But the guy I saw would probably be as useless as a fart in a hurricane if anything really started to go down."

Despite the gravity of the situation, Delia couldn't help smiling at that comparison. "Duly noted. But still...."

Caleb swallowed some more wine, then said, "If it was the demons messing with me, then they wouldn't have had to do anything as obvious as slide under the car with a pair of wire cutters or something. I guess now all I can do is wait to see what the mechanics have to say tomorrow morning."

She nodded. "Well, I'm glad you're safe and sound. How'd you get here?"

A grimace. "I took a taxi. I suppose that's how I'll have to get around for a while until I can get all this straightened out. Even then...." He let the words trail off, his expression now sour. "Almost a hundred and fifty grand for that car, and I can't even drive it."

Privately, Delia thought maybe that was a good

thing. It was awfully flashy, and it seemed as though it had already attracted way too much attention.

"Maybe you should get something nice and anonymous, like a silver Honda Accord or something," she suggested, and Caleb made a face that reminded her of a toddler being force-fed a spoonful of peas.

"I'd rather keep taking taxis," he said. "An econobox isn't exactly my style."

Now she allowed herself to chuckle. "My mother has an Accord. It's actually a really nice car. But if you want something a little higher-end, then you could still get yourself a Mercedes or a BMW. There are plenty of those in Vegas, so you'd be a lot harder to track down if you were driving a car like that."

His dubious expression told her he wasn't too thrilled with any of those alternatives, so she decided to let it go for now. It wasn't really worthwhile to start planning for contingencies like that until they knew for sure what had happened to the brakes on his Porsche.

Thinking it might be a good idea to change the subject, she said, "How was the tournament?"

The familiar glint was back in Caleb's warm brown eyes. "'Other than that, Mrs. Lincoln, how did you like the play?'"

Delia couldn't quite stop herself from laughing outright. "Okay, you got me," she replied. "But—"

"Oh, the tournament was fine," he cut in. "I'm moving on to the third elimination round tomorrow."

The words came out sounding almost too casual, so she could tell he was very proud that he'd managed to advance to the next round, especially since he was trying so hard to win without using any of his powers.

"That's awesome," she said, then paused delicately. She probably shouldn't say anything, but she couldn't quite prevent the thought from circulating in her head.

Had he won fair and square, or had he helped things along a little bit?

"Totally on the up and up," he told her, correctly gauging the reason for her hesitation. "No hanky-panky. But once again, it sure felt to me like one of the other players was using some sort of magic to manipulate things."

"Like those shimmery cards you noticed in the first round?" she asked, even as she tried to ignore the sinking sensation in her stomach.

Just how many supernatural beings were hanging around the Desert Paradise casino's poker tournament, anyway?

Caleb shook his head. "No, this felt different. Almost like some kind of mind control, like the guy—or someone he was working with—was trying to make the rest of us fold even if we had the cards to stay in."

This was sounding worse and worse. "You think there was more than one of them?"

A shrug, and Caleb swallowed some more of his wine. "I can't say for sure. I got this weird feeling that the guy playing was in some kind of mental contact with an older man who was with the rest of the spectators, but I don't know. It's possible we're dealing with some sort of possession by proxy here or something like that."

"Is that even a thing?" Delia said. Although she'd learned way more about demons and their behavior over the past couple of months than she'd ever wanted to know, she still understood that there were huge holes in her knowledge of the subject.

"It can be." Caleb set his near-empty glass on a coaster, then settled against the back of the couch once again. "Rather than inhabit a body directly, a demon can cast its influence on the person it wants to control. In a way, it's sort of an insurance policy for the demon, since when it's doing something like that, it can't be exorcised. Technically, it isn't possessing anyone, just making them do what it wants."

Well, that was just lovely. Delia swallowed some of her wine, thinking they were probably going to need more than the remnants of that one bottle to get them through this conversation. "Does that happen very often?"

"No," Caleb replied at once, reassuring her somewhat. "You need a pretty senior demon to do the possessing, and the person it's trying to control needs to be sufficiently weak-minded to allow that kind of control to even happen." He paused there, and a knowing gleam entered his dark eyes. "If you were wondering whether something like that could happen to you, don't worry about it. You're way too strong for a demon to take command of your brain."

Those words made Delia absurdly pleased. Not just because she apparently wouldn't have to worry about some random demon getting its nasty fingers on her mind, but because Caleb thought she was strong...and obviously didn't have a problem with it, unlike a few other men she'd dated.

Not that she was dating Caleb. Their relationship was friendly, nothing more. All the same, she was glad that once again he'd thought to come to her in a moment of crisis. True, it didn't seem as if he had many friends he could turn to, but still, after nearly getting in a car accident, he hadn't gone straight home, had instead dropped by her house, as if he'd known he'd be sure to find a sympathetic ear there.

She gave a neutral nod, then said, "So...what's next?"

"I wait to see what the mechanics at the Porsche dealership have to say," he responded at once. "Luckily, they work a half day on Saturdays, because otherwise, I'd be left hanging until Monday morning before I learned anything. And go back to the tournament and see what happens next, of course."

Well, at least this time, she'd be there to offer moral support. When it came to fighting demons, she couldn't do much except fling holy water and hope for the best, but it was still better than nothing.

She'd make sure to bring one of her larger purses so she could fit plenty of the little vials in there...and hope that security wouldn't inspect her bag too closely.

"Of course," she echoed, and paused. It was getting around the time when she would have started scrounging in the fridge to see what she could put together for dinner, but she kind of doubted that Caleb would be satisfied with a salad and some cold chicken, especially after everything he'd just been through.

And if he didn't want to stay, that was fine, too. But as his friend, she should make the offer.

"Want to get some takeout?" she asked, and he smiled.

"Absolutely."

Delia had offered to drive him home, but Caleb told her that wouldn't be necessary, that he'd just call another taxi. Sure, he could have teleported, and yet he liked the idea of acting like a regular guy and not using his powers to get around. The decision to take a cab seemed to resonate with his vow not to use any demonic abilities in the poker tournament.

But it had been good to spend those couple of hours with her, to sit down with their Chinese takeout and talk about the possibility of selling his old house quickly, or discuss a couple of listings she'd seen pop up on the MLS that might be candidates for flipping. Everything relentlessly normal, as if she understood that he didn't want to dwell on what had happened earlier tonight, the way his shiny new toy had betrayed him out of the blue.

If it was even the car's fault at all. The more he pondered the problem, the more he realized there must have been some kind of tampering involved, whether demonic or just good old-fashioned human mayhem.

But the taxi got him home without incident, and when he went inside the house, Caleb couldn't see any evidence that anyone had tried to come by and mess with the place. It was peaceful and quiet, the air faintly scented with vanilla, thanks to the plug-in fragrance vaporizer near the front door.

Delia's idea, obviously. She'd told him she always liked to smell something friendly when she first walked into a house, and he had to admit that it helped relax him a bit.

They'd opened another bottle of wine with dinner, since neither of them had to worry about driving. Because of that, Caleb didn't bother to pour himself a glass of brandy the way he might otherwise have, but instead went straight out to the backyard so he could get some fresh air to clear his head.

The pool glowed blue-green in the darkness, and the strategically placed landscape lights kept the yard from being too moody and mysterious. To the east, a nearly full moon rose above Frenchman Mountain, warm yellow and somehow friendly, making him feel a little less alone.

Come to think of it, he didn't feel alone at all. Not when he'd just come from Delia's house, where she'd welcomed him in and offered a sympathetic ear—and some much-needed wine.

After all, that was what friends did for each other, wasn't it?

He supposed so. Oh, sure, he'd had friends back in Greencastle...not just the other quarter demons, but people he'd gone to high school and college with...and yet for some reason, none of them had felt as reliable as Delia did. Caleb couldn't even say exactly why, but he somehow knew deep down that even if he showed up in the middle of the night after suffering one crisis or another, she'd still let him in and offer whatever help she could.

More precious than rubies?

In his mind, absolutely.

He went back inside and made sure the big bifold glass door was shut firmly behind him. No, there hadn't been any sign that someone had tried to tamper with the house in his absence, but he hadn't noticed that anyone had messed with the Porsche, either.

Well, not until he'd tried to drive it, anyway.

The faint sense of well-being he'd experienced after going outside evaporated immediately, replaced by a growing feeling of outrage. Bad enough that he could have been seriously injured— that innocent drivers could have been hurt—but to have his brand-new car messed with?

That annoyed the crap out of him.

Unfortunately, unless he was able to pin down the culprit, there wasn't much he could do about the situation. One part of him hoped it had just been a fluke, a one-in-a-million mechanical failure, but he didn't think so.

When demons were in the mix, it was almost always smarter to pin the blame on them.

So, okay. If demons were involved, just what were they trying to accomplish? Revenge for discovering that "Robert Hendricks" hadn't been a man at all and then banishing the demon who'd taken over his body?

Maybe. In general, demons didn't like mortals meddling with their schemes and would retaliate whenever possible.

Still, they'd had the greater part of two months to go after him. Why now? Simply because he'd made himself visible by participating in the Desert Paradise poker tournament?

He supposed that explanation made as much sense as anything else. Still, they were going to discover soon enough that they should have kept their ugly hands to themselves.

That brandy was sure sounding tempting right about now.

But no, he wouldn't indulge himself. His demon blood might have given him a better tolerance for alcohol than any regular human being, and yet, he couldn't see the wisdom in tying one on right now, not when he had no idea when the next attack might occur.

Or where.

Chapter Eight

—‹‹‹·☾·›››—

BLESSEDLY, DELIA HAD ONLY ONE HOUSE showing that Saturday, and it was scheduled for eleven in the morning, meaning she shouldn't have anything to prevent her from going to the tournament in the afternoon to provide moral support for Caleb.

God knows he needed it.

Even though she knew he was safe, she couldn't quite prevent herself from thinking what a close call it had been. Good thing he'd had the driving skills to pull himself out of what could have been an utter disaster...or worse.

After she got that morning's pot of coffee going, she pulled out her phone to make sure she hadn't missed anything too momentous overnight. Not so long ago, she'd kept the phone on her nightstand and checked it far too often, but after she realized her sleep was degrading at a rapid rate, she'd made some changes. No phone or TV in the bedroom, light-darkening shades exchanged for blackout ones. She knew she should also avoid watching television or being on her computer close to the time when she went to bed. However, that had seemed like a bridge too far, and since she was sleeping much better now that the phone remained safely in the living room during the overnight hours, she figured that was good enough.

Two messages had come in after Caleb left around eight-thirty the night before. One from Marcy, just a courtesy note that she'd be showing his property around two that afternoon. Since the house was on a lockbox, Delia knew she didn't have to concern herself with that too much...except to hope that the buyers loved the place and she'd have an offer on her desk first thing Monday morning. Even though nothing untoward seemed to have occurred at the property, she couldn't help thinking it would be better for everyone involved once it was off her hands.

The second one was from Aaron Sanchez.

I know this is last minute, but one of my clients gave me tickets to "O" for Saturday night, and I was wondering if you'd be interested in having dinner and going to the show afterward. If you're busy, I understand. Just LMK.

Delia couldn't quite keep her eyes from

widening as she absorbed the message. All right, she'd gotten a few vibes from Aaron that he might be interested in something a little more than a professional relationship, but she'd figured if he was going to go for it at all, he'd start small, like maybe meeting for coffee somewhere and then progressing from there. The thought had never even entered her mind that he might jump straight to dinner and a fancy show.

True, a show he hadn't paid for, since the tickets had been a gift, but still.

A few months ago, she would have said yes almost immediately. Not because she thought anything major would develop between her and Aaron, but because she understood that if she ever wanted to settle down and have a real long-term relationship, she would have to start somewhere.

Besides, if she was at least casually dating someone, then she wouldn't have to put up with her mother's oblique but still somehow pointed comments about how Mr. Right wasn't going to just waltz into her office one day.

Which she supposed was true enough. However, now that Caleb was a part of Delia's life, things had gotten just a little more complicated. They weren't dating or anything close to it, but she'd been relentlessly single when they met and during the several months that had passed since then.

How would he react to knowing she was seeing someone?

Okay, you're getting way ahead of yourself. Going out with Aaron Sanchez for dinner and a show doesn't exactly mean you're in anything close to a committed relationship.

No, but it might be the first step toward one.

Frowning, she got a mug out of the cupboard and poured herself some coffee, then went to the fridge to get her favorite hazelnut creamer. She didn't drink it every day, but she thought it might help her puzzle through the conundrum.

As far as she'd been able to tell, each round of the poker tournament Caleb was playing in seemed to end around five-thirty or maybe a quarter to six at the latest. There was no reason in the world why she couldn't be his cheering section and still have time to go out with Aaron.

But what if Caleb advanced to the quarterfinals? Surely he'd want to go out afterward and celebrate?

Considering how he didn't need much of an excuse to go out to eat, Delia thought that was a likely possibility. Could she leave him hanging like that to go on a date with a guy she barely knew?

The more she thought about it, the less she liked the idea. Yes, she and Caleb were only friends and nothing more, but still, friends didn't leave friends hanging when they'd just accomplished a major milestone.

Even more so when they didn't. If his luck didn't hold, then he'd need some consoling.

Besides, neither of them knew yet what had happened with his Porsche. If someone was trying to get at him, really hurt him, then she thought she should be there to offer whatever help she could.

On the other hand, being supportive didn't mean she couldn't make some sort of compromise.

It was too early to reply to Aaron's text—just in case he was the kind of guy who did leave his phone next to the bed—but Delia already knew what she was going to say.

I already have plans Saturday night...but maybe you'd be up for drinks on Sunday?

Caleb generally didn't climb out of bed before nine on the weekend, but he made a special effort today, getting up a little before six and showering and prepping himself to leave the house. No breakfast, just coffee, and then the taxi he'd booked was at the curb, waiting so he could head over to the Porsche dealership and try to find out just what the hell was going on with the Cabriolet.

Even at seven-thirty, the day was bright and sunny, promising mild temperatures and clear skies. However, he couldn't find much to be cheerful about. No matter what the mechanics found, it wouldn't be good. Either the brake lines had been tampered with or they'd failed spontaneously, and both options presented their own set of problems.

However, he thought he'd prefer simple mechanical failure. At least that way, the vehicle warranty would take care of the problem.

But if demons were involved, the solution wouldn't be quite that easy.

The drive to the dealership was quiet enough, though, and after he'd paid the driver and gotten out of the car, Caleb tried to reassure himself that he'd get this handled eventually. Just another hiccup, one he could get straightened out one way or another.

He had a sneaking suspicion that Delia was right, however. The Porsche was a gorgeous car and exhilarating to drive—well, when he wasn't trying to weave his way through a crowded intersection with failed brakes—but it would probably be smarter to drive something that didn't attract every eye in a hundred-yard radius.

First things first, though.

The service department wasn't as busy as he'd feared, so he was able to talk to the manager right away.

"We're looking at her right now," the man said.

He looked like he was probably around forty-five or maybe a little older, dark-haired, not very tall but with the kind of shoulders that made it seem like he could lift a Porsche using brute strength and nothing else. "Give us about twenty minutes or so. There's coffee and tea and snacks in the waiting room."

Caleb thanked the manager and headed into the space reserved for the people whose vehicles were being worked on. At the moment, it had only one other occupant, a tall guy with a shaved head and heavy eyebrows. He sent Caleb a sideways look but didn't say anything before returning his attention to his phone.

Well, he hadn't come here to socialize, so no biggie.

And while he'd already had coffee this morning, he figured a second cup couldn't hurt, especially when he could accompany it with a large, luscious-looking bear claw. After putting together his impromptu breakfast, Caleb sat down in a chair nowhere near the bald guy, just to make it clear that he had no intention of intruding on the man's absorption with his phone.

Once he was done with the bear claw and had wiped his fingers on one of the paper napkins provided, he pulled out his phone to see if he'd missed anything important.

Nothing.

His brows drew together, but he told himself it wasn't a big deal, not when he'd already made his plans with Delia the night before. She'd be at the casino at four o'clock to cheer him, just as they'd arranged. Honestly, the lack of any contact was probably a good thing.

The last thing he wanted was a text from her telling him she needed to cancel at the last minute because something real estate–related had popped up.

He checked the weather, and then, just for shits and giggles, he went over to Facebook to see what the Greencastle gang was up to. Even though he was supposedly deceased, his mother hadn't thought to deactivate his Facebook account, and he guessed that if anyone noticed he was active on the site, they'd probably just think it was Brooke logging in to keep up with her son's old friends.

Not much was going on that he could see. Well, Tiffany Adams, who'd been about to get engaged to one of Caleb's fellow quarter demons when they were all dragged to Hell, had just announced to everyone that she was engaged for real this time, to a man Caleb vaguely remembered from his high school days. A quiet, studious guy, about the polar opposite of Sean.

But it seemed that Jon had just finished his doctorate and been hired as an associate professor at DePauw University, the college all of them had attended, so Tiffany had probably decided it was safe to start thinking about getting settled down and starting a family. Judging by all the congratulations Caleb saw in the group, no one seemed to think it strange that she'd moved on so quickly.

Except it hadn't been all that quick, had it? More than two and a half years had passed since that fateful night at Rubel Castle in Glendora when all the Greencastle half demons and quarter demons had been banished from this plane, even though it felt like the blink of an eye to Caleb.

Actually, scratch that. Every moment spent in Hell had been an excruciating eternity, and yet it was hard to remind himself that lives had moved on during those two years, and people were building the futures they wanted to see for themselves.

While he...?

Caleb wasn't sure he wanted to think about that too hard. Yes, he'd gotten out of Hell and had begun to build a life for himself—a life on the surface that looked pretty damn good—but he was already beginning to understand that he didn't want to continue in this same vein indefinitely.

And a whole lot of that depended on what Delia decided to do.

Deep down, he knew that wasn't entirely fair. She'd been nothing but friendly and supportive, and he knew he shouldn't be looking to her to make his life complete, or whatever. At the same time, though, he couldn't quite bring himself to start dating anyone. Delia knew the truth about him and accepted it, warts and all, while Caleb couldn't convince himself that he'd ever feel comfortable enough with someone else to tell them exactly who—or what—he was, where he'd come from.

Luckily, he was saved from having to ponder that thorny topic any further, since the service manager paused in the door to the waiting room and said, "Mr. Lowe?"

Good thing he was used to answering to that name by now. He got up from the chair where he'd been sitting. "Yes?"

"Let's go into the garage."

That request sounded somehow ominous. He'd always gotten the impression that mechanics didn't want people hanging around their cars while they were being worked on, but it didn't seem as if the service manager had too much of a problem with him being back there.

He followed the man into the engine bay, where the Porsche was already being rolled off the lift where the techs had been inspecting the vehicle.

"What did you find?" he asked, and the service manager shook his head.

"Nothing."

"'Nothing'?" Caleb repeated. It wasn't that he hadn't heard the guy clearly, but more that his brain didn't want to acknowledge that single word.

"There's nothing mechanically wrong with the car," the man said, enunciating each word clearly, as though he wanted to make sure they all adequately penetrated his client's brain. "We checked her from top to bottom. The brake lines are intact, and there's plenty of brake fluid. The traction-control system is working flawlessly. So I don't know exactly what happened to you yesterday evening. All I do know is that it had nothing to do with the vehicle."

The news Caleb hadn't wanted to hear, even though he'd known in the back of his mind that it was the most likely outcome. Of course the car hadn't failed. It was a piece of engineering genius, flawless in every way.

No, this was all about demons sticking their ugly fingers where they shouldn't.

Obviously, he couldn't say anything about that to the service manager.

"The road wasn't wet or anything, was it?" the guy asked next. It seemed clear to Caleb that he was looking to give him some kind of out, a way to save face rather than admit he'd screwed up, that maybe his foot had hit the gas pedal instead of the brake pedal and he hadn't wanted to cop to making such a rookie mistake.

"No," he said evenly. "I was driving home from

a poker tournament, and the thing just went haywire."

Something about the service manager's expression relaxed then. He'd probably been thinking that Caleb must have been drinking to make such a huge mistake, but since alcohol wasn't allowed during competition, his explanation about where he'd been put the kibosh on that notion.

"Well, there's nothing wrong with the car," the guy said. "So you're safe to drive it home."

Driving it anywhere was about the last thing Caleb wanted to do. However, he could only imagine the raised eyebrows if he said he would prefer to leave it here.

But just because he wouldn't abandon the thing here at the dealership, that didn't mean he planned to keep it, either.

After thanking the service manager, he climbed into the Porsche and turned on the engine. The low, sexy growl of the motor made him want to rethink his decision, but he knew Delia was right.

The Cabriolet was too conspicuous...and that meant he needed to get rid of it.

A quick search on his phone located a used car dealership that specialized in exotic vehicles. He knew he was going to take a hit because of the way a car always lost value as soon as you drove it off the lot, but better to make sure it was well out of his life.

The guy at the used car dealership seemed a little skeptical that someone would want to sell a brand-new Porsche with barely fifty miles on the odometer, but even though Caleb only had the temporary registration, the title came back clean. Ten minutes later, he was walking out of the man's office with a cashier's check for a hundred and twenty grand in his pocket.

But his main bank was open until one, so he took a cab over there, deposited the check, and then called a different cab to take him to the Mercedes dealership.

Nothing flashy, he told himself as he got out of the taxi, since his gaze immediately went to a red roadster sitting near the front of the lot. All right, it wasn't quite as conspicuous as his late, lamented metallic green Cabriolet, but he was trying to be practical here.

All the same, he was buying a coupe, dammit. He wasn't quite ready to settle for a sedan.

A salesman approached, and Caleb explained what he was looking for. After a few minutes of walking around the various vehicles, he decided a smoke-gray CLE would be a good choice. It was certainly a pretty car, but one that shouldn't attract too much attention.

They took a test drive, although he'd already made up his mind. Still, it was good to note that the car was very smooth and had plenty of power, and should be more than adequate for his needs.

Plus, it was about eighty grand cheaper than his Porsche.

Even though he was paying cash, the paperwork still took about an hour. Finally, he was done and driving off in his new acquisition.

He could only hope it would last a bit longer than his previous vehicle. Having to continually trade in cars was going to get old real fast.

As he drove home, he wondered what Delia was up to.

It was hard to read emotion from a text—especially when you were communicating with someone you didn't know very well—but it seemed as if Aaron was cool with her not being able to go to Cirque du Soleil tonight.

Drinks tomorrow is fine. I know it was sort of a gamble to expect you'd be free at such late notice.

They agreed to meet in the lounge at the Hard Rock...Delia figured they couldn't get much more public than that...and the matter seemed to be settled.

She'd just put down her phone and was getting ready to transfer a load of laundry from the washer into the dryer when her phone rang.

Aaron getting back to her and saying he couldn't make it for drinks tomorrow after all?

That didn't make much sense, though. They'd been messaging the whole time, so she didn't see why he'd suddenly decide to call instead.

When she hurried out of the laundry room and into the kitchen, she realized those worries had been for nothing.

The caller was Caleb.

"I took your advice," he said without preamble, and she blinked.

"'Advice'?"

"About the Porsche," he explained. "The mechanics at the dealership couldn't find anything wrong with it, so that means our little friends were having fun at my expense. Anyway, I sold it and bought a Mercedes. Nice and low-key."

Delia wanted to smile at the idea of a Mercedes somehow being low-key, but she thought she knew what he was trying to say. "I assume it isn't red or bright yellow?"

"Nope," Caleb said cheerfully. "Dark gray. And it's a mid-level model, which means there should be plenty of others driving around town. I sold the Porsche at one dealership and then took a cab to buy the Mercedes, and it doesn't look as if anyone was paying attention to what I was doing. So I think we might have given them the slip."

She certainly hoped so. Spending half your time looking over your shoulder was no way to live.

"That's good news," she replied. "And I'm taking care of all my chores now, so I'll be a complete free agent this afternoon."

"Great." A pause, and then he asked, "Do you want me to come pick you up?"

Maybe it would have been safer for them to take separate vehicles. On the other hand, she wanted to see his new car—partly so she could determine for herself that it was as inconspicuous as Caleb claimed—and she had to admit there hadn't been any sign of the demons poking around her house, or his new one. Having him drive seemed innocuous enough.

"That would be great. What time?"

"I'll come by around three-thirty, since I need to be at the casino a little before the official start time to sign in and do that kind of stuff."

Delia knew she'd have the laundry finished by then—she'd slipped in the first load on her way out to her house showing—so she only said, "Sounds good. I'll be ready."

"See you then."

He ended the call, and she put her phone back down on the counter. While they were speaking, she'd wondered if she should have said anything about Aegis Holdings and what Pru had been able to dig up so far.

Which admittedly wasn't much.

All the same, there didn't seem to be much point in mentioning any of it unless Aegis ended up making the highest offer on the house. And since Delia hadn't heard a peep out of Evan Matthews for several days, it seemed much more likely that someone else would snap up the place.

As with so many other things in life, real estate was more of a waiting game than anything else. And until she had something concrete to give Caleb, she figured she might as well leave it alone.

With the last qualifying round coming up in just a few hours, she knew he had much more important things to occupy his mind.

Chapter Nine

— ‹‹‹ ‹ ☾ › ››› —

ALTHOUGH HE HADN'T SAID ANYTHING TO
Delia about what she should wear to the tournament, he should have known she'd pick exactly the
right thing. Skinny jeans, a silky top in a soft blue-
green that only made her red hair stand out that
much more, sandals with a bit of a heel but not
enough to make her look as if she was tottering
around the way some women did when they
slipped on a pair of stilettos that were way too high.

No, she was just effortlessly beautiful in a way
that made him want to stand there and stare and
drink in every single detail of her appearance.

However, he had a feeling that doing so
wouldn't win him any points, not when she was so
relentlessly trying to keep him in the friend zone.

"What do you think?" he asked as she followed

him out to the driveway where the new Mercedes was parked.

"Very nice," she observed. "Beautiful, but understated."

"And not rare in the slightest," he said as he opened the passenger door for her. "In fact, I saw two of this same model while I was driving over here."

A smile tugged at the corner of her mouth. "Same color?"

He couldn't help smiling in return. "Well, one of them was."

She chuckled, and he went around to the driver's side of the car and lowered himself into the seat. A brief pause while he checked the mirrors—he'd already set up the automatic seat position at the dealership, but he didn't think he'd gotten the mirror angles just right—and then he backed out of her driveway and headed toward the feeder road that led out of the development where she lived.

From there, it was about a fifteen-minute trip to the casino. During the drive, they talked about cars...she wanted to know why he'd opted for a Mercedes over a BMW, and although he didn't have a very good explanation as to why he'd made the decision, he found himself saying, "I suppose it's because there was a Mercedes dealership closer to the place where I sold the Porsche. Trying to keep those cab fares as low as I can."

At that comment, she only shook her head, although he noted how another smile lifted the corners of her mouth.

She seemed in a mellow mood today. Whether that was because she truly was more relaxed, or whether she was just trying to do what she could to make sure he wasn't too stressed out heading into the tournament, he couldn't say for certain.

Either way, he'd take it. Right then, he was just glad of the chance to spend a little more time in her company, considering how busy she'd been lately.

"Any news on the house?" he asked, and she shook her head.

"Well, not news, news," she replied. "I know at least one broker was showing the place today, but I haven't heard anything from her."

"But someone else could have viewed it?"

Delia nodded. "Usually, an agent will tell me out of courtesy if they're going to show a property, but they don't have to, not when the house is on a lockbox."

Right. Caleb knew the lockbox code would be available on a home's real estate listing, since he'd seen that for himself when he was cruising the MLS looking for any viable candidates for a house flip. However, since he'd never sold a house or even shown one, he wasn't completely clear on the etiquette involved.

"I suppose if that's the case, then it's just a nice

surprise when someone calls out of the blue with an offer."

She was looking forward, her face in profile to him, but he could still see the way her lips curved in amusement. "That's a good way of looking at it."

By that point, they were almost at the casino, so they both went silent as he pulled into the parking lot. Today he didn't have quite as good luck finding a parking space, and they had to settle for something at the end of one row. However, Caleb told himself that might be a good thing, since the spot he'd found was just isolated enough that no one was around to see them get out of the car.

Since this was his third day in a row doing basically the same thing, this had begun to feel like a routine, like some kind of job he was going to. Not old hat, though, not with Delia at his side. The same tension tightened his stomach, however, and he knew he definitely didn't want to fail this time.

This time, Delia would be watching him play, and that had made a huge difference in how he viewed the proceedings.

After he checked in, they had to part ways, with her going to join the spectators while he went to take a seat at the table he'd been assigned to. On this last day of qualifying rounds, the number of players had been diminished significantly from more than eighty to just thirty-two. By the time the day was over, though, only sixteen would be continuing to the quarterfinals.

Today's table held three other players Caleb hadn't encountered in the previous rounds: a middle-aged woman with close-cropped gray hair who introduced herself as Margaret Howard, a heavy-set man with thick Coke-bottle glasses named Paul Reeves, and a reed-thin guy who called himself Dave Wheeler but whose Eastern European accent suggested that probably wasn't his real name.

As Caleb took his seat, he caught sight of Ty Carter lurking near the velvet rope, ostensibly watching someone at another table. Maybe he was just there to pick up a few tricks from the players who'd made it to the final qualifying round, considering how he'd had to drop out very early on.

But something about Ty's presence made Caleb's supernatural senses prickle in an unfamiliar way. Not the dark, hungry energy he associated with demon blood, but something else—something almost luminous, like sunlight through stained glass, a sensation he'd never experienced before. The way Ty's attention kept returning to this table suggested he had more than a casual interest in the proceedings, and Caleb felt himself tensing, even if he couldn't say exactly why.

The dealer—another new face—began shuffling with practiced efficiency. From his position at the table, Caleb could see Delia in the crowd, her red hair making her easy to spot. She gave him an encouraging smile, and the tension that had been tightening his neck and shoulders eased ever so slightly as he sent her an answering grin. He also noticed a tall Hispanic man standing among the spectators, though his attention seemed more focused on Delia than the tournament, his dark eyes watching her closely.

Did she have a stalker? A boyfriend?

No, that didn't feel right. He and Delia might not have been dating, but he knew they were good enough friends that she would have told him if she was seeing someone.

Well, whoever the guy was, Caleb knew he couldn't let the man's presence rattle him. Not when he was here to compete...and to win.

The first few hands played out cautiously, with Margaret taking an early pot and Dave folding more often than not. But it was Paul Reeves who drew Caleb's attention—there was something about the way his chips moved across the felt, their movement not quite natural, as if they were being guided by more than just his fingers.

Then came the hand that changed everything. Caleb looked down at an ace and a king, both spades—the kind of hand that would normally have him reaching for his powers, just to ensure he got the flush he needed. But no. He'd made it this far playing straight, and he wasn't about to change now.

"Raise," he said, pushing forward a substantial stack of chips.

Margaret folded immediately, but Dave called with barely a hesitation. Paul's chips seemed to whisper across the felt as he called as well, and Caleb noticed Ty Carter shift his position at the velvet rope, his presence casting what felt almost like a protective aura over the proceedings, even though Caleb guessed the impression must have been his imagination and nothing more.

The flop came down: king of hearts, seven of hearts, two of diamonds.

Top pair, top kicker. Strong, but not unbeatable. Dave checked, and Paul bet big—almost too big, as if he was trying to buy the pot right there. The chips moved with that same uncanny precision, and now Caleb was sure he wasn't imagining things...even though he kind of wished all this was his imagination and nothing more.

He called, watching as Dave mucked his cards with a disgusted expression.

The turn brought the jack of hearts. Three hearts on board now, giving Caleb the nut flush draw to go with his pair of kings. Paul's bet was smaller this time, almost tentative, but there was nothing tentative about the way his chips seemed to arrange themselves perfectly as they slid forward.

Caleb felt the familiar itch to use his powers, just a peek to see what he was up against. But then he caught a glimpse of Delia in the crowd, her expression confident, encouraging, and the urge faded. He called.

The river card was the ace of clubs.

Two pair now, aces and kings with a jack kicker. Strong, but that flush draw hadn't gotten there. Paul pushed forward nearly all his remaining chips, and this time Caleb knew he saw them move the last half-inch on their own.

He glanced toward the rail and caught a glimpse of Ty Carter watching intently, his expression unreadable, but something about his presence radiated a strong sense of disapproval. Whatever was going on here, Ty knew about it—and seemed to be monitoring not just the supernatural manipulation, but Caleb's response to it.

Paul's face remained impassive behind his thick glasses, but there was something in his eyes that didn't feel quite right, a gleam of satisfaction that seemed sort of premature, given that Caleb hadn't even called yet.

"All in," Caleb said quietly, pushing his stack forward.

Paul's composure cracked for just a moment,

revealing a flash of darker emotions underneath, like the sullen glow of magma beneath a crust of hardened lava. He called instantly, turning over pocket aces for three of a kind.

Caleb showed his ace-king. "Two pair, aces and kings," he announced. "Jack kicker."

Paul's face went slack with shock. At the velvet rope, something like approval flickered across Ty's even, model-handsome features, and he gave a very faint nod. The chips seemed to shiver on the felt, as if whatever power that had been controlling them was suddenly uncertain.

"Hand to seat three," the dealer announced, pushing the massive pot toward Caleb. "Player in seat two is eliminated."

As Paul stood, looking slightly dazed, Caleb noticed how Ty's attention had sharpened. For the briefest second, it almost seemed as if a faint glow surrounded the man, but then it disappeared as if it had never been there at all.

Maybe all the stress was making him imagine things.

Paul paused by Caleb's chair. "Good hand," he said, but his tone suggested anything but congratulations. "Watch yourself. Some of us don't like surprises."

"No surprises here," Caleb replied evenly. "Just poker."

But as Paul walked away, Caleb saw him

exchange a look with the Hispanic man who'd been watching Delia, a glance that seemed heavy with meaning. Meanwhile, Ty Carter had shifted position again, placing himself where he could see both the table and the two men who'd just shared some sort of silent communication. Whatever game they were playing, it wasn't just poker anymore—and Caleb had a feeling the real stakes were just beginning to show themselves.

Margaret Howard was already focused on the next hand, but Dave Wheeler was watching the crowd with knowing eyes. Maybe Caleb wasn't the only one who'd noticed something odd about this tournament.

He looked over at Delia again, relieved to see that she seemed unaware of the undercurrents swirling around the table. Better that way. He had enough to worry about without trying to explain why some of his fellow players seemed to be operating under supernatural influences—or why Ty Carter, who'd dropped out early, was watching him with the intensity of an avenging angel.

The dealer began shuffling for the next hand, but Caleb's attention was divided now between the cards and the complex web of supernatural forces gathering around the tournament. He'd made it to the final qualifying round by playing it straight, but he had a feeling the real challenge wasn't going to be poker at all.

Despite being a native of Las Vegas, Delia had never had much interest in poker. Sure, she'd play blackjack every once in a while if her date was so inclined or if some of her relatives from Chicago were visiting town and wanted to spend some time at the casinos. But she'd never learned the rules of Texas Hold 'Em, which meant most of what she was watching was arcane at best and incomprehensible at the worst.

She wasn't here to track all the various ins and outs and ups and downs of the game, though. No, she'd come here to support Caleb, and it didn't really matter if she couldn't understand everything that was happening at his table.

However, even a person as clueless as she was could see that he'd won the first hand. His dark eyes, bright with triumph, met her gaze for a moment, and she smiled back at him and flashed a thumbs-up to show her happiness at his victory.

Now he'd just have to do that enough times to make it to the quarterfinals.

The dealer began shuffling her cards again and placed two in front of the three remaining players. From this angle, Delia couldn't see what Caleb had been dealt, and since his features remained utterly impassive, it was impossible to tell whether he'd been given something he could actually work with or whether he was just maintaining a cool façade so the other players would have no idea what was going on in his mind.

In a way, it was sort of odd to see him looking so stoic, because most of the time, his emotions were easy to read, his face animated, those cola-hued eyes full of energy and life.

She knew she liked him better when he was being himself.

"Delia?" said a startled voice just then, and she looked up in shock.

"Aaron?" she responded, knowing she sounded just as surprised. "What're you doing here?"

Even as the words left her mouth, she wondered if they sounded too much like an accusation, as though she was implying he'd been stalking her or something by being here. But it was a public place, after all, and she knew the event had been advertised on local television, so it wasn't as if no one knew about it.

Aaron Sanchez smiled. Today he wore a loose black camp shirt over a pair of jeans and looked much more relaxed than he had when she'd seen him in his work attire of a dress shirt and slacks only a few days earlier.

"Oh, a friend of mine is playing," he replied, then pointed to a man who looked like he might be in his mid-thirties, fair-haired and just as poker-faced as Caleb, sitting at the farthest table. "Since I didn't have any house showings this afternoon, I thought I'd drop by and see how he was doing." Aaron paused there, one eyebrow lifting ever so slightly. "How about you?"

"The same," she said, and inclined her head toward Caleb's table, although she didn't elaborate which of the players was her friend. Aaron would probably be able to guess, but still, she didn't see the need to reveal all to someone she barely knew.

Even if she had agreed to have drinks with him tomorrow night.

"So I guess these were the 'plans' you mentioned?" he continued, then glanced down at his watch.

The meaning was clear enough. She'd declined a date that probably wouldn't have started until six-thirty at the very earliest, but this round of the tournament would be over long before then.

"Yes," Delia said calmly. Even though she knew she didn't owe Aaron any explanations, she figured it couldn't hurt to add, "We'd already decided to go out to eat after today's rounds were over."

To her relief, he didn't challenge her on the comment. "Makes sense," he said.

A round of clapping interrupted them, and she looked over to see another player getting up from Caleb's table. Now it was just him and an intense-looking woman with gray hair in a pixie cut that wouldn't have worked on most people, but perfectly complemented her high cheekbones and strong brows. She sort of reminded Delia of her junior high P.E. teacher, and she wondered with some amusement if the woman would pull out a whistle and blow hard on it if Caleb made a move she didn't like.

Nothing like that happened, of course. No, the piles of chips in front of both players grew incrementally taller, and even though what Delia knew about Texas Hold 'Em could probably fit in her shoe, she got the feeling that both competitors were pretty evenly matched. In the past, Caleb probably would have employed some of his demonic abilities to ensure a win, but he'd sworn he wasn't going to rely on anything except his brains in this competition.

He was smart, but he hadn't been playing poker for very long. Would his sharp mind and good instincts be enough to squeak out a win?

Apparently, they were, because about five minutes later, the woman called, and Caleb revealed a flush, easily beating her three of a kind. She reached across the table to shake his hand, and he smiled at her, murmuring something that Delia couldn't possibly hear over all the applause.

Some sort of congratulations, she assumed.

But a few minutes later—after he'd shaken hands with the others who'd made it through this round of the competition and would soon be his direct opponents—he came over to the spot where Delia was standing next to Aaron. Caleb's smile slipped just a little as he seemed to realize she wasn't alone, but it was back full force when he stopped near them.

"Hi, there," he said as he extended a hand. "I'm Caleb Lowe."

"Aaron Sanchez," Aaron replied easily. "I'm a friend of Delia's—a fellow real estate agent."

Those words seemed to make Caleb relax a little...or at least, he appeared to be glad that Aaron and Delia were work colleagues in a way, and that he wasn't just some rando who'd approached her in the crowd because he thought she was attractive.

"Big into poker?" Caleb inquired, and at once, Aaron shook his head.

"Not really. I'm just here to provide moral support." He paused there and looked past Delia, toward the table where he'd said his friend had been playing. "It looks like Bryce is going on to the next round, too, so I think I need to go offer my congratulations. Nice meeting you, Caleb." Another hesitation, one so small, she almost missed it. "And I'll see you tomorrow night, Delia."

And then he was off, weaving his way through the crowd so he could go meet his friend.

As soon as Aaron was out of eyeshot, Caleb's smile abruptly faded. "'Tomorrow night'?" he echoed.

A flush heated Delia's cheeks, and she found herself devoutly hoping that the lighting in the casino was dim enough that Caleb wouldn't be able to see it.

"We're meeting for drinks," she said lightly. "He wanted to take me to see Cirque du Soleil tonight, but I told him I already had plans." She stopped there and gave her companion a piercing look. While Caleb wasn't quite as impassive as he'd been while he was playing poker, she still got the feeling that he was doing whatever he could to hide what was going on in his head. "At least, I assumed we did. Or was it wrong to think you'd want to go out to eat after you were done here?"

At once, the blank expression vanished, and Caleb sent her one of his signature smiles. "Oh, sure," he replied at once. "Playing poker can really work up an appetite. Just give me a minute to check in with the competition officials, and then we can get out of here."

"Sounds good."

He wove his way through the crowd and paused to speak to a woman with highlighted hair who could have been anything between forty-five and sixty-five, thanks to her obvious Botox and plumped lips. But he was back soon enough, saying, "Okay, I have my marching orders for next week, so I guess now all I need to do now is go out and have some fun."

That sounded like a great idea to Delia. Nothing crazy, of course, but something about the air in the casino felt almost oppressive, as if it was carrying the burden of too many people hoping for a big win and couldn't quite let it vent.

"Yes," she said. "Let's get out of here."

Chapter Ten

—‹‹‹‹·۞·›››·—

WHILE THEY WERE WALKING BACK TO THE car, Caleb's thoughts roiled. Should he say something to Delia, let her know that her friend...fellow realtor...whatever...might be connected to some bad guys?

Or had he totally misinterpreted what he'd seen pass between Aaron Sanchez and Paul Reeves, and they weren't working together at all?

Even if they were, maybe it had everything to do with real estate and nothing else. For all he knew, Paul had been counting on a big win in the tournament to help him put a down payment on a property or something.

That didn't make much sense, though. The tournament wouldn't even be over until a week from today, so it wasn't as if Paul Reeves would have gotten a payout on the spot or anything close to it.

Also, he had a feeling that if he made a negative comment, Delia might think he was jealous. Okay, he kind of was, even if she'd said she and Aaron were only meeting for drinks. Nothing in her tone or her expression seemed to suggest she was all that into Aaron Sanchez, and maybe she'd accepted his offer as a way of being polite.

Downgrading from a dinner date to go see "O" or whichever show he had tickets for to merely having drinks did send kind of a message.

The car looked fine when they got to it. Okay, nothing about his Porsche's outward appearance had indicated it had been tampered with, either, but Caleb got the feeling the Mercedes was just fine, that either the forces that had messed with the Cabriolet's brake lines hadn't been able to track his new vehicle, or they'd just decided they needed to go after him in a different way now that he was on the alert.

Delia might have hesitated for just a second before she got in the passenger seat, but now she was calmly fastening her seatbelt as if she had absolutely nothing to worry about.

Still, Caleb made sure to drive slowly, keeping his speed right at the limit or even a couple of miles per hour under. That behavior irritated the drivers behind him to no end, and multiple people pulled out and passed them, with a couple making rude gestures as they went by.

"Is there some reason you're driving like my grandmother?" Delia asked with a grin, and he found himself smiling in return.

"Just being careful, I guess," he said. "Even if the brakes fail, I'll be able to recover in time if I'm not driving like a maniac."

She nodded. "Do you think they're going to fail?"

All his instincts told him they'd be just fine... but his instincts had lied to him before.

"I doubt it," he replied. "For whatever reason, I don't think they've messed with this car." He paused there, wondering how much he should say, if anything.

After all, sometimes it was just better to keep your mouth shut.

"I'm sensing a big 'but' there," she remarked, and now he found himself grinning.

"No, the car is fine." He turned left onto Paradise Avenue, and the vehicle performed flawlessly, no sign of the brakes not cooperating, no reason to think he should have anything but supreme confidence in its ability to keep him safe.

Then again, he'd thought pretty much the same thing about the Porsche.

"But...?"

"That guy you were talking to. Aaron Sanchez."

Her expression was now almost amused. "What about him?"

"I'm not sure he's on the up and up."

She shifted in her seat so she was more or less facing him. The faint smile that had touched her lips was now gone, so at least it didn't seem as if any thoughts of jealousy were dancing in her mind. "What makes you say that?"

"Just a feeling." Briefly, he explained how he'd sensed that Paul was using some kind of supernatural powers to try to influence the game—a gambit that hadn't worked out so well for him, thank God or whoever else might have been watching. "And I saw him making the kind of eye contact with Aaron Sanchez that you just wouldn't make unless you knew the other person pretty well."

Delia looked thoughtful. "Real estate agents tend to know a lot of people."

Caleb supposed he couldn't really argue with that assertion. All the same, he couldn't shake the feeling that something much more than a client/agent relationship was going on here.

"True," he allowed. "What do you know about him?"

She played with the strap of her purse, which now rested in her lap. "Aaron? Not a whole lot. I think he came on the Las Vegas real estate scene about three or four months ago. He's sold a few properties. I wouldn't describe him as a barn-burner or anything, but he's definitely doing enough to make a decent living."

Something about that timeframe made alarm bells go off in Caleb's mind. On the surface, he supposed there was nothing too strange about someone relocating to Las Vegas in the winter, when the weather would be positively mild compared to most of the country, but the way he'd shown up here not too long after Caleb had decided to make the desert town his home base?

It didn't smell right.

"So, you don't know the guy very well, but you agreed to have drinks with him."

The words came out much harsher than he'd intended. Too bad there was no way to take them back.

However, Delia didn't look offended. Tone mild, she said, "Well, going out for drinks is a good way to get to know someone a little better." She stopped there and sent him a sideways glance. "Do you think I should cancel?"

For some reason, the question made an unexpected warmth go through him. He'd expected her to accuse him of being jealous, of intruding where he had no right to, and instead she was asking him seriously whether she should back out of her date with Aaron Sanchez.

Caleb's first instinct was to say that yes, of course she should cancel the whole thing. However, he thought that might be overstepping a bit.

Besides, if Aaron let his guard down around her, then maybe she'd be able to pick up a few things he might unintentionally let slip.

"No," he said. "I mean, that's your decision. It's not my place to tell you what to do. And it could be that I'm imagining things."

"I doubt it," Delia said at once. "You're not the sort of person to conjure this kind of stuff out of thin air. If something's got your spidey-sense tingling, then I believe you when you say there might be something kind of dodgy about Aaron Sanchez."

"Maybe all you need to do is find out a little more about him before you go on the date," Caleb suggested. "Have your friend Pru check him out."

The suggestion seemed to make sense to her, because Delia nodded. "That's easy enough. I doubt she'll find much, though—Aaron is working for a pretty solid agency, and I know they wouldn't have hired him without a thorough background check."

Possibly not. On the other hand, a standard check like that wouldn't pull up the sorts of things Caleb was looking for.

"Still, it's worth a try," he said. "Ask Pru to

check and see if he's moved around a lot, or if his employment history has holes in it. That's not the sort of thing the agency might care about, as long as his real estate liccnsc is up to date and he doesn't have any kind of criminal background. But if something about his residences and his work feels flimsy, then there's a good chance he's manufactured the whole thing to make it look as if he's been living on this plane for a while."

"As opposed to popping up here straight out of Hell," Delia commented. She shifted once again so she could look at him directly. "You don't *really* think he's a demon, do you?"

Right then, Caleb didn't know what to think. The only thing he did know was that something about the situation didn't feel right.

"I don't know," he said. "It could be that Paul is the demon, and he has Aaron under his control."

Delia's brows drew together. "But for what reason? Why would a demon be controlling a real estate agent?"

The answer was right there in front of them, even if she didn't want to acknowledge it. "To get closer to you, of course," Caleb replied. "They know we've been working together, even if they've been leaving you alone lately. That's the thing with demons—they're playing the long game, so it's not too hard for them to sit back and wait for a situation to resolve itself in one way or another."

"Well, that's reassuring," she remarked, and he couldn't help chuckling.

"No, in a way, it's good, because they've already found out what happens when they try to confront us directly. Calach wasn't some minor-level demon, so the simple fact that we were able to banish him is enough to give any of them pause."

All right, maybe he was being a little optimistic. But Delia was looking worried, and he didn't want her to think the situation was utterly dire. The two of them had managed to send Calach back to Hell, after all, and she kept so much holy water on hand that even a powerful demon might think twice about confronting her directly...especially since she'd already used it once in combat and knew just how effective it was.

"So you're not worried."

"No, I'm not worried," Caleb lied. "All the same, it couldn't hurt to have Pru look into the guy."

Just in case.

Their conversation on the way to the restaurant hadn't been the most reassuring thing in the world, but Delia told herself they needed to celebrate Caleb's big win. He was going on to the quarterfinals, and he'd managed that accomplishment with only his brains and skill, and absolutely no demonic powers at all.

He needed to be rewarded for that accomplishment.

How he'd even gotten a reservation for this place on a Saturday night, she had no idea. Primal Steakhouse was one of the hottest tickets in town, and when she and Pru had investigated the possibility of going there on a weeknight when it wouldn't be so crowded, she'd been told there wasn't an opening for over a month.

In her humble opinion, no place was *that* good.

Maybe Caleb hadn't used his demonic powers to get ahead in the poker tournament and instead had brought them all to bear on making sure there'd be a timely cancellation at Primal just when they needed one.

She waited as their server pulled out a chair for her, then sat down, wishing Caleb had warned her about where they were going. Her silky top and heeled sandals and dark jeans were probably all right for most dining destinations around town, but if she'd known they were coming here, she would have put on a dress.

Then again, it was Las Vegas, and even the fanciest restaurants didn't have much of a dress code beyond banning baseball caps and flip-flops and pants that slipped down far enough to reveal your underwear. With that in mind, her pretty teal sleeveless blouse and Caleb's rust-colored camp shirt were probably just fine.

No prices on the menu, but she already had a pretty good idea of what things cost, thanks to the way she'd researched the place when she'd thought she and Pru would have a girls' night out here. Depending on what kind of wine Caleb selected, Delia was pretty sure the meal would set him back at least five hundred bucks, maybe more.

Somehow, she doubted he would care much too much about that.

Since neither of them knew what they were ordering yet, they both agreed on a bottle of merlot, figuring that would go with a lot of different things. Once their waiter went off to fetch the wine, Caleb settled against the back of his chair, although he was still looking down at the menu, eyes narrowed slightly as he absorbed the various offerings.

"Excited about making it to the quarterfinals?" she asked, and he set the menu on the table next to his place setting.

"I suppose so," he replied. "To be honest, I wasn't sure whether I was going to make it this far. Either all that studying paid off more than I thought, or the rest of the people in the competition just aren't that good."

Delia grinned. "I have a feeling it's probably the former."

"If you say so."

The waiter came back with the wine, which he expertly uncorked—not that she'd expected anything less in an establishment like this —before tipping a scant quarter-inch into Caleb's glass so he could taste it. He pronounced the wine excellent, so their server poured a decent amount for her before going back to top off Caleb's drink.

She'd already decided on the duck, figuring it wouldn't be as heavy as a steak but would still go well with the wine. Caleb ordered a porterhouse, and soon enough, they were left to their own devices again.

Not that Delia thought they'd be able to discuss anything too sensitive here. Maybe they weren't elbow to elbow with the people at the neighboring tables, but still, the restaurant was crowded enough that they'd need to watch what they said.

"Has Aaron shown the house?" Caleb inquired, his tone a little too casual.

Was he worried that the realtor might go poking around where he shouldn't? She supposed real estate agents ran that risk whenever they left a house on a lockbox, but it was just easier to let other agents view a property on their own schedules rather than having to handle the whole setup themselves.

"No," Delia replied. "Or at least, while he told

me he had some clients who might be interested in the place, he hasn't said anything about actually giving them a tour yet."

"Good," Caleb said, and she lifted an eyebrow.

"I thought you wanted to get out from under that property."

"I do," he said calmly. "But I'd much rather it went to someone who's represented by a different agent."

Fair enough. It was his house, after all, and his was the final determination as to who would actually end up with it.

"Well, another agent showed it this morning," Delia told him. "And I know Marcy can really get things moving if she thinks a house is perfect for someone, so it could be that we have an offer as soon as Monday morning."

"That would be good," Caleb responded. "It would be one less thing to worry about."

Yes, he did have quite a lot on his plate right now. True, until escrow closed—well, unless Marcy's buyers were paying cash, which Delia sort of doubted—all sorts of things could go wrong and the deal could still fall apart, but even though horror stories abounded in the real estate industry, she'd only had that happen twice in the entire time she'd been selling houses.

"Then let's drink to that," she said as she lifted her glass.

Caleb obligingly raised his as well and clinked it against hers. Once they'd both had a swallow of merlot, however, he glanced around and said in an undertone, "But your realtor friend and his possible accomplice weren't the only strange thing about the tournament."

Pausing, Delia sent a quick glance to either side. No one seemed to be paying them much attention, and yet she still didn't know if it was the best idea to be discussing this sort of stuff right now.

He'd obviously noted her wariness, because one corner of his mouth quirked as he remarked, "It's okay. I'm not mentioning the big D-word. But still, there's this one guy—Ty Carter. He was knocked out in the first qualifying round. I saw him at the casino today, though, which seemed strange."

"Strange how?" Delia asked. "I mean, I don't think it's too weird that he might have come back to watch the competition. Maybe he was trying to study everyone's strategies, see if he could pick up some tricks."

A shrug, and Caleb swallowed some wine. "Under other circumstances, I might say maybe that's all it was. But the guy's vibe is…weird."

"Like, big D-word?" After all, if anyone could sense a demon, it would be someone with demon blood in their veins.

His expression grew cloudy, as if he wasn't quite sure he could explain what he was thinking. "Not exactly. The energy was off, but not off in that particular way." He stopped there, brows pulling together, and then he shook his head. "I know I'm not explaining myself very well."

Delia could tell he was frustrated, so she did her best to look sympathetic, even if she couldn't quite understand what had set him off. "It's okay," she said. "Did this Ty Carter person do anything to disrupt the tournament or cause some other kind of problem?"

"Nothing like that," Caleb replied immediately. "I suppose that's part of the reason why I can't figure out what's going on with the guy. He's just...watching."

Which was sort of what spectators were supposed to do at a poker tournament. However, the man had definitely pinged Caleb's radar, which meant something was going on even if he couldn't explain what it was.

"Well, I can try to keep an eye on him when I come to watch you on Thursday," she said, and at once, Caleb's brows lifted.

"You don't have to work?"

"I do," she replied calmly. "But I started rearranging my schedule as best I could so I'd be free from three onward on those afternoons next week."

"Even before you knew whether I'd be advancing to the quarterfinals?"

"Even before then," she said. Yes, maybe it had been counting Caleb's chickens before they hatched, but after his first win this past Thursday, she'd quietly begun moving whatever appointments she could to earlier in the day, and moving to the week after the competition any that absolutely had to happen after three in the afternoon. Then she added, "I had a feeling you'd make it out of the qualifying rounds."

He smiled at her, the kind of genuine, unforced smile she guessed didn't make an appearance very often. Or rather, while she'd seen that look on his face once or twice, she had a feeling he hadn't worn it too often before he'd come to Las Vegas. Although he'd been reticent about his past, she could still tell that the life he'd left behind in Greencastle hadn't been an entirely happy one, even though he'd lived in what sounded to her like a world of privilege.

"I appreciate that."

The words were spoken simply, but Delia could sense the world of meaning behind them. For a moment, she wondered what would happen if she reached over to take his hand...if she gave herself permission to see where all this might lead.

But something held her back, and the moment passed.

However, she didn't want to sound dismissive by saying it was nothing, so she summoned a smile of her own and said, "Everyone needs someone to cheer them on."

"Well, I'll make sure to be there for you when you need a cheering section."

She didn't know if that would be anytime soon —it wasn't as if she was planning on entering a poker tournament or even a pickleball competition —but she appreciated the sentiment anyway.

They both seemed to realize they should move on to topics that were a little less fraught, so Delia told him how she planned to have an open house late on Wednesday afternoon...well, unless either Marcy or Aaron or one of the other brokers who'd viewed the property came up with a qualified buyer before then...and Caleb said he planned to visit several different casinos over the next couple of days so he could keep burnishing his Texas Hold 'Em skills.

"I probably won't want to play another game for at least six months after this is all over," he said with a grin. "But I also don't want to lose my edge by just sitting around and waiting for the quarterfinals to start. So picking up a hand or two in the meantime seems like the best way to stay sharp."

"That does sound like a good plan," she agreed, then paused. The question that had been floating around in her mind might have sounded rude, but she hoped Caleb wouldn't take it that way.

And she was genuinely curious.

"So...what do you plan to do with yourself after the tournament?" she asked. "I mean, the house is done, so what's next?"

He flashed her another of those patented Caleb Lockwood grins. "What, you mean sitting around the house and watching basketball isn't an option?"

Delia reached for her wine and took a sip. "I think you should do whatever you want to do. But somehow, you don't seem like the couch potato type."

Another smile flickered around the corners of his mouth, but he had to wait to reply since the server finally showed up with their entrees. A minute or two was consumed by making sure they had everything they needed, but then he disappeared again.

"No, I'm not a couch potato," Caleb agreed, as if their conversation had never been interrupted. "I'm not sure what to do, to be honest. I suppose I'll keep looking for a likely flip. It was fun working on my house."

"Doing a flip you don't plan to live in is kind of a different beast," Delia said, and his shoulders lifted.

"Oh, I know that. I know I'll have to keep an

eye on costs and not go crazy, or I won't have any kind of return on my investment. But watching a house get transformed…there's something fun about that. I didn't think I'd enjoy it as much as I did."

Which was about the same way Delia had felt about those sorts of projects. She'd genuinely regretted it when she and her mother had decided to get out of the flipping business, but the market had shifted since the time they'd determined the returns weren't worth the investment, and now there were more likely prospects for those sorts of projects than there had been even six months ago.

"Then I'll keep looking and let you know if anything promising turns up," she said.

"Oh, I'm looking, too," he replied as he cut off a chunk of porterhouse. Before he popped it in his mouth, he added, "But you probably have a better eye for what might work than I would."

Most likely, just because she'd gone through the process a rough dozen times, and he only had one flip under his belt. To be honest, Delia wasn't even sure whether they could call it that, since he hadn't sold the house and instead had moved right in.

"I'm sure with the two of us looking, we'll find the right project," she told him, and something about his expression now seemed almost relieved, as if he hadn't been sure whether she'd truly be on board with continuing to assist him in his house-flipping journey.

But Delia knew she was. If nothing else, she'd get to experience the process vicariously through him...and she had a feeling he'd want her design input going forward.

Fine by her. She loved shopping for fixtures and lighting and whatnot, especially if she wasn't spending her own money.

"Then we should drink to our next project together," he suggested.

They lifted their glasses again and made a ceremonial clink, sealing the deal.

It seemed that no matter what, both her personal and professional lives were going to be entwined with Caleb Lockwood's for the foreseeable future.

Chapter Eleven

When Caleb opened his eyes the next morning, it was to an overwhelming sense of well-being. No, he and Delia hadn't shared a goodnight kiss—she'd offered him a friendly thanks for dinner and a promise to keep in touch right before she got out of the car—but he knew he was going on to the quarterfinals, she'd all but promised to work with him on his next flip...whenever that happened... and the brakes on his new Mercedes hadn't failed and the car hadn't blown up as they were driving home from the restaurant.

He thought he could count all of that as a win.

A pause to throw back the covers, and then he got out of bed and padded downstairs in his underwear to get a pot of coffee going. Sure, he supposed he could have paused to pull on a T-shirt, but with the thermostat set at a steady seventy-two degrees no matter what, he didn't have to worry about getting cold.

As he waited for the coffee to finish brewing, though, he found his upbeat mood starting to slip away. Yes, he'd secured a place in the quarterfinals, but he had absolutely no idea what had been going on with Ty Carter or Aaron Sanchez, who might prove to be the more problematic of the two men.

At least Delia wasn't going out for drinks with Ty.

Unfortunately, there didn't seem to be much Caleb could do about it, except hope that Delia's friend Prudence dug up some good dirt today in enough time for the date to be canceled.

Of course, if Pru did happen to find something incriminating, then that would add yet another person to his "do not trust" list...and it was starting to get pretty long.

First things first, though. He drank his coffee and then nuked a breakfast sandwich he'd bought at Sprouts before heading upstairs to take a long, hot shower. Once he was dressed and ready for the day, he checked his phone to make sure he hadn't missed any calls or texts.

Nothing there, and he found himself frowning. Okay, it was still early enough—a little before ten—that Delia might not even be out of bed yet, although he found that hard to believe. When someone had that many plates spinning in the air, they tended not to spend half their weekend asleep.

But he knew next to nothing about Prudence and her work habits, except a few comments Delia had dropped here and there that made it sound as if her friend tended to be kind of a night owl. If Delia hadn't texted Pru right after she got home the night before, none of that research into Aaron Sanchez probably would have even started yet.

Well, just because they were going to dig up dirt on Aaron, that didn't mean Caleb couldn't start looking into some of the other players, especially Ty Carter and Paul Reeves, the man who seemed as though he might have some connection to Aaron, even if Caleb hadn't been able to puzzle it out yet. He didn't have a private detective license the way Pru did, but he could still try poking around at the surface-level stuff to see if any of it pinged his radar.

After all, it wasn't as if he had much else to do with his time.

Delia woke up to a message from Pru.

Aaron Sanchez seems on the up and up. Got his real estate license about five years ago. Before that, he was a manager at an Italian restaurant in Bullhead City.

That did seem pretty innocuous, and Delia could see why he'd wanted to move into a different career. The food service industry was not for the faint of heart...and had even crazier hours than the real estate business.

Pru's text continued after that.

Went to UNLV, grew up in Laughlin. Parents still live there, younger sister is in Reno. I'll keep poking around, but as far as I can tell, he isn't anyone except who he seems to be.

Those words should have reassured her, but Delia knew that Robert Hendricks had seemed to be your ordinary, run-of-the-mill casino executive... right up until the moment when he'd turned into a demon and tried to kill both her and Caleb.

But as good as Pru was at digging up all sorts of interesting information about a person, there was no way she'd be able to tell just from looking at some online data whether a certain individual had been co-opted by a demon.

No, you had to have done something to provoke said demon, the sort of situation Delia was trying desperately to avoid.

Based on the information at hand, she had absolutely no reason to cancel her date with Aaron, even though all her instincts were telling her she should still back out.

Clearly, she needed coffee to figure out this particular conundrum.

She pulled on a robe and went downstairs, then started a pot. A few years earlier, her mother had asked if she wanted a Keurig for a birthday or Christmas present, but Delia had decided she could get along just fine with her trusty old Black & Decker coffeemaker. Maybe it wasn't as fancy, but at least she didn't have to worry about what all those K-cups were doing to the environment.

Cup of coffee in hand, she went back to the living room to sit down on the sofa and get that sweet caffeine flowing through her bloodstream. Sometimes, she'd turn on the local news while she had her morning drink, but since it was nine o'clock on a Sunday, most of those channels would have already switched over to religious programming.

No, thanks. The only evidence of Heaven and Hell she needed had already taken her out to dinner the night before.

The coffee helped, though, and by the time she was finished with her cup, she'd decided she wasn't going to chicken out of her date with Aaron. Maybe that was a big mistake, but if it turned out he was just a regular guy, then she would feel like an idiot, even if she didn't have any intention of letting things get serious between them. He was good-looking enough, but she could tell they didn't have the chemistry she needed to let things get past a first date.

And no, she wasn't going to think about the chemistry she had with Caleb, because that would only lead her into a place she didn't want to go.

Some fruit and yogurt and water, and then she went upstairs to shower and wash her hair. No point in getting dressed up this early in the day, so she put on yoga pants and a slouchy shirt, the kind of ensemble that was just perfect for wiping down the countertops and running the vacuum in the main living areas.

Then her phone pinged. She hurried to pick it up, thinking it might be another text from Pru, or possibly Caleb getting in touch, even though they'd already basically agreed that they wouldn't see each other until Thursday unless some sort of emergency came along.

She didn't recognize the number, although it had a local 702 area code.

I heard from a friend that you provide a particular kind of help. Do you have any time today to look at a property for me? It's not too far from downtown.

Nothing else in the message...not that she needed too much more clarification. "Particular help" had to be code for her ghost-clearing sideline, although things had been pretty quiet on that front for the past month or so. However, since she knew that part of her business had its ups and downs just like everything else, she hadn't been too worried about the current lull.

Especially since the last time someone had hired her for that sort of work, he'd turned out to be a demon in disguise.

She wanted to think the odds of that happening again were pretty low, but she couldn't know for sure. And while part of her wanted to tell the unknown texter that she was busy today, she also knew she couldn't turn down someone in need.

So she picked up her phone.

I have some time this afternoon. Would two o'clock work for you? I'll need the address.

Two o'clock is fine. The house is at 1412 Desert Wind Drive.

Got it. I'll see you there.

Thank you.

That was the end of the exchange. Delia gazed down at her phone's screen for a moment and wanted to shake her head. A lot of people would have suspected the whole thing was a setup for human trafficking or something equally vile, but she knew that people who reached out to her for ghost-whispering help were often on edge and nervous, and tended to forget important pieces of information.

Like their name, for example.

Anyway, she had a police whistle on her keychain and kept a canister of pepper spray in her purse, so she wasn't too worried. Also, she and Pru had taken a *krav maga* class at the local community college a few years ago, and while Delia knew she'd forgotten a chunk of what she'd learned, she still thought she had enough moves in her arsenal to fend off any would-be rapists or traffickers.

She wasn't worried about the ghost itself. Ghosts—and now demons—were the reason why she always carried holy water with her.

However, those precautions didn't mean she wouldn't also take out some cheap insurance, just to be safe. She went back to the text thread with Pru.

Thanks for the info on Aaron. BTW, I'm doing the ghost thing this afternoon at two. 1412 Desert Wind Dr. If I don't check in with you by three, can you follow up?

Apparently, Pru was already awake, because her text came back right away.

No problem. It's been a while, right?

A little over a month. But sometimes it just works out that way.

Which was fine by her. Yes, once she'd figured out her unusual talent and what exactly she could do with it, she'd tried to make herself available to the people who needed their homes—prospective or otherwise—emptied of any spirits, but that didn't mean she wanted to be freeing houses from their resident ghosts day in and day out. Even when a ghost turned out to be mostly benign...

unlike the serial killer who'd haunted Caleb's house...working with them could still be a taxing process.

A nice, long break was just fine by her.

That break appeared to be over, though.

She headed into her office and woke up her iMac, then checked the address against the MLS database. Yes, the property was currently in escrow and was repped by an agent Delia had worked with in the past, Jackie Villanueva. Since Jackie knew exactly what Delia could do with haunted properties, it seemed odd that she hadn't sent her client over much earlier in the process, before any money had exchanged hands.

Then again, she had no real idea what might have happened. For all she knew, the spirit had been quiescent as long as it knew the house was standing empty, but now that it had realized someone would be moving in soon, it had decided to make its presence known.

Whatever was going on, she supposed she'd find out soon enough.

So far, Caleb's internet sleuthing had turned up a big, fat zero. No, he hadn't thought that any of the people he was investigating would have a flashing red "demon" on their driver's licenses or something, but he'd at least hoped to find something slightly anomalous.

But he hadn't seen anything to make him think that Paul Reeves or Ty Carter were anything out of the ordinary. Maybe if he had access to the sorts of databases that Prudence did, he'd be able to locate something incriminating. Right now, though, those men looked like a couple of upstanding citizens and nothing more. Paul Reeves owned a carpet cleaning business based in Summerlin, and Ty Carter was a tennis pro at DragonRidge Country Club, a very high-end establishment.

No doubt all those bored, Botoxed rich men's wives were lined up to get lessons from the guy. Caleb still didn't like the vibe he'd gotten from the man—or at least, it had managed to somehow disturb him without actually feeling sinister—but bad vibes weren't a crime, or even an indication that someone might be a demon.

That didn't mean he was about to give up. After all, he knew better than anyone else that demons were awfully good at coming up with fake mortal identities when necessary, so this surface-level stuff wasn't anything close to conclusive.

Except that there wasn't much else he could do, not without outside help. He supposed he could have looked up Prudence Nelson online—the woman was a P.I., after all, and must have some kind of website—but for some reason, that felt like horning in on Delia's territory. He thought it better to talk to her first before he hired Pru to investigate those two men.

Especially when it seemed as if there might not be a whole lot to find.

Annoyed, Caleb closed his laptop. He knew part of his current irritation stemmed from feeling utterly at loose ends, but he figured he could cure that easily enough.

It was still early, but in a town where the casinos ran 24/7, that wasn't much of an impediment.

He grabbed his keys and headed out.

The house looked just about the way it had online—a pretty Mediterranean-style two-story that had been built in the early 1990s but had been subtly updated on the outside, just enough to show that the interior had also been renovated and wouldn't be a '90s flashback of white tile countertops and popcorn ceilings.

A sleek black motorcycle—a Ducati, she noted as she passed it by—was parked in the driveway, so Delia assumed her new client, whoever he was, waited for her inside.

Or at least, she thought it was probably a he. Sure, there was no reason to believe that a woman might not ride a sporty bike like the Ducati, but the vibe she was getting didn't come across that way.

The front door was unlocked, so she let herself in. Standing in the empty living room was a man she thought she recognized.

Ty Carter, one of Caleb's erstwhile competitors...and an individual who'd definitely pinged his demonic radar.

"Mr. Carter?" she blurted in shock, then realized she probably shouldn't have let it slip that she already knew who he was.

However, he only smiled, as if summoning her like this was the most ordinary thing in the world. "You can call me Ty," he said. "No need to stand on formality."

He looked like he was probably a few years older than Caleb, so in his mid-thirties. His dark hair was pulled back into a ponytail, and she guessed it would be a bit longer than his shoulders if he let it fall free. In contrast to his near-black tresses, his eyes were a bright blue, clear as desert skies at the peak of summer.

If she hadn't been so preoccupied with more important matters, she might have thought Ty Carter was pretty spectacular. As it was, she could only stare at him in consternation.

"Why did you call me here?"

"To look at the house, of course," he said imperturbably.

"You bought this house?" she returned, not sure whether he was joking.

"Not exactly."

His expression remained utterly calm, so Delia had no idea what might be going through his head.

"If you didn't 'exactly' buy it, then what are you doing here?"

"It's haunted," he said. "The buyers don't know that, of course, but this place does have a resident spirit." Ty paused there, those sky-colored eyes fixed on her face, as if to gauge her reaction. "I wanted to see how you work."

This was insane. "If you're not the buyer, then we're trespassing."

He shrugged. "There was still a lockbox on the door. I suppose the listing agent wanted to keep all her options open until escrow closed."

Delia had to admit that sounded like something Jackie Villanueva would do. And since the house had a lockbox, that meant a licensed realtor could come in without any repercussions.

"So...you have a real estate license?" she asked next. "Because otherwise, how did you get the code to the lockbox?"

His expression remained neutral. Caleb hadn't gone into details about how Ty Carter had lost in the qualifying rounds, but she guessed it hadn't been due to his lack of a good poker face. For some reason, that annoyed her, probably because she would know better how to react if she could get even some sort of read of his emotions.

"It's not so difficult to get that information if you know where to look," he replied. "Anyway, I wanted to know if you could sense the ghost here."

Delia planted her hands on her hips. "Not so far," she said. "But the vibes in this room might be interfering with my ability to tell if there's a ghost in the house or not."

Maybe his lips quirked ever so slightly. "I'm sorry about the vibes, then. I'll wait here in the living room while you explore."

This was insane. Part of her wanted to turn around and walk right out of the house...but a bigger part wanted to see if there really was a ghost, or whether this was just some elaborate joke on Ty Carter's part.

Except...why would he even do such a thing? He didn't know her from Eve, so what was the point?

To put Caleb off-balance, she thought then, although that theory didn't feel quite right, either. It would be one thing if Ty was still in the tournament, but he'd dropped out the first day. There wouldn't be much point in making Caleb lose when there was no chance in the world that Ty could win.

Then again, maybe this was just some sort of petty revenge. If Ty couldn't win, then possibly he thought that playing head games with Caleb was one way to make sure his former opponent didn't get any farther than the quarterfinals.

She didn't see that happening, though. For all his mercurial nature, Caleb Lockwood could be *very* focused when he needed to.

So she gave a very visible shrug, then walked out of the living room toward the back of the house, where the kitchen and attached family room were located. Homes had been a lot more compartmentalized back when this place was built, and clearly, whoever had spent money on upgrading the flooring and the lighting hadn't wanted to pop for the expensive beams required to tear out walls and still keep the structure from collapsing in on itself.

More signs of updating here, from the quartz countertops and backsplash to the smoothly plastered fireplace. However, she wasn't here to look at the improvements...even though her real estate agent's eye went unerringly to those very details.

No, she needed to see if this house truly was haunted.

So far, she hadn't felt a single thing. But she'd been focused on Ty Carter for the past couple of minutes, which could explain why she hadn't sensed any ghostly vibes in the house.

There, out of the corner of her eye. Just the faintest hint of movement, something that disappeared just as soon as she tried to turn and see what was there.

At the same time, though, an icy little chill ran down her spine, and she knew she wasn't alone back here. Ty had remained in the front room, and Delia hadn't heard a peep from over there, so she knew that odd little blip at the edge of her vision hadn't been him.

"I'm here," she said quietly. The entity she'd just barely sensed already knew that, of course, but sometimes it was better to open these dialogues with something neutral, something a spirit wouldn't see as threatening.

Now she knew she wasn't imagining things, since that odd little shimmer of movement became more solid, resolving itself into the form of a girl who looked like she'd probably been in her early teens when she died. Judging by the shirt slipping off one shoulder and the baggy rolled-up jeans, she must have left this plane soon after the house was built. That outfit just screamed early nineties.

What had happened? The girl looked healthy and whole—well, for someone who was halfway transparent. Then again, not all ghosts manifested the cause of their deaths, unlike the people who walked the afterlife in the *Beetlejuice* movies...the same movies that had provided the inspiration for Delia's name.

"Was this your home?" she asked next.

To her surprise, the ghost shook her head. She pointed toward the second floor and the stairs, and then put her hands against the side of her cheek as if to mimic someone sleeping.

Clear as mud. But Delia knew she had to do her best to puzzle out what the spirit was attempting to communicate. "You were at a...sleep-over here?"

A nod, and the ghost girl pointed at the stairs again.

Now this was starting to make sense. "And you...wanted to come downstairs for something?"

Another nod, followed by the ghost lifting her hand to her lips, then tipping it backward as if in imitation of someone drinking from a glass.

All right, now they were getting somewhere. "You got up in the middle of the night to get a glass of water, but you tripped on the stairs?"

While the ghost didn't smile, something about her expression seemed brighter, as if she was glad she had finally found someone who understood. She rolled her two index fingers around themselves, making a motion like someone tumbling head over foot. Then she leaned her head to one side at an angle that should have been impossible for anyone who was still alive, and for just a second, Delia thought she could see a bone sticking out of the back of her neck.

Ouch.

So she'd come to a slumber party not long after the family who'd lived here back then had moved in, and, moving around in the darkness in an unfamiliar house, she'd lost her footing on the stairs and fallen to her death.

"Did anyone know you were here?"

A very small shake of the ghost's head. It seemed she'd been the quiet sort of spirit, the kind that hovered in the background but didn't participate in any kind of actual haunting.

So how in the world had Ty Carter been aware of her presence in the home?

A mystery that would need to be cleared up later. For now, it seemed better to focus on helping the girl's spirit to go on to a better plane of existence.

Very gently, Delia asked, "Do you want to stay here?"

Another shake, more emphatic this time.

"I can help you move on."

The girl's gaze met hers, hopeless and sad, and her shoulders lifted.

"No, really," Delia said, even as she thought that no one so young...even a ghost...should be wearing that expression. "I've done this for a lot of other spirits. You just have to give yourself permission to cross over to the next life. This wasn't your house, and there's no real reason for you to stay here. You need to accept that this life is over, but something new and wonderful is waiting for you on the other side."

A parting of lips, as if the spirit wanted to ask a question and then realized it would be impossible, given that she couldn't speak.

However, Delia thought she understood what the ghost was trying to ask.

"I can't tell you what's there," she said quietly. "I'm not the kind of psychic who can travel in that realm. But everything I've read and heard tells me it won't be so different from this world, except that it will be easier to become your higher self, the person you were always meant to be."

As she listened, the girl looked almost solid for a moment. Her big eyes—Delia thought they'd probably been blue when she was alive—widened even further, and a smile played around her mouth for a second.

And then she was gone.

"Very good," said Ty Carter, who'd appeared out of nowhere and now stood a few feet away from the kitchen. Probably, he'd come down the hall while she was busy talking to the ghost, but it was still a little disconcerting that he'd been able to approach so quietly.

Delia turned back toward him. He stood there

looking oh-so-casual, arms hanging loosely at his sides, something in his expression almost satisfied, as if he'd been hoping for this particular outcome.

"You heard all that?" she replied. She didn't think she'd been speaking very loudly, but it wasn't as if there was any other noise in the house to conceal the sound of her voice.

"Enough," Tyler said. He came a little closer, although not so close that it felt anything like an invasion of her space. "I wanted to see what you'd be able to do with Becky."

"That was her name?"

He nodded. "She came here for a slumber party and fell down the stairs in the middle of the night, and she's been here ever since." A pause, and he added, "Or rather, she was here up until a few minutes ago. But she was a quiet girl in life, and she was quiet in death. None of the families who lived in this house even knew it was haunted."

Since this was what Delia had already pretty much pieced together, she only said, "But somehow you knew."

"I did," Ty replied, still with that almost Buddha-like calm surrounding him. "And I wanted to see how you would handle it." He stopped there, expression now approving. "It seems your reputation is well-deserved. I also think you might discover you have talents you didn't even know existed."

She put her hands on her hips and sent him a flat stare. Okay, he'd been right about the spirit who'd inhabited this house for thirty-plus years, but she still wasn't sure she liked hearing him make those sorts of pronouncements. "Such as?"

A smile that would have done the Mona Lisa proud. "Oh, I think I'll leave you to figure that out for yourself."

Before she could reply, he'd turned away from her and was walking swiftly down the hallway to the entryway. A moment later, she heard the door shut—not slammed, but closed firmly enough that it was clear there wasn't much point going after him. Another second or two passed, and the sound of his motorcycle revving came clearly from the driveway.

Delia let out her breath and looked around. The house was utterly calm, and she knew no other spirits dwelled here.

All the same....

"Well, that was weird," she said aloud, then headed for the front door so she could let herself out.

Chapter Twelve

— ‹‹‹ · ☼ · ››› —

An afternoon wandering the gaming floor at Caesar's Palace told Caleb that his wins at the Desert Paradise poker tournament hadn't been a fluke. Sure, he lost here and there, but his wins more than made up for that. Not huge wins—he wasn't about to start attracting any real attention to himself, so manipulating the cards to pull in another quarter-mil or so definitely wasn't in the plan—and yet he thought he was staying sharp enough.

Still, even though he was able to walk out of there with a fresh five grand in his pocket, he knew he had been just a wee bit distracted.

And that, he thought, was all Delia's fault.

Okay, maybe that was pushing things a little. All the same, he hated the idea of her going out with that Aaron Sanchez guy. Even if he hadn't been able to pull up any incriminating evidence about the man, Caleb still knew deep down there was something very wrong about him, and that he was obviously working with the equally dodgy Paul Reeves despite the lack of any real evidence to prove such a connection.

Caleb drove home in his new Mercedes, which had continued to work flawlessly. Either the demons hadn't been able to determine what his new wheels looked like—or where he was living now—or they were holding back and plotting some new mischief that they planned to unleash at the worst possible time.

Considering his previous dealings with them, he thought both scenarios were equally likely.

Once he was inside, he found himself wishing he knew where Delia was meeting Aaron for drinks. Someplace very public and very crowded, he assumed, since Caleb knew she was smart enough to set up a first date in a venue where she'd be surrounded by people.

Unfortunately, there were hundreds of bars and restaurants in Las Vegas which fit that particular description.

Maybe he should hire a private detective of his own. Not Prudence, of course, but Caleb knew there were probably plenty of P.I.s operating in the area who'd be more than happy to take his money and dig up all sorts of dirt on Aaron Sanchez and Paul Reeves.

And probably Ty Carter as well, although Caleb had a feeling he might be a bit harder to investigate. Also, even if the guy seemed not quite right to him, he didn't give off the overwhelming sense of malevolence that inevitably surrounded a demon.

Unless he was hiding it. Any demon operating in this town would probably know Caleb was here, and therefore would do its best to mask the sulfurous stink that usually emanated from one of their kind.

Well, even if he didn't end up hiring a private investigator, it might not be a bad idea to collect the names of some likely prospects.

Half an hour later, he had a list of ten people who sounded as if they'd be able to do the job he would hire them to do. He'd run across Prudence Nelson's name multiple times, but obviously, she couldn't make the final list, not if he wanted to keep all this hidden from Delia.

By that point, the hour was well past six, a time when he'd usually start thinking about whether he wanted to go out and pick something up for dinner, or whether it would be better to just stay home and have DoorDash bring his food over.

He'd done that multiple times in the past, so he knew it would be safe enough.

But for whatever reason, he couldn't get his brain to settle down long enough to focus on what he wanted to eat. No, he kept thinking about Delia's meeting with Aaron, and how things would go. What if they really hit it off? What if they actually started dating?

She's a big girl, he told himself. *She can handle this. And you're not her boyfriend. You don't have a say in what she does with her personal life.*

No, he definitely didn't. But he was her friend, and obviously, he didn't want her to be in any kind of danger.

If there was any danger at all, except maybe the normal first date kind of either being bored to death or realizing she had absolutely no chemistry with the man.

Still....

Frowning, he went back into his office and studied the list of private detectives he'd compiled. When he picked up the phone, however, he stood there for a long moment with it waiting in his hand before he carefully put it back down again.

He didn't know what was going to happen between Delia and Aaron Sanchez. The only thing he did know was that if he started investigating her maybe-boyfriend without telling her what he was up to, then he'd be in a world of hurt once she found out.

No matter how hinky he was feeling right then, he wasn't about to betray her trust like that.

———

Even though it was a Sunday and nowhere near a holiday—Easter was almost a month off—spring break crowds still packed the bar at the Hard Rock casino. Delia hadn't thought about that, mostly because she tried to avoid the touristy places and it had been years since she'd had to worry about spring break, but she supposed the crowds had their use.

It would be pretty hard to get up to any real mischief when surrounded by this many people.

Aaron had gotten there before her and had even managed to snag a high-top table not too far away from the bar. He must have been watching to see her enter, because as soon as she had paused at the entrance to scan the crowd, he'd lifted a hand to wave her over.

"What kind of voodoo did you have to perform to get a table like this?" she asked as she sat down, and he grinned.

"No chicken sacrifices necessary. Someone was leaving just as I came in, and I was able to get one of the busboys to clean it off for me."

She thought sacrificing chickens was more of a Santería kind of thing, but she decided to let it go. "That's some good luck."

Despite how busy the bar was, one of the waiters must have noticed the way they'd snagged the table and were now waiting for drinks, so he came over to take their order.

Since this wasn't really about having dinner— Delia guessed they might decide to share an appetizer later on, but that would be it—she decided to skip the wine and have a margarita. Aaron ordered a Kiltlifter pale ale, and once that was handled, he said, "I have some good news."

"Oh?"

"One of my clients thinks the Piñon Drive house would be a great fit, so I'm showing it to her and her husband tomorrow afternoon. It doesn't have any offers on it yet, does it?"

Unfortunately, no. But Delia summoned a smile and said, "Not yet. I know Marcy Talbott showed it yesterday afternoon, but I haven't heard anything from her. It's likely her clients are taking the weekend to mull it over. Until I have an offer on the table, though, it's open season."

Aaron nodded. "Good to know. I saw you're having an open house on Wednesday, too?"

"I am," she said, then paused, since the waiter had returned with their drinks. Once he'd set them on the table, though—and once they'd put in a quickie order for some nachos—she added, "I thought it couldn't hurt to have a weekday open house late in the afternoon to catch those people whose schedules won't allow them to attend one on the weekend."

Of course, the real reason she'd scheduled the open house for Wednesday and not the following Saturday was that she'd be at the poker tournament, cheering Caleb on. However, even though Aaron knew she'd been there in that capacity yesterday, she didn't see the need to point out that she planned to attend all three days this coming week.

They certainly weren't well-acquainted enough to entitle him to know everything she planned to do and everywhere she intended to go.

Besides, plenty of agents had open houses during the week to accommodate people's often crazy work schedules. In a town like Las Vegas, where many businesses were open 24/7...or at least seven days a week...there were plenty of residents who didn't work anything close to a standard Monday-through-Friday and nine-to-five schedule.

"Good idea," he said. "Although I assume you'll cancel it if you get an offer before then."

"Maybe not," she replied at once. "It never hurts to have some contingencies, right?"

Another smile, one that was warm enough, even if it didn't quite reach his eyes. Was he hoping his client would love the house so much that she would make an offer that very same day?

Well, Delia couldn't blame him for that, not when it was the sort of outcome everyone involved in those sorts of transactions hoped for.

"Let's drink to contingencies," he said, and lifted his pint glass.

The customary *clink,* and then they both drank. It was a good margarita, not watered down the way so many of the bars here in town tended to do. By this point, she was used to it, and had the "good" bars on a mental list she updated as necessary, but even so, part of the reason why she drank wine so often when she went out was that then she wouldn't have to worry about getting a wimpy cocktail.

Not much chance of that here, it seemed, so she was glad she'd already mentally resolved to have no more than two drinks tonight. True, it would be easy enough to take a cab or an Uber home if she thought she'd overindulged, but still, it just felt better to keep her wits about her when she was out with someone she barely knew.

"So...what made you go into real estate?" she asked, figuring that was a logical enough question for a first date. The information Pru had provided had already told Delia about where Aaron was from and where he'd gone to school, but obviously, those bare bones of facts hadn't revealed anything about why he'd made the switch from managing restaurants to selling houses.

He smiled, one finger playing with the condensation on the outside of his tall glass. "A couple of different things. I was a restaurant manager for a while—I got my degree in business with a focus on the hospitality industry—but it was kind of grueling, and I knew I wanted to try something else."

"Real estate can also be a bit overwhelming," Delia responded, but he only chuckled.

"I suppose it's a different kind of overwhelming," he said. "Now I have more control over my schedule, even when you count the late night hand-holding when you're trying to reassure a nervous client that their mortgage really is going to fund."

Since Delia had been in that position more than once over the years, she smiled. "Yes, that part can be kind of rough. But I suppose it's better than dealing with customers who keep sending their food back because their pasta is cold, or whatever."

She'd meant that as a sort of throwaway line, but something in Aaron's posture seemed to stiffen.

Was he wondering how she'd known that he'd worked for an Italian restaurant down in Bullhead City?

No, that was silly. Italian food was pretty much universally loved, so making an off-hand comment about pasta wasn't that out of line.

But then he appeared to relax, saying, "Or letting their kids run wild in the restaurant, or dining and dashing, or—" He stopped there, a rueful smile touching his lips. "Anyway, there are lots of things that can go wrong in a restaurant. I suppose you can say the same thing about a house or how it's getting funded, but I still feel like it's a lot more rewarding. You're helping someone find their forever home. That's pretty cool, don't you think?"

Delia did. At the same time, though, she couldn't help thinking that something about his reply had seemed almost too pat, as if he'd said what he thought she wanted to hear rather than what he was actually thinking.

Or she could be reading way too much into all of this. It had been a while since she'd been on a first date, so maybe she was just rusty and was over-analyzing everything because she couldn't remember how to act in these sorts of situations.

She'd never felt awkward with Caleb, though, not when they'd first met, not even when they'd gotten into increasingly crazy circumstances.

Because she'd approached him as a client first and then as a friend. There hadn't been the kind of expectations that inevitably floated around when you were out on a first date.

"I think it's really rewarding," she said, and hoped she didn't sound like someone on a job interview...or maybe answering questions during a beauty pageant. "But then, I grew up around it. My mother's been a real estate agent for, like, forever."

"I know," Aaron replied, and Delia lifted an eyebrow. He didn't seem fazed, however, and added, "Your mom is kind of a legend in the Las Vegas real estate community. So of course I heard about her when I moved here and set up shop."

Delia didn't know about a "legend," but she had to admit that her mother had been at this for nearly thirty years, which was sort of legendary in itself when you considered how many people came and went in the local real estate industry every year. And because she sold everything from multimillion-dollar penthouse condos to three-bedroom starter homes, she had an excellent idea of everything that was out there for a potential buyer, no matter what their budget might be.

Wherever this date ended up going, she knew she'd need to tell her mother about this part of it. Linda Dunne would be tickled pink to know that some people regarded her as a legend.

The nachos arrived then, so Delia and Aaron dug into them, exchanging snippets about the local real estate market, trading stories about the oddest things they'd ever seen.

"No kidding, I repped a guy who'd installed carpet on all the ceilings," Aaron said as he reached for a loaded nacho, barely getting it into his mouth before some of the ground beef and olives and chunks of tomato began to slide right off.

"Why in the world would he do something like that?" Delia asked. She was getting to the bottom of her margarita and figured she should be okay to have another one. The hardest part would be flagging down the waiter, who seemed to have disappeared to another section of the bar.

"He said it was all about noise reduction," Aaron replied, now that he'd finished chewing.

"Was the guy a musician or something?"

A shake of the head. "Nope. He just said he was sensitive to noise. But it ended up costing him a chunk, because the person who decided to buy the house asked for it to either be removed or to have a reduction in price to cover the cost of repairs."

Which couldn't have been cheap, since Delia didn't even want to think what that kind of installation might have done to the ceiling drywall. "What did he decide to do?"

"He took the money hit," Aaron said, then swallowed some of his pale ale. "Told me he didn't want to waste his time looking for contractors. But the cheapest bid came in at around twenty thousand, so it still hurt a good bit."

That was for sure. Delia guessed that a lot of people might wonder why the repairs would cost so much, but if they'd had to replace all that drywall and repaint throughout the house, then the price of those repairs would add up really fast.

"I never had anyone with carpet on the ceiling," she said. "Plenty of bathroom carpet, though. You gotta love the eighties."

Or maybe the seventies. She wasn't sure when the trend for putting carpet in bathrooms...especially master baths...had first begun, but she was glad it had died out with bell-bottoms and acid wash.

They continued to chat, and when the waiter finally came by and asked if they wanted another round of drinks, neither Delia nor Aaron hesitated in saying yes. In fact, she had to admit to herself that she was having a pretty decent time.

Nothing earth-shattering, of course, but that was all right. She just hadn't wanted the evening to be an unmitigated disaster, which it certainly was not.

Aaron also talked a little about his family, and since everything he said matched what Prudence had already told her, Delia was rapidly coming to the conclusion that the man had nothing to hide.

And she supposed she should be relieved about that.

The second margarita was even stronger than the first, so she was glad she and Aaron had ordered the plate of nachos, which was huge and served as a decent substitution for an actual meal. Without it, she would have felt downright tipsy rather than being just a little elevated.

Once they were done eating and had finished their drinks, Aaron insisted on walking Delia to her car.

"I know they have security guards, of course," he told her as they made their way over to the parking garage. "But my mother would have my head if I didn't make sure that a lady made it to her car safely after a date."

"Old-fashioned, huh?" Delia asked with a grin, and he nodded.

"She was born in Veracruz and didn't move to the States until she was around fifteen, when my grandparents on that side of the family emigrated to Nevada. And her grandmother—my great-grandmother—helped raise her, so she's kind of old-fashioned."

In a way, Delia liked that idea, of learning from your forebears, of being steeped in tradition and old family customs. Both her parents had moved here from elsewhere, her father from Chicago and her mother from Seattle, and her grandparents still lived out of state. They came to visit when they could...usually in the depths of winter, so they could escape the snow and the rain for a week or maybe two...but it wasn't anything like being raised with all of them around all the time.

"Well, I appreciate the company," she said. "I've never had a problem in one of these parking garages, but a friend of mine was mugged at Treasure Island a couple of years ago."

And of course, Caleb had been attacked by a couple of minion demons in the Bellagio's parking structure back in January, but she supposed that wasn't quite the same thing as a regular old mugging.

Not that she had any intention of mentioning that particular episode to Aaron Sanchez.

He looked sufficiently sympathetic after learning about her friend's incident. "I hate hearing stuff like that. Was she okay?"

"Yes, just shaken up," Delia replied. "The mugger got her purse, but because she had 'Find My Phone' enabled on her iPhone, the police caught up with the guy just a couple of hours later. He wasn't exactly the sharpest tack in the box, or maybe all the meth had just fried his brains."

That was why he'd attacked Megan. She'd seemed like an easy mark, one who hopefully had enough cash on her that the man could buy himself another hit.

Ever since then, Megan had carried pepper spray with her. Delia didn't bring up that particular detail, though, or mention that she had the same defensive weapon in her own purse. Of course, she would have no need to use it tonight—

Aaron seemed like a perfect gentleman—but at the same time, it never felt smart to reveal all your cards.

"Here we are," she said as they approached her white Kona SUV. A silver BMW occupied the spot to its right, but the one on the left was empty, giving them an easy angle of approach to the driver's-side door.

They paused there, Aaron now looking a little awkward. But this was always the fraught part of a first date, wasn't it? The tense little pause while they tried to decide whether the time was right for a kiss, all the mental calculus that went into determining if this would be a first date with no follow-up or maybe something more.

In this case, though, Delia already knew how she felt about the situation. Yes, Aaron seemed like a nice guy, and they'd certainly had a pleasant conversation over drinks. However, she hadn't experienced a single spark while she was with him, letting her know the chemistry just wasn't there.

And that was fine. She'd tell him she'd had a good time...even as she was inwardly grateful that they'd agreed to split the check, so at least there shouldn't be any entitlement issues to deal with... and then that would be the end of it. True, she'd still have to see him on a professional basis going forward, but they were both adults.

Sometimes things were meant to be, and sometimes they just weren't.

"Thanks for meeting me here," Aaron said. His tone had softened a little, and his dark eyes now seemed almost too piercing, almost black, very different from Caleb's warm brown.

That direct gaze put Delia instantly on alert. She'd seen that same look on other men's faces before, and it usually meant they were about to lean in for a kiss.

Which was the last thing she wanted. Aaron was physically appealing enough, she supposed, but he wasn't the guy for her.

And that was why this needed to end here.

"It was fun," she said. "But I need to get going. Early day tomorrow."

The statement wasn't an exaggeration; she really did have a client meeting her at the office at eight-thirty, the only time the man could squeeze out of his schedule before he had to get to work.

However, Aaron didn't seem too happy to hear about her professional commitments. His eyes narrowed slightly, and his voice turned coaxing.

"Oh, come on," he replied. "It's not that late. I was kind of hoping we could go back to my place for a nightcap."

A nightcap? Did people even say that anymore?

But Aaron looked serious enough, which meant she needed to tread cautiously...even as she thought he had some pretty big *cojones* if he thought she was going to go back to his place on a first date. She wasn't a prude or anything, and yet she had never once gone to bed with a guy after just a couple of drinks.

"Thanks, but I really need to get home."

For just a moment, his eyes remained narrowed, but then he appeared to shake off his irritation, saying, "Okay, sure."

And then he leaned in toward her, one hand reaching for the small of her waist.

Instinctively, she moved away, and a flash of anger showed in his features.

"So...not even a goodnight kiss?"

In the grand scheme of things, Delia knew it wasn't that huge a deal. But something inside her was recoiling, and if she'd learned anything over the years, it was to trust her gut.

"I don't kiss on the first date," she said, her tone deliberately light.

You really think you're all that?

The words sounded clear in her mind as a bell, and for a second, she just stood there, not sure what the hell was going on.

Had she just heard Aaron Sanchez's thoughts?

Before she could even begin to process what had just happened, he spoke again.

"I get it. You have a nice night, Delia."

He turned and walked away, his stride fast,

angry. For just a second, she wondered if she should say something to stop him, then realized this was the best possible outcome. At least he'd gotten the message.

And although she knew she had a lot she needed to sort out, one thing was crystal clear.

She didn't think she'd have to worry about Aaron Sanchez anymore.

Chapter Thirteen

—·‹‹‹·◎·›››·—

A VERY WELCOME MESSAGE PINGED Caleb's phone early Monday afternoon.

Can we meet for dinner at my place? I'll order takeout.

He honestly hadn't expected to hear from Delia today, since he knew she had a full schedule, what with balancing both her mother's clients and her own. She hadn't said exactly when her parents would be back from their anniversary trip to Hawaii, but it sounded as if they were going to be gone all this week as well.

Not the greatest timing in the world, considering how their vacation lined up with the tournament, but sometimes you just couldn't do much about those sorts of coincidences.

At least Delia had reached out, though, which

seemed to indicate she had something important to discuss. She was friendly, sure, but she also didn't generally invite him to hang out just because.

Whatever her motivations, he wasn't about to turn down the invitation.

Sure. I'll bring the wine.

Her reply came back almost at once, so even if she wasn't camped on her phone, she must have had it somewhere nearby.

Seven o'clock okay? I've got a house showing at five-thirty, and I have to go to the office to do some paperwork afterward.

It's fine. See you at 7.

She replied with a thumbs-up, which seemed to indicate that was the end of the convo.

He didn't mind, however. Now he had unexpected dinner plans with Delia, so he only had to worry about filling up the remainder of the afternoon.

Which wouldn't be a problem, since he'd already decided to hit the poker tables again and keep that part of his brain sharp. He'd been watching reruns of past poker tournaments to get some more insight into strategy, but there was a lot to be said for actual in-person interactions.

But he had a few things he wanted to handle first. Although he'd gone back and forth with himself, trying to decide whether he should even bother with a private investigator, in the end, he'd figured it couldn't hurt to have a professional take over his admittedly slapdash sleuthing. Maybe the guy wouldn't find anything at all, but at least then Caleb could tell himself that he'd tried and that it seemed his suspicions hadn't amounted to much in the end.

Just Paul Reeves and Ty Carter, though. Delia hadn't said a peep about Aaron Sanchez in her text, but Caleb had still been able to read between the lines. He sort of doubted that Delia would have asked him to come over for takeout the very next night if her evening with Aaron had gone well. No, they probably would have tried to go on another date right away.

That obviously hadn't happened, though, and Caleb didn't even bother to quell the sense of satisfaction the insight gave him. He didn't have any say as to who Delia dated—they were friends, but he knew doing something like that would be stepping way over the line—but that didn't mean he couldn't be happy when it seemed pretty clear she was going to stay safely single for now.

Since it was now a little past one in the afternoon, he figured he shouldn't have any trouble reaching out to one of the private detectives he'd looked up the day before. All of them seemed about equally qualified, so it came down to just putting his finger next to one of the names and hoping for the best.

The man he called, though—a guy named Jim Whitaker—sounded competent enough on the phone. Caleb explained that he was about to enter into a real estate deal with Paul Reeves and Ty Carter, but he wanted to do his due diligence first and make sure they were on the up and up before he signed on the dotted line.

Jim Whitaker didn't seem to have a problem with any of this. "I'll look into them," he said. "My rate is two hundred a day, plus expenses."

"'Expenses'?" Caleb repeated. Not that he couldn't afford the man's fees, but he didn't want to be paying for the guy to be slipping five-dollar bills into a stripper's G-string or something just because he'd decided to follow a lead at a "gentleman's" club.

"Gas and food, mostly," Jim replied. "I'll provide receipts, of course."

Well, that seemed reasonable enough. "Sounds good."

"Then I'll go ahead and email you my standard contract. Once that's signed and you've paid the retainer, I'll get started."

"Got it."

They ended the call, and only a moment later, Jim Whitaker's contract landed in Caleb's inbox.

Since he guessed it would be easier to read through and sign on his laptop, he went into his office, downloaded the document and looked it over, and then used the auto-sign feature in Adobe Acrobat to fill it out. Afterward, all he had to do was pay the electronic invoice for the retainer—five hundred bucks, no big deal—and send the signed contract back to Jim.

A few minutes later, the man replied, saying he'd gotten everything and that he'd start his investigation tomorrow morning.

Very efficient. Quite possibly, he wouldn't turn up anything at all, but now Caleb felt as though he'd done pretty much everything he could.

Now he just needed to wait.

That Monday was quiet enough, which made Delia happy. Sure, she'd been busy from basically the second she set foot in the office until she walked out the door at a little past six, but it was a normal kind of busy, whether signing up new clients, looking over offers, or sending information on listings that had popped up over the weekend to those who still hadn't found their dream homes.

No voices in her head, nothing to show that anything weird had occurred the night before.

Except it had. Or at least, she thought it had. With almost twenty-four hours elapsed since that strange moment when she could have sworn she'd heard Aaron Sanchez's voice in her head, she was ready to say the whole thing had been nothing more than her imagination.

But she still wanted to talk to Caleb and see what he thought.

A few months ago, she would never have believed that Caleb Lockwood would turn out to be her sounding board and confidant. And sure, there were plenty of matters she would prefer to talk over with Pru, but when it came to anything remotely supernatural other than Delia's ghost-whispering sideline, Caleb was her go-to guy.

She also wanted to talk to him about what had happened at the home Ty Carter had summoned her to on Sunday afternoon. Yes, sending ghosts to the next plane so they wouldn't hang around a house was kind of her bailiwick, but something about that encounter still felt not quite right.

Maybe Caleb could help her untangle all the weirdness of the past couple of days.

He rang the doorbell promptly at seven, and she hurried over to answer it. Because she'd only gotten home a few minutes earlier, she hadn't bothered to change out of her work clothes, although she'd switched her heels for a pair of much more comfortable flats. Maybe one of these days, she'd say the hell with it and wear more practical shoes all the time, but her mother still wore three-inch heels to the office every day, and Delia wasn't sure if she wanted to let her mom show her up.

"Come on in," she told Caleb, who stepped into the foyer and waited as she closed the door. As promised, he held a bottle of wine, although since it was in a fabric gift bag sort of thing, she couldn't tell what it was.

Probably a blend of some sort. They hadn't decided what kind of takeout they wanted, so it made sense that he would have brought something to drink that could go with a variety of dishes.

"What're you in the mood for?" she asked as they headed into the living room.

"Anything," he said with a grin. "Lunch was a while ago, so I'm open."

That made things easier. So far, it didn't seem as if there was any particular type of cuisine he actively avoided, so she felt okay with suggesting a Mediterranean place that wasn't too far away, one that offered DoorDash.

Caleb was amenable to that, so soon enough, they'd placed their order and then opened the bottle of wine he brought. As she'd guessed, it was a red blend from California, and the first sip told her it should go perfectly with their kabob and shawarma.

They sat down in the living room to wait for the food to arrive. After he'd sipped some wine, he said, "So, what happened?"

She blinked at him. Was he asking about her date?

"Something must have happened," he said reasonably. "Or you wouldn't have called me over to have takeout on a Monday night."

"You've been here for takeout before," she pointed out, but his mouth only quirked.

"True, but usually not after you've had such a full day at work. So I figure something must have gone down yesterday, something you didn't want to wait to talk about."

Well, he had her there. "A couple of things, actually," she replied. "But now I'm starting to wonder if it was just my mind playing tricks on me."

He drank some more wine before he responded. "From what I've been able to tell, you're not the kind of person whose brain messes with them too much. So...what happened?"

Where to start? With that unexpected summons from Ty Carter, of all people...not that she'd known at the time who had sent the text...or the weird way she'd possibly heard Aaron Sanchez's thoughts after what had seemed like an utterly prosaic first date?

She decided that talking about the ghost in the

updated '90s house was probably a better place to start, simply because that incident had occurred earlier in the day.

And also because it seemed much less fraught than discussing her date with Aaron, for whatever reason.

However, she'd barely opened her mouth to answer Caleb's question when the doorbell rang.

"Let me get that," she said, then set down her glass of wine so she could go to the door.

He rose as well—not to follow her, but to pick up her glass and carry it and the one he already held over to the table so the wine would be waiting for them when they sat down to eat. They'd already left the partially full bottle in the dining room, so they wouldn't have to worry about that part.

Soon enough, they'd both seated themselves and started portioning out all the goodies they'd ordered—kabob and rice and grilled vegetables, shawarma and fresh pita bread and this amazing creamy dip that looked sort of like hummus but was made with puréed potatoes and garlic. Once they were done with that, however, Caleb settled himself against the back of his chair and gave her a very direct look.

"Well?"

No point in trying to wiggle out of it, especially since she was the one who'd asked him over here specifically so she'd have a sympathetic ear for her tales of supernatural woe.

All right, maybe "woe" wasn't exactly the right word, but she had to admit that yesterday had been weird by anyone's standards...even a quarter demon's.

"I got a text from someone who needed a house cleared," she said.

Caleb looked nonplussed by that revelation. "And?" he responded, then put a forkful of chicken kabob in his mouth.

"The text was from Ty Carter," she said.

Both Caleb's brown brows—several shades darker than his hair—lifted in surprise. "His house is haunted?"

"I don't think it's his house," Delia replied. "I think he just called me there because he wanted to watch me in action, so to speak."

"But there was a ghost."

"Definitely," she said, then paused. Although she was glad that the spirit of the girl had finally been able to move on after spending so many years haunting the property, it was still sad to think of all the milestones she'd missed, from learning how to drive to attending prom, or going to college and discovering her passion as she moved into the world of adults.

All that gone, simply because of a trip and fall in the dark.

"What did you think of him?" Caleb asked, which Delia found telling. He hadn't pressed for further details about the ghost she'd encountered, but instead was far more interested in the man who'd summoned her to the house in the first place.

"I'm not sure," she said slowly. "There's something about the guy that just feels off, even though I can't really put my finger on it."

"That's the same vibe I've gotten," Caleb replied. "I can't explain it, either. But that's why I'm having a private investigator look into him and that other guy from the tournament, Paul Reeves. They both ping my radar, but for different reasons."

For a second or two, Delia could only stare back at him. His revelation had come from so far out of left field, she wasn't sure what to make of it.

"A P.I.?" she managed at last.

He nodded. "Some guy named Jim Whitaker. Seems pretty solid. Anyway, I just have to hope he can find a lot more than I was able to look up online."

A sip of wine sounded like a good idea right about then. After the mellow red blend had slipped down her throat, she said, "You could have called my friend Pru."

"Nope," Caleb responded. "I mean, I'm sure she's good at what she does, but having me hire her for something like this didn't feel right. It just seems smarter for each of us to stay in our lanes, if you know what I mean."

Oddly, Delia thought she did. Or at least, even though there was no real reason why Pru couldn't be working for both her and Caleb, it did feel less complicated for Prudence to stay safely out of his orbit as much as possible.

"If you think so," Delia said, figuring she should leave it there. "What do you think the detective will find?"

"I have no idea," Caleb said. Still holding his wine glass, he leaned against the back of the chair, his expression now almost rueful. "I did my best to find what I could about the two of them, but it wasn't much, and certainly nothing incriminating. So I suppose I was just hoping that a professional might have better luck."

"What did you find, though?" she asked. Ty Carter seemed like such a cipher to her that she thought he could be almost anything from a hairstylist to a martial arts instructor.

"Like I said, not a lot. Paul owns a carpet cleaning business, and Ty is a tennis instructor at DragonRidge Country Club."

Now it was Delia's turn to raise her brows. Of course, she wasn't a member of the country club, but she had clients who were, so she knew it was at least a sixty grand initial membership fee before you could even set foot in the place, and the greens fees were nothing to sneeze at, either.

Anyway, she had to believe that any of the pros who worked there—whether they taught tennis or golf—were probably paid pretty well for their services.

At the same time, though, she had a hard time imagining Ty Carter teaching the backhand to a bunch of trophy wives or out-of-shape executives. He seemed a little too high vibe...and a bit too odd, to put it bluntly, for that kind of career.

"But I couldn't find anything more than that about either of them," Caleb went on. "Which is why I reached out to a private detective. If he can't dig up much more than what I did, then I'll know my spidey-sense is broken and can just move on."

Delia didn't think there was anything wrong with Caleb's instincts. So far, they seemed to have served him pretty well.

All the same, it would be nice to have some hard evidence to back up his suspicions that something was going on with those two.

"One weird thing," she said, and now he grinned.

"Just one?"

"Well, okay, we're dealing with more than that, but we'll stick with the one for now. How did Ty Carter know that house was haunted when people have been living there for more than thirty years with not a single peep that they thought a ghost might be hanging around the place?"

"How do you know someone didn't know about the ghost?" Caleb asked reasonably.

In most cases, that was a logical enough question to ask. But Delia had been clearing haunted houses in the greater Las Vegas area for the past ten-plus years, so she knew better than anyone else which ones had their resident spirits and which were clean as a whistle.

"Because I looked up the property records when I was at the office today," she said. "The house has changed hands four times since it was built in 1991. Even if one of the families that lived there vibed well enough with the ghost that they never detected her presence—and that happens more often than you might think—the odds are pretty damn low that none of the others ever noticed anything wrong. And as far as I can tell, no one ever called in a psychic or a priest or whatever to scope out the place."

Caleb appeared to absorb all this, brows pulling together as he helped himself to a bite of grilled bell pepper. "That does seem a little weird."

"Exactly. But Ty Carter knew the house was haunted, and he had me come there because he wanted to see for himself how I worked."

"Were you able to banish the ghost?"

"It's not really a banishing," Delia replied. A

fine point, but one she would always argue, because it mattered. "I send those spirits to the next plane —or at least, I help them understand that it's better for them to move on, and they do it for themselves. It's not like sending a demon to Hell."

"But that's what I did with the ghost of the serial killer who was hanging around my house," Caleb returned, and she shrugged.

"He'd been avoiding Hell by staying on this plane. Most ghosts are a lot more benign than that, so they just need a nudge to go on to the next world."

Maybe that wasn't precisely a curl of Caleb's lip, but she could tell he wasn't entirely impressed. "Heaven?"

"I don't usually like to call it that," Delia said, knowing she sounded way too prim. "It's possible Heaven exists, but—"

"Oh, it exists," he cut in. "You can't have Hell without Heaven. But I suppose I can see how there might be other planes between Heaven and here."

It seemed he was okay with conceding the point, and she could only be glad of that. After the past couple of days and all their assorted weirdnesses, she wasn't sure whether she was in the right mental place to be arguing for the existence of Heaven.

"Well, then," she said, and reached for her glass of wine.

She knew she needed a drink.

"But there's something else, right?" Caleb probed. "What happened with Ty Carter was a little strange, but I get the feeling that's not the only thing you wanted to talk about."

To be honest, she wasn't sure she wanted to talk about it at all, even with someone as sympathetic about supernatural goings-on as Caleb Lockwood tended to be. But she'd invited him over for dinner, so it would be pretty stupid to turn evasive now.

"It kind of starts with Ty Carter, though," Delia said. "Just as we were wrapping things up at the haunted house, he told me, 'I think you might discover you have talents you didn't even know existed.' At the time, I didn't make much of it, but later that night...."

She let the words trail off, since she wasn't sure how she could even begin to explain the way she might have heard Aaron Sanchez's thoughts as they were standing next to her car in the parking garage.

"What happened?" Caleb asked. He sounded almost gentle, and she wondered what her face looked like right then.

Worried, probably.

"It was...strange," she said. "We were done with our drinks and appetizers, and then Aaron walked me to my car. Up until then, the evening had been almost too normal, but...."

Once again, she found herself wondering if she should complete the sentence, especially since she couldn't really describe what Aaron had been thinking if she didn't also add at least a few details about what had led up to that moment.

Caleb still sat there quietly, one hand resting on the tabletop near his wine glass, although he didn't reach for it. "But...?"

"We had a nice time, I suppose," she said. "I mean, we got along okay, but I could tell there wasn't any real spark, so I knew we wouldn't be having a follow-up date. When Aaron walked me to my car, I got the feeling he wanted a goodnight kiss, and I was thinking about how to fend him off. So I told him I didn't kiss on the first date, and then I heard it in my head, clear as if he'd said it to me directly. 'You really think you're all that?'"

Just uttering the words out loud made heat rush to her cheeks, but at least she'd gotten the worst part over with.

"Is that really true?" Caleb asked. His expression was so neutral right then that she couldn't tell what he was thinking.

Which maybe was a good thing.

"Is what true?" Delia returned. "Because yes, I heard Aaron Sanchez's voice in my head as clear as if he'd spoken to me."

Caleb's mouth quirked. "No, I mean that you don't kiss on the first date."

She set down her fork and shot him what she hoped was a sufficiently withering stare. "I don't see how that's relevant."

"I don't know about 'relevant,'" he said easily. "But it's interesting."

Deciding she really didn't want to go down that road with Caleb Lockwood, she said, "So, you don't have an opinion about the way I heard his thoughts?"

"I'm not denying that it's a little odd," he replied. "Or maybe not. That is, I've heard of things like this happening before."

"'Things'?" she echoed.

"Psychic powers developing out of nowhere, that kind of stuff," he said, calm as if they were merely talking about allergies developing in midlife, the way they had for Delia's mother.

"I'm not psychic," Delia said. The words might have come out a little too harsh, but she didn't think anyone would blame her for that.

Caleb appeared singularly unconvinced. He scooped some more shawarma onto his plate from the takeout container before saying, "Some people would argue that of course you're psychic. Otherwise, you wouldn't be able to communicate with ghosts the way you do."

"It's not like we're having full-on conversations," she returned. "I just sort of...persuade them."

"It's still a kind of communication," he responded. "So maybe it's not so strange that it's started to...branch out, for lack of a better way to put it."

Delia didn't think she liked the sound of that idea at all. Over the years, she'd gotten used to her quirky little talent, especially since she thought she could do some good with it. But she'd prefer to stay out of other people's heads, thank you very much.

"I don't know," she said, knowing she probably sounded way too stubborn. On the other hand, she guessed that a lot of people might have an issue with psychic talents popping up out of nowhere, so her defensiveness on the topic probably wasn't so strange. "I guess I find it hard to believe that my gift...if you want to call it that...could suddenly start morphing into something else."

For a moment, Caleb didn't reply. Instead, he ate a bite of shawarma, washed it down with some wine, and then said, "Back in California, there was this woman named Audrey Barrett."

"An ex-girlfriend?" Delia asked with a curl of her lip.

"No," he said, now looking amused. "She's married to a guy named Michael Covenant. He's a demonologist."

"Ah," Delia said, although she couldn't really see where Caleb was going with this.

"Anyway," he went on, expression undaunted,

"she was a marriage and family counselor when she met Michael. Not a single drop of psychic blood, as far as she knew. But after she was around Michael and was exposed to a pretty crazy demon infestation, her talents began to develop. These days, she's a powerful psychic."

For a moment, Delia could only stare back at Caleb. "So, what," she said slowly, "you're saying that because I've spent all this time around you, my latent psychic powers are beginning to emerge?"

"Something like that," he replied. "I mean, I wouldn't say they were totally latent, not when you've been communicating with spirits on some level for years. But it's possible that being around me has made them stronger, made them something a little different from how they started out."

Well, that was just fabulous. Her life had been humming along smoothly enough, maybe with a little weirdness thanks to the whole talking to ghosts thing, but overall just fine, and now she was supposed to accept that she could sometimes hear people's thoughts?

"It's obviously not constant," he added, as though trying to comfort her. "I mean, can you hear what I'm thinking right now?"

Delia stared across the table at him. His whole attitude was utterly casual, so she didn't think she'd be able to discern his thoughts merely from his posture.

"No," she said after a moment.

"Well, then," he replied, as if that solved everything, and then picked up the bottle of wine and poured them each a little more.

She didn't think he'd proved anything at all. "What were you thinking?"

"That we should have ordered some baklava for dessert."

For a second, she only gazed at him blankly, and then an unwilling chuckle emerged from her throat. "I suppose you have a point there."

He grinned in response. "I'm sure what happened last night was kind of disconcerting. But it doesn't look as if you've had some sort of 'always on' mind-reading talent descend on you, so I don't think it's so bad. And it could come in handy one day."

Possible, like if the thoughts of one of the people he was trying to investigate came through loud and clear when she was standing nearby. However, Delia thought the odds of that happening were fairly low, especially when you considered she'd been near Ty Carter for the greater part of fifteen minutes and hadn't heard a single one of his thoughts.

Or maybe this weird offshoot of her supposed talent only worked properly after she'd had a couple of margaritas. With so many variables involved, it was really hard to say for sure what had caused her to hear Aaron Sanchez's voice in her head...or what it would take for that mental power to wake up again.

"I suppose so," she said, but wasn't willing to allow anything more than that.

Caleb smiled again. "I guess we'll just have to see what happens next."

Chapter Fourteen

———·‹‹(·۞·)››·———

ALTHOUGH HE COULD TELL DELIA WAS
rattled by the sudden shift in her psychic abilities,
Caleb thought it was a promising development. Of
course he'd never ask her to listen to his opponents'
thoughts when he was playing poker—if he wasn't
going to use his demon gifts for that sort of activity, then he obviously wouldn't ask his friend to do
something so morally gray—but still, there was
always the chance that she'd be able to see into
someone's head at exactly the right moment and
possibly give them an advantage they hadn't been
expecting.

By the time he left her house, she seemed a little
less on edge, so he figured he'd done his best. At
least she appeared to understand that, while
unusual, this sort of thing wasn't utterly unprece-
dented, and since she hadn't heard a single blip

from him the entire evening, then she probably wouldn't have to worry about other people's thoughts intruding on her at odd times.

He'd gotten her to promise to reach out if anything else strange happened, and then he'd headed home. That drive had been uneventful as usual, so he wondered if maybe the demons had done their worst and he could let down his guard a bit.

Or maybe they'd backed off precisely so he'd get careless.

Well, that wasn't going to happen. He still checked to make sure he wasn't being followed, and before he'd left Delia's house, she'd loaded him up with another half-dozen bottles of holy water.

"I got a refill from Father Bryce," she'd told him with a laughing glint in her blue-gray eyes as she named the Episcopalian priest who was her source for the blessed liquid, and Caleb could only be glad she was doing her best to handle the situation with as much good humor as she could summon.

Even though he knew logically that she was just as protected as he was—maybe more, since she had a lot of holy water on hand—he found himself wishing she'd asked him to stay. In the guest room, obviously, because she wouldn't have allowed anything else, but if he was right there, he would have been able to come to her rescue immediately if something weird happened.

You can do that anyway, he reminded himself. Lately, he'd been careful not to use his teleportation powers too much, just because popping up in places without any real evidence as to how he'd gotten there was sure to attract attention, but that didn't mean he wouldn't blink himself right over to Delia's house at the first sign of trouble.

No, there wasn't any real reason for him to have stayed.

He just wished she'd asked.

The situation wasn't extreme enough yet for her to have done such a thing, however, so he was left to remind himself that she was a big girl and could take care of herself. Still, a pretty important component of being a grown-up was knowing when it was time to reach out for help.

Even though Jim Whitaker had said he wasn't going to start looking into Paul Reeves and Ty Carter until tomorrow morning, Caleb couldn't help checking his email and his texts, just to make sure he hadn't missed anything while he was over at Delia's. But his inbox didn't have anything except a bunch of notices for various online sales...not for the first time, he wondered how the hell he'd even gotten on all those lists...and he knew he was going to have to wait for the week to really get started before there were any further developments.

Annoying, but there it was.

So he made himself watch some TV, and then eventually he headed upstairs to go to bed. Even as he did so, however, he couldn't help thinking about Delia. Was she doing okay, or had she chided herself for letting him go rather than keeping him around for a while longer to help settle her head?

He had a feeling he'd never know.

Because she hadn't been bombarded all night with random brain waves from her neighbors, Delia was feeling a bit more cheerful when she woke up the next morning. Not all the way, because she still wasn't sure how any of this worked, and she supposed it was possible that a person needed to be much closer than just next door for her to pick up on their thoughts, but still.

Part of her didn't want to look at her phone—she hadn't heard a peep from Aaron Sanchez after that uncomfortable exchange at the end of their date on Sunday evening—but she knew avoiding her voicemails and texts wasn't an option, not when a client could have reached out overnight. Although she tried to be as firm as she could about boundaries, she inevitably would still have that one person who didn't think it was a big deal to call after ten or before eight, which was why she'd made the decision to turn off her alerts at night and make sure the phone stayed in a different room.

However, the only message she'd missed was a text from Prudence.

So far I haven't found anything incriminating about Aaron Sanchez. The one thing that stuck out to me was that he suddenly paid off all his student loans about five months ago. But then I saw that his grandmother died around the same time, so I figured that he'd used his inheritance to pay them off.

On the surface, that theory sounded logical enough. Nothing Aaron had said about his grandmother had made it sound as if she was a woman of means, but maybe she'd been hiding cash in her mattress for decades. Delia knew he'd gone to UNLV, so it wasn't as if he'd been carrying the kind of loan debt he would have racked up at a private college. All the same, if he'd had to finance all four years and didn't have any grants or scholarships to take some of the load off, then he still would have been in the hole around fifty grand, maybe more if he hadn't been living at home while he was going to school. Since he hadn't brought up that particular detail about his college years, she couldn't say for sure.

Also, Pru could have been talking about Aaron's paternal grandmother, and Delia knew absolutely nothing about the woman. He hadn't mentioned her at dinner, most likely because there hadn't been any reason to.

A second text bubble continued Pru's message.

I'll keep looking. It might be hard to find out exactly how Aaron paid off those loans, but that doesn't mean I won't try. And if I dig up anything else, I'll let you know.

Nothing beyond that, but Delia knew her friend was doing her best. If there wasn't anything to find, then obviously, they wouldn't find it.

In the meantime, though, she needed to get ready for work. Her schedule today was just as crammed as it had been on Monday, so she wouldn't have a lot of time to be chasing after various conspiracy theories anyway. No, she needed to keep her head down and get the tasks done that had to be done, and to let Prudence—and the private detective Caleb had hired, she supposed—do the footwork necessary to see if any of the people they were investigating actually had something to hide.

She had several house showings, two new listings to put together, and a client coming in to sign all the paperwork the mortgage company was supposed to send over—they'd promised it the day before but it hadn't materialized, and she was praying it would show up today—so she was sort of glad that the next text from Pru didn't come through until late in the afternoon.

Found something else. Aaron bought a brand-new BMW right around the same time he paid off his student loans. Since I can't get into his bank records, I can't say for sure where the money for the down payment came from. Still, it seems a little fishy.

Yes, it did. Again, he could have just gotten a chunky inheritance, but it still felt like a red flag firmly planted in the ground.

Any other big expenditures around that time?

He moved from a one-bedroom apartment to a condo in Henderson. Much fancier. I think he's just renting it, though, because the county recorder shows the place as being owned by a company called Aegis Holdings.

Cold trickled down Delia's spine as she absorbed that piece of information. Sure, some people probably would have said it wasn't so surprising that Aegis owned Aaron's condo, considering how they were actively acquiring properties in the greater Las Vegas area, and yet she couldn't help thinking this was a lot more than a simple coincidence.

Thanks, Pru. That's...interesting.

Interesting how?

I'm not sure yet. But it's one more piece of the puzzle.

Well, like I said, if I find anything else, I'll let you know.

Delia sent her friend a smiley-face emoji in response to that comment, although she was feeling anything but cheerful right then.

Why was Aaron Sanchez living in a condo owned by the Aegis Group? A mere accident of fate, or something more?

While it seemed like the company tended to focus on vacation homes, they also had a smattering of long-term rentals. She supposed it was possible that they'd just started branching out into that section of the market and Aaron had merely lucked into one of their early offerings.

Or maybe the condo was partial payment for services rendered, although she had no idea what those services might be.

And exactly why had he been at the Desert Paradise poker tournament, anyway? His explanation that he'd been providing moral support for a friend now sounded pretty weak, even if that had been Delia's sole reason for attending.

Well, whatever was going on, she needed to talk to Caleb again. Having him over at her house two nights in a row didn't feel exactly kosher, for reasons she probably couldn't have defined even to herself, but she also didn't want to angle for an invitation to his place.

However, he solved that problem for her by calling a little after five, right before she was about to head out of the office.

"I found out some more stuff," he said, sounding cheerful. Then again, he tended to generally be upbeat, not the kind of disposition she would have expected from someone who had demon blood running through their veins.

"So did I," she replied.

"Perfect. Then why don't you come over and we'll talk about it? I'll order pizza."

She could work with that. Because her day had been so busy, she hadn't even eaten lunch, only wolfed down a protein bar and drank some water during a brief lull between clients. Making up the calorie deficit with a couple of slices of pepperoni sounded like a great idea.

"Okay," she said. "I just need to finish closing up shop over here, so I can be at your place in about twenty minutes."

"See you then."

Delia finished locking up the office and then headed out to her car. Traffic was awful, of course, but eventually she pulled into the driveway of the Pueblo Street house. The whole way over, she'd kept checking her rearview mirrors and being as vigilant as possible, and yet she didn't think anyone had followed her.

Of course, she'd taken extra precautions. Maybe it was crazy, but she'd carefully daubed all the door handles of her SUV with holy water, figuring if any of the demons lurking out there tried to mess with her car, they'd be in for a rude shock. For all she knew, that application of holy water had also allowed her to fly under the radar, so to speak.

There was so much about how all this worked that she just didn't know.

But there was Caleb, smiling and inviting her in, and an open bottle of chianti already waited on the kitchen counter.

"I went ahead and ordered the pizza," he told her as he handed over a glass. "From the way you sounded on the phone, I figured you wouldn't want to wait. Pepperoni and black olives and bell peppers, right?"

They'd hung out together enough that he knew just what she liked. Sending him a grateful smile, she said, "Absolutely right. And thanks for ordering the pizza. I didn't have a chance to eat lunch, so I'm starving."

"Well, it'll be here in a couple of minutes." Caleb paused there, warm brown eyes carefully surveying her. "Do you want to talk about it now, or wait for the pizza to get here?"

"Let's wait," she replied. "It won't be too much longer, right?"

"Probably not. I called them ten minutes ago."

They used up the remaining time by getting the table set and putting some neutral, almost New Age music on in the background. Delia would have thought Caleb was more of a head-banger, but it seemed she was wrong about that...or he'd simply decided it would be better to play something that wasn't quite so intrusive.

The food arrived right on time, which meant they were sitting at the dining room table soon enough. Caleb topped off their glasses of chianti and waited while she put a slice of pizza on her plate.

"So," he said, and gave her an expectant look.

"Maybe this is all nothing," she began, and his eyebrow lifted.

"If it was 'nothing,' then you wouldn't be so worried about it."

Had she really been so obvious? Yes, she'd been keyed up ever since she'd gotten Pru's text, but she didn't think her agitation had been that plain.

Caleb was more perceptive than he let on, though. And since he'd already known something was up, he'd probably been looking at her with a more critical eye than usual.

"Aaron Sanchez," she said, then allowed herself a fortifying sip of chianti. "Pru discovered that he paid off all his student loans around six months ago. He also bought a brand-new BMW for cash right around the same time...and he moved into a fancy condo, one that's apparently owned by Aegis Holdings, if the information on the county recorder's site is to be believed."

"That's a whole lot of coincidences," Caleb remarked before biting off a piece of loaded pizza.

"I thought so, too," Delia replied. Her stomach wouldn't allow her to ignore the toothsome aroma rising from the slice on her plate any longer, so she picked it up and allowed herself a few bites.

Seeming to understand that she needed to eat in peace, he was quiet for a moment as she chewed. But once she'd washed down the pizza with some more wine, he said, "Have you heard anything from that guy at Aegis Holdings?"

"No," she said. "I guess he decided the property wasn't the right fit."

"Or maybe he's just waiting for the right moment."

That possibility had crossed her mind, but in the world of real estate, hanging back and waiting wasn't always the best strategy. "To see if we come down in price?"

"Maybe," Caleb replied. "I mean, I don't have any plans to do that, but—"

"I don't think you'll need to," Delia said quickly. "Marcy Talbott messaged me this morning and said her buyers were very interested but that they were still thinking it over. And there's the open house tomorrow."

The smile he sent her after she delivered that statement was almost indulgent. "I'm not worried about the house selling. Sure, it would be nice to not have so much money tied up in it, but since I'm not paying a mortgage and won't have to worry about property taxes for almost a year, it's not that big a deal."

She'd already known that, and yet it was good to have confirmation from Caleb that he didn't expect her to have the place sold by the end of the week.

"So, it's fairly obvious that Sanchez is sus, even if we don't really know the depth of his involvement with Aegis Holdings," he went on. "It's too bad you weren't able to pick up more of what he was thinking when you were with him."

The thought of having to muck around in Aaron Sanchez's mind wasn't remotely appealing. Delia shrugged, then said, "Well, next time I'll try the full Vulcan mind meld."

Caleb chuckled, as she'd sort of hoped he would. "With any luck, there won't be a next time. It's probably better for you to give him as wide a berth as possible. I know that won't be completely easy, not when you might have to interact with him professionally, but I suppose as long as you're not alone together, you should be okay."

She wouldn't argue, not when doing everything she could to avoid being alone with Aaron Sanchez sounded like a pretty good idea. Since she didn't have too much more to offer on that subject, she said, "Sooo…you have some news, too?"

"I do," Caleb replied, clearly not deterred by the obvious change in topic. "Jim Whitaker—the P.I. I hired—found some pretty sketchy stuff about Paul Reeves. Supposedly, he owns a carpet-cleaning business, but Jim says he's pretty sure it's a front of some kind. The company was created about eight years ago, and yet it only has a handful of Google reviews."

"Well, maybe people don't see the same need to review a carpet-cleaning business as they do a restaurant or something," Delia responded. Taken on its own, that particular data point didn't seem too significant.

"Maybe not," Caleb said. "But then Jim told me he copied and pasted a couple of the reviews he did find into Google to see if they popped up anywhere else, and sure enough, they were originally posted about other carpet-cleaning companies across the country. The name of the business was changed, obviously, but otherwise, they were identical."

All right, that sounded pretty fishy. And Delia had to admit that a carpet-cleaning outfit might be the perfect cover for all sorts of shady activities. No one paid much attention to a van with a business logo on it, whether it was driving around town...or parked in front of a particular property for a lengthy amount of time, the way a carpet cleaner would need to be.

"Did he find anything else?"

"Not yet," Caleb said. He'd finished his first slice of pizza, so he reached into the box to get another.

"Does Paul Reeves own or rent his home?" Delia asked next, since she'd certainly hit pay dirt on Aaron Sanchez when looking at him from that angle.

Or at least, Prudence had.

"Own," Caleb said briefly. He swallowed some chianti, then added, "Nothing weird there, as far as Jim was able to tell. Regular mortgage, one he took out about ten years ago. No defaults or late payments or anything like that."

Well, if he really was using his carpet-cleaning business to launder money, then Delia supposed Mr. Reeves would do whatever he could to look like an honest, upstanding member of society.

"Okay, so he's someone we definitely need to keep an eye on," she said. "What about Ty Carter?"

He was the one she was really interested in, although she kept that thought to herself.

She didn't want Caleb getting jealous.

Something that sounded suspiciously like a sigh, and he set down his wine glass. "Clean as a whistle, according to Jim. The guy's worked as a tennis pro at DragonRidge Country Club for about five years, and before that, he worked at another tennis club in Brentwood, California. He's renting a townhouse not too far from the place where he works now. No complaints, nothing out of the ordinary."

Nothing except the way he'd summoned her to a house he'd somehow known was haunted, even if the people who'd actually lived there apparently didn't have a clue.

Or the way he might or might not have awakened some latent psychic powers that had been buried deep within her. Caleb seemed to think that was a natural consequence of spending time around him, but Delia wasn't sure whether she bought that idea. After all, she'd known him for several months now, so why had that strange ability to read minds appeared only recently instead of soon after they'd met?

She had no idea...and she had a feeling that if she pressed him on the subject, he probably wouldn't know, either.

"But you of all people know it isn't that hard to hide information about your identity," she pointed out, and Caleb gave a reluctant nod.

"True," he replied. "On the other hand, I'm pretty sure if someone really started looking into my past, they'd discover this life I've constructed for myself doesn't hold up under close scrutiny."

He didn't sound too worried as he spoke those words. Bravado, or the simple understanding that he'd always be able to bounce back no matter what the world might throw at him?

Delia thought it would be nice to have that kind of confidence.

This wasn't about him, though.

No, it was about Ty Carter...how something about him simply didn't add up, even if she couldn't have explained why she felt that way.

"What if Ty is like you?" she asked.

"You mean, a quarter demon?"

She nodded.

"Definitely not," Caleb said at once. "I'd be able to sense that. True demons are harder, just because they know how to mask their identities when it suits their purposes. Whereas we quarter demons always knew who each other were." He paused there, his expression almost sad. But then he straightened and added in a much brisker tone, "Anyway, I already told you that the only quarter demons in existence were the guys I knew from Greencastle, and they're all in Hell right now."

"And there aren't any other hybrid people out there?" Delia asked next, remembering how he'd told her there was a family of psychics in California whose father was an angel. She still had a hard time wrapping her brain around the concept, but what would have been the point in making up something like that?

"The McGuires," he said.

"The ones who are half angel?"

"Yes," he replied. Something about his tone sounded almost reluctant, but that didn't stop him from adding, "Rosemary and her two sisters."

"No brothers?" she asked, doing her best to puzzle her way through all this, and Caleb shook his head. "Does that mean angels can only have female children, just like demons only have males?"

"I'm not sure about that part," he said. "But, based on a couple of things my father said, I have a feeling that there are more angelic offspring in the world than any of us knew about." Another hesitation, and he added, "What, you think Ty Carter is part angel or something?"

"I don't know," Delia responded. Right then, she thought what she didn't know definitely outweighed anything she did, especially when it came to the supernatural stuff. "All I know is that he summoned me to a haunted house I'd never even heard of, and after I was around him, suddenly I could hear other people's thoughts."

Caleb took a bite from his piece of pizza and chewed in a meditative way as he appeared to ponder the conundrum. "But you've only heard Aaron thinking. No one else, right?"

Well, that question was easy enough to answer. "No. And I've had plenty of clients coming and going since then, so you'd think I should have been able to pick up on at least some of their thoughts."

"Maybe, maybe not." Caleb set down his half-eaten slice of pizza and wiped his fingers on the napkin in his lap. "All this stuff...it's not cut and dried. It's possible that Aaron Sanchez presented some kind of threat, and that was why you could hear what he was thinking. Your clients weren't a threat, so there was no reason for the gift to kick into gear."

Had Aaron even been a threat? At the time, she'd just thought he was being a little pushy and entitled, but certainly not dangerous. However, that was before she knew that he'd had a chunk of money appear out of nowhere...before she'd discovered that the condo where he lived just happened to be owned by Aegis Holdings.

All of which could still be a coincidence and nothing more. After the way they'd parted, she sure as hell wasn't going to call him and inquire about his living arrangements or where he'd gotten the money to pay off his student loans and buy himself a luxury car, so she supposed it would all have to remain a mystery for now.

"But even though Ty Carter looks perfectly normal on paper, that doesn't mean there still couldn't be something supernatural going on with the guy," Caleb continued. "If he actually is part angel, then sure, I suppose being around him could have had just as much to do with the expansion of your psychic talents as anything else. What that doesn't explain is why he would care whether you were able to hear other people's thoughts."

Delia wasn't sure about that, either, although she had a few ideas on the subject. What if Ty Carter was unable to directly intervene with the demons that might possibly be roaming around Las Vegas? What if the only thing he could do to help was try to beef up her defenses so she'd be better able to spot trouble coming?

Possibly. It was hard to say what any of this meant.

Now Caleb was almost smiling. "Have you tried to listen to my thoughts?"

"Of course not," she replied, knowing she sounded indignant. "That would be rude."

"I suppose so," he said. "Still, I think you should give it a try."

Was he joking? His expression was faintly amused, although Delia didn't get the impression that he was teasing her.

"I don't know how," she said. That might have sounded like a cop-out, but it was the simple truth. When Aaron's thoughts had invaded her mind, she hadn't been consciously trying to listen to him. It had just...happened.

Maybe Caleb's shoulders lifted ever so slightly. It was hard to say, because he'd reached for his slice of pizza at the same time. "I'm going to pull a Yoda here and say you shouldn't try. Just...let it happen."

Easy for him to say. Also, Caleb Lockwood was about as opposite from the little green Jedi master as any person could possibly be, but she thought he had a point.

All right. She closed her eyes, mostly because she thought the fewer distractions she had preying on her mind, the better. Yes, she could still smell the rich scent of melted cheese and crisp pepperoni, but it wasn't too intrusive.

Of course, she'd always completely sucked at meditating since she could never get her hamster wheel of a brain to let things go and Zen out, so if that was a prerequisite for reading other people's minds, then she was doomed to failure before she even got started.

But that wasn't a very healthy point of view to maintain regarding the situation, so she did her best to banish it as well.

For a fraction of a second, her mind went utterly blank. And in that blankness, she thought she heard a whisper of a notion, one she was pretty sure hadn't originated in her own brain.

I really hope that guy isn't an angel.

That was it, come and gone before Delia could barely begin to grasp the words. Still, she was almost positive that had been Caleb, not her.

"Were you just hoping that Ty Carter isn't really an angel?" she blurted, and Caleb sat up in his chair, eyes widening slightly before he got control of himself.

Then he smiled.

"Yes, I was. So...you picked up on that?"

"I guess I did." She hesitated, wondering if she should press him on the issue, and then figured the hell with it. "Why is it such a problem if Ty is an angel, or part one? Wouldn't he be an ally?"

"It would be nice if that were the case," Caleb replied. "But even if you put aside the problem of him helping a quarter demon like me, angels aren't always the most reliable beings in the universe. They like to stand back and observe, which I suppose makes sense when you're someone who takes the long view but isn't so great if you need some immediate help."

Delia supposed he had a point there. "But you don't think he's consciously interfering."

"No. In his own way, he might be trying to help. I just don't think we can rely on him."

Well, she hadn't been planning to. "It's fine," she said, and Caleb lifted an eyebrow.

"Really."

"Sure," she replied, and found herself grinning back at him. "After all, we beat these demons before...and we can beat them again."

Chapter Fifteen

—·«《·☽·》»·—

WHILE CALEB WAS GLAD TO SEE THAT
Delia remained undaunted, he wasn't sure whether
he shared her entirely optimistic view of the situation. There were so many threads going on here
that he was pretty sure all it would take was one
sharp tug, and the whole thing would unravel.

But since she seemed cheerful as he said good
night and then remained in the doorway to make
sure she got safely in her car, he didn't say anything
else. Once he closed the door, though, he found
himself frowning.

All of the men they'd investigated had been
involved with the poker tournament in some way.
True, Aaron Sanchez had claimed to only be there
to watch and help out a friend, but that could have
been a convenient lie. And Ty had washed out
pretty early on, making Caleb wonder why the

man...part angel, whatever he might turn out to be...had been there at all.

Unless he'd played in the tournament simply to provide himself with an excuse to hang around even if he wasn't competing.

That theory didn't make a lot of sense, though. It wasn't as if the competition was closed to spectators, so Ty Carter could have been there simply as an onlooker and no one would have paid him any particular attention.

But maybe he'd wanted to be an actual competitor so he could see how Caleb operated up close. Maybe he'd needed to find out if Caleb was using his power to win.

In that case, Mr. Carter would have been sorely disappointed. Even though Caleb had been tempted from time to time, he hadn't used one iota of his demonic abilities to influence the cards. Was that why Ty had allowed himself to be disqualified so soon? Had he learned there wasn't much to see, so he didn't need to hang around?

Maybe.

Or maybe angels were just crappy poker players.

But Caleb had to admit that things had been quiet enough today, and Delia hadn't reported any weirdness at work, either, so maybe they didn't have much to worry about. For all he knew, Paul Reeves was a sort of watchdog, either in league with the demons or unconsciously influenced by them, and they were standing back because when he was playing in a tournament, he wasn't off at a different casino winning way too much money through magical underhanded means.

Although if their real intent was to keep him away from the gaming tables, one would have thought they would have tried to drive him off when he was making the rounds yesterday, still winning, if not nearly so much.

None of this was making a whole lot of sense.

Because he didn't think he'd get to the bottom of the whole mess by standing there and brooding, he instead busied himself with putting the leftover pizza—not that there was much, only two pieces, which he planned to eat for breakfast—in the fridge and then clearing away the plates and glasses and loading them in the dishwasher.

The modest amount of cleanup didn't take very long, however, so soon enough, he found himself standing in the living room, wondering if he should try to watch some TV, maybe the reruns of the poker championships he'd stored on his DVR. That didn't feel right, though...especially since he planned to make one last run at the casinos tomorrow afternoon while Delia was holding her open house...so instead he headed upstairs and returned to some of the websites he'd bookmarked during his initial research into his poker competitors.

Ty Carter's face stared at him from the Dragon-Ridge Country Club site, handsome, smiling, but with eyes that still seemed to hold a lot of secrets.

Or maybe that was just Caleb's imagination. He had to admit something about the guy rubbed him the wrong way, but he supposed he was mostly irritated about the way Ty had made Delia meet him at that haunted house just so he could awaken her latent psychic powers.

If that was even what had happened at all. As he'd already pointed out, Caleb thought it just as likely that those gifts had begun to awaken because Delia had been spending time around him. With a regular person, it wouldn't matter how long they spent in the company of a partial demon...or angel, he supposed. But because she already had her own psychic power, the one that allowed her to communicate with ghosts, it hadn't taken too much to get other parts of her brain to begin to wake up.

She'd certainly heard him earlier tonight when he'd coaxed her to try listening to his thoughts. Just a small bit of what had been going through his mind, true, but it still proved she would probably be able to develop her talent further now that she understood how much it might be capable of.

But if Ty was much more than he'd pretended

to be, why was it that Jim Whitaker hadn't been able to find anything inconsistent about his background? There seemed to be clear evidence that Paul Reeves wasn't the simple carpet cleaner he pretended to be, and yet that didn't seem to be the case with Ty Carter. Was it simply that the side of the angels was a lot better at hacking government databases and employee records?

Caleb didn't have the answer to any of those questions. Not for the first time, he thought that his sheltered upbringing in Greencastle hadn't prepared him for any of this kind of stuff. He'd gotten a very small taste of the real world when he'd gone to California to look for the missing *Project Demon Hunters* footage, but even though he'd had to lie through his teeth the whole time about who he really was and where he'd come from, it wasn't as if he'd been tasked with figuring out whether the people he'd been dealing with were who they pretended to be.

Also, back then, he'd been the bad guy. He probably wouldn't have thought of the situation in those terms, but he'd been doing his father's bidding, following along with Daniel Lockwood's wishes because that was what he'd always done.

And his father had never been on the side of the angels.

In a way, the demon hunters had done him a

huge favor by banishing the whole Greencastle gang to Hell. At the time, he'd been furious and despairing, thinking there was no way he'd ever be able to free himself from that godforsaken place.

But because he'd been able to escape and the rest of them hadn't, he could now say he was finally free of his father and his terrible edicts.

Caleb ran a hand through his hair, then closed his laptop. He still didn't have a lot of answers, but for the moment, he seemed safe enough, and so did Delia.

For now, he'd have to be content with that.

Getting ready for open houses was always kind of crazy. Sure, this wasn't Delia's first rodeo...or even her fiftieth...but still, there were so many little things that needed to be handled, from making sure all the signs were placed on the right street corners to ensure the most visibility to deciding which treats would tempt buyers the best, from arriving early to do any last-minute tidying up to reminding herself for what felt like the hundredth time not to forget the flyers she'd picked up from the printer just the day before.

Of course, she didn't have to worry too much about straightening up the place, just because it was empty and there hadn't been anyone around to drop crumbs on the shining floors or leave their mail on the table near the entryway. All the same, she found herself roaming around the house, adjusting a picture here or plumping a pillow there, just so the place would look as perfect as possible when the buyers started to arrive.

If anyone came at all. She'd had a few open houses like that, awful wastes of time while she stood there in her uncomfortable stilettos and wondered if events such as those were outmoded in an era of video walk-throughs and 3D models, which were included on most online listings these days.

But Delia reassured herself that the market was very different now, and although inventory was up slightly from its lows of more than a year ago, there were still more interested buyers than there were houses available. That didn't mean people would snap things up sight unseen, and yet she had a feeling Caleb's former home wouldn't be up for sale for too much longer.

That inner pep talk seemed to be just what she needed, especially since several cars pulled up in front of the house and parked just as the hour ticked over to four-thirty, telling her they'd probably been waiting somewhere else to avoid arriving too early.

From then on, she had a steady stream of people coming and going. She handed out refreshments and answered questions, including the ones where people asked if there were any offers on the house. Of course she had to respond, "Not yet, but there's been a lot of interest," which seemed to be sufficient to let everyone know that they shouldn't sit on this one indefinitely.

At six o'clock, Evan Matthews walked in, just as the last of the browsers was leaving.

Because Delia hadn't heard a single word from the man since she'd shown him the house the week before, to say she was startled was probably an understatement. However, she recovered her composure as quickly as she could and offered him a smile she hoped looked genuine.

"Mr. Matthews," she said. "I could have given you another private showing if you needed a second look at the house."

He returned her smile, although something about it didn't quite seem to reach his eyes. "Well, when I saw you were having an open house, I thought I'd just drop by rather than take up more of your time by making another appointment."

She wasn't sufficiently annoyed by his unexpected—and late—arrival to point out that she'd been just about to start closing up the house, and therefore he was intruding on her time almost as much as he would have been if he'd come here for a real showing.

"That's fine," she said, glad that years of experience in the industry had taught her how to put on a friendly public face no matter what she might be thinking. "I was just about to tidy up in the kitchen, but feel free to take a look around."

He nodded. "This won't take very long."

Then why come by at all? she wanted to ask, but instead she only inclined her head toward him. "Of course. Just let me know if you need anything."

"I will."

As she was heading into the kitchen, she noticed that he'd pulled a phone out of his jacket pocket and was starting to take pictures of the living room and the downstairs powder room. Technically, he wasn't supposed to take photos without her express permission, but because the house was vacant and he wasn't really intruding on anyone's privacy, she decided to let it slide.

Especially if his unexpected return signaled that the Aegis Group was about to make an offer.

Caleb might have some words to say about that, though, especially in light of what they'd discovered over the past couple of days. It wasn't as if they'd found that the Aegis Group had been doing anything technically illegal, but the connection to Aaron Sanchez still stank to high heaven no matter how she tried to explain it away.

Well, then maybe she should be praying that Marcy Prescott's buyers would finally get off the pot and make an offer. That would cut out Evan Matthews and Aegis altogether, and, with any luck, Delia would never have to deal with them again.

She put the leftover brownies and chocolate chip cookies in a Tupperware container and sealed it up, then got a sponge from underneath the sink and began wiping down the island. By the time she was done, Evan Matthews had reappeared from his tour of the home, looking almost pleased with himself.

"I'm glad I came back for a second look," he said. "The other members of the board weren't as keen about the property, since it's fairly far from the Strip, but I think I have enough information now to convince them that this house is just what we've been looking for."

Exactly what information he now possessed that he didn't have in hand last week, Delia wasn't sure. The online listing for the property had more than sixty pictures and a detailed write-up, but if a few amateur snaps were what the Aegis board required to reassure them the house would be a good investment, then so be it.

That didn't mean she didn't plan to send Marcy a quick text after Evan was gone to let her know the sharks were circling and that her buyers needed to make a decision, stat, if they wanted to buy the place after all.

Some people might have viewed such a move as slightly unethical. Delia didn't look at it that way, though, especially since Marcy's buyers were the ones who'd viewed the house first.

And also because Caleb would much prefer to sell the house to a private party.

"I'm glad to help." She paused there before adding, "If there's anything else...."

"No, you've been very helpful. Thank you again."

Evan let himself out the front door, and Delia hurried over to lock it. She wasn't expecting anyone else to come by, but still, the last thing she wanted to deal with right now was a couple of stragglers.

Also, she wanted to make one final pass of the property before she left. Although she didn't think Evan had meddled with anything, she still needed to check and see that everything was where it was supposed to be.

But the furniture and the other decor appeared completely untouched, and if Mr. Matthews had scribbled pentagrams on the ceiling or done something else to the house, it certainly wasn't evident to her.

Too bad her supposed psychic gifts hadn't kicked in while he was here. A quick peek into his mind might have provided some of the information she needed.

But her telepathy...or whatever you wanted to call it...seemed to have taken a powder for the moment, and there didn't seem to be much she could do about it.

Well, except gather her things and make a quick call to Caleb, just as she'd promised him she would, so he'd know how the open house had gone.

She went back downstairs and put the extra sales flyers in the leather satchel she used as a briefcase, then got her phone out of her purse. He picked up on the second ring, a sure signal that he'd been waiting to hear from her.

"How'd it go?"

"Pretty good," she replied. "We had about twenty people come through." Then she paused, realizing she should just go ahead and blurt it out. "Evan Matthews stopped by."

"He did?" Caleb sounded genuinely surprised. "I thought he'd bailed on the place."

Not that strange an assumption, considering how they hadn't heard from the man in days. "So did I," Delia said. "But he said the board was still considering the property, and he wanted to come over and take a second look."

Caleb was silent for a moment. "That seems kind of fishy to me."

"I thought so, too," she responded. "But that

could just be because neither of us is too disposed to think the best of Aegis Holdings right now. Problem is, we don't have any real evidence to suggest they're anything more than what they appear to be."

"Maybe not, but...."

He didn't finish the sentence; he didn't need to. What with Aaron's suspicious behavior and the way his current home was owned by Aegis, it didn't take a huge leap of logic to guess that something sinister might be percolating under the surface, even if they had no idea what it might be.

"I know," Delia said. "And honestly, I'm going to text Marcy and let her know interest in the property has picked up, so she needs to light a fire under her clients. I can't do much more than that, though."

"And I appreciate it." A sigh came through the phone's speaker, and Caleb added, "But I can always refuse to sell to Aegis, right?"

"Of course," she replied immediately. "It's your property, so you're the one calling the shots. The only issue with that is if word gets around town that you're difficult to deal with, you might have a harder time selling the house."

Now he chuckled. "I'm not too worried about that part. I'm sure if you let it be known that I wasn't interested in selling to some conglomerate that wanted to turn the place into a vacation rental, I'd be viewed as a hero in some circles."

He was probably right about that. While plenty of people had made lots of money turning private residences into temporary vacation homes, the other residents in the neighborhoods involved often had a few choice words to say on that topic, none of which could be safely printed in a newspaper article.

"Then keep thinking good thoughts that Marcy's buyers will come through," Delia said lightly.

"I will." Caleb paused for a beat or two before saying, "And I'll see you at the tournament tomorrow, right?"

"Wouldn't miss it," she reassured him. "Three o'clock?"

"Yep," he said. "Actual play doesn't start until three-thirty, but you'll want to get a good spot so you can see all the action."

At least half of which she wouldn't be able to understand. That was all right, though. The important thing was that she'd be there to lend her support.

"Sounds like a plan, then. I'll see you at three."

"Thanks for updating me on the open house."

They both ended the call there, and Delia shoved her phone in her purse and started gathering all her things. When she got to the front door, however, she stood in the entryway for a moment, glancing around, double-checking that everything was in place and that you'd never know some twenty-odd people had tromped through the house just a little while earlier.

She'd done her best. Now they'd just have to see who was willing to put an offer on the property first.

God willing, it wouldn't be Evan Matthews.

Chapter Sixteen

—·‹‹‹ ‹ ◯ ‹ ››› ·—

Delia was right on time, pushing her way through the crowds at the Desert Paradise casino to the spot where Caleb stood. As far as he could remember, she'd told him that she was still going to work a half day today, but she must have gone home to change since she was now wearing slim jeans and sandals and a pretty embroidered top in a pale sage color that perfectly complemented her copper-red hair.

Just the sight of her was enough to buoy his spirits. He didn't quite know why he'd been feeling so anxious this morning, but he supposed that was mostly because, while they guessed some sort of supernatural shenanigans had been going on this whole time, neither of them really knew what the end game was...or what form it might take.

"Hey," she said as she stopped near him. "Parking was crazy. I hope I'm not late."

"No, you're right on time."

If they'd had a very different sort of relationship, he might have bent down to give her a kiss, or she might have come over and put her arms around him and given him an encouraging hug. But since they were still floating uncomfortably in the friend zone, he knew neither of those things was going to happen.

Well, it was uncomfortable for him, anyway. If Delia wanted things to progress further, then she was doing an awfully good job of hiding her feelings.

He couldn't worry about any of that right now. This afternoon, his sole focus was on surviving until the semifinals tomorrow...and, with any luck, the finals on Saturday.

And while he thought it would be great to win the whole thing, he was okay with only advancing a little further. Just accomplishing that much would let him know that he could hold his own with some serious poker players, even if he didn't use any of his demonic gifts to help him along. By this point, a lot of the real amateurs had been knocked out of the competition, leaving people who, if they weren't on the pro circuit, still definitely knew what they were doing.

"So...how does this work, exactly?" she asked.

"It's pretty simple," he said. "We're down to eight tables of four people each. Eliminations will take that down to four tables of four during the semifinals. And the final will just be the last four who survived the semis."

"Funny how you have half the people competing today, but it feels twice as crowded."

Her observation was correct; the place looked positively packed this afternoon, even with two more rounds to go. It seemed as if a lot of people must have gotten off work early so they could hang out on the sidelines and watch.

"Guess there's not much else going on today," he said with a grin.

Delia only shook her head. "Guess not. Do you know which table you'll be playing at?"

Because he'd already checked in with Hank Bowers a few minutes earlier, Caleb had an easy answer to that question. "The one over there," he replied, pointing to the one set up on the opposite side of the gaming area.

Maybe her lips pursed a little. "It's going to be hard to see anything that's going on."

The same thought had passed through his mind, and yet there wasn't much he could do about it. He didn't know how the event organizers arrived at the seating arrangements—did they pull the names out of a hat, or maybe use some sort of computer randomization system?—but he guessed he and Delia would just have to roll with it.

"I know," he said. "About all I can do is hope that I survive today and that I get a better table assignment tomorrow. I suppose the good thing is that there'll be a lot fewer of us in the semifinals, so it should be easier to get close to the action."

"Oh, you'll survive," she said, tone supremely confident.

He lifted an eyebrow. "Did you have a vision or something?"

"Nothing like that," Delia replied, a flicker of worry passing across her features. It seemed pretty clear that she didn't like to talk about her psychic powers, even in jest.

Not that she'd exhibited even the slightest hint of precognition or whatever it was that people called it when you could see the future, so Caleb didn't think she'd added that particular talent to her psychic grab bag.

At least, not yet.

"No, it's just that you always seem to have luck on your side," Delia said, and Caleb chuckled.

"I wouldn't exactly call it 'lucky' to have been trapped in Hell for two years."

No one was paying any attention to what they were saying, which was why he'd felt safe making that remark.

Besides, even if someone had overheard him, they would have thought he was speaking metaphorically, like maybe being stuck in Barstow or something, not the actual real-life Hell.

"But you got out," Delia replied, and now her expression was very earnest. "That has to mean something, right?"

He supposed it did. Whether it had any bearing on him making it into the semifinals...or the final round...remained to be seen.

A woman's voice sounded over the P.A. system. "Players, please take your assigned seats. Play will begin in five minutes."

"Guess I need to go," Caleb said. He knew he sounded calm enough, and he realized he now felt pretty steady on the inside, too. No nervous butterflies like he'd experienced during the first rounds of the competition, and he wondered if he was getting jaded.

Or maybe his modest wins at the gaming tables on Wednesday afternoon while Delia was conducting the open house at his old property had been enough to reassure him that he still had it, and that there wasn't any material reason why he shouldn't do well during the quarterfinals.

Delia flashed him an encouraging grin, and he made his way over to his table. Although he'd seen some of the other people who'd been assigned there during earlier rounds of the competition, he hadn't formally met any of them.

Today, they were all men—an older guy with gray hair combed straight back from his face who introduced himself as Ken Steele, and then two who looked as if they were in their late thirties or early forties, Lou Bishop and Daniel Fields. Everyone shook hands and then sat down to wait for the dealer to arrive.

Caleb hadn't felt anything strange from any of the guys when they'd exchanged handshakes, which didn't necessarily mean much. Sometimes he was able to detect whether someone was a demon in disguise, and sometimes he wasn't. He still didn't know for sure whether it was because his own instincts weren't as great at that particular task as they should have been, or simply because some demons were better at masking their origins than others.

After the dealer—a woman maybe around thirty, with platinum hair and near-black roots— arrived and began shuffling the cards, Caleb settled into his seat, letting his awareness expand across the room. Just at the edge of his peripheral vision, he spotted Ty Carter standing near the bar, his attention fixed not on any particular table but seeming to scan the entire tournament floor with methodical precision.

Had Delia noticed him? She remained where she'd been when she first arrived, straining a little to keep her eyes on the action, so Caleb had a feeling she hadn't noticed their otherworldly visitor.

If Ty Carter was even otherworldly at all. He could just be an oddball. God only knew that Las Vegas had plenty of those.

The first few hands were played conservatively, with everyone feeling each other out, getting a sense of their limits and, with any luck, their vulnerabilities. Caleb won a small pot with a pair of queens, Daniel folded twice in a row, and Lou took down a decent pot with trip sevens. Nothing unusual...yet.

It was during the fourth hand that Caleb first noticed something funky was going on.

Ken Steele, who'd been sitting almost motionless since the game began, suddenly twitched his left hand when Caleb raised pre-flop. A small gesture, barely perceptible, but in that moment, something strange rippled through the air, reminding him again of heat waves rising from hot asphalt. The cards in the deck seemed to shimmer for just an instant.

Two tables over, a player—a middle-aged man Caleb recognized from the previous rounds, even though he didn't know the guy's name—made exactly the same twitch.

The flop came: Jack of hearts, nine of spades, ten of diamonds. A dangerous board with a possible straight in play.

"Check," Ken said, his voice carefully neutral.

Lou bet aggressively, and Daniel folded at once.

When Caleb called, he felt it again—that strange ripple of energy, like something unseen passing between the tables. His demon senses tingled, picking up patterns he hadn't noticed before: three players at three different tables all shifting their chips in precisely the same way. Four others maintaining the identical posture.

It was all way too coordinated to be a coincidence, and his back tensed.

"Raise," Ken announced, pushing a substantial stack forward. The chips slid across the felt with unnatural precision.

As Ken made his move, Caleb caught sight of Hank Bowers standing behind the rail, watching intently. The tournament organizer still wore his usual friendly expression, but something calculated seemed to lurk behind his gaze as it darted from table to table, player to player, in a pattern too deliberate to be random observation.

The turn brought the queen of hearts.

"Check," Ken said again, but this time his eyes flicked briefly toward Lou, who immediately bet half his stack.

Caleb hesitated. The straight was there if he

had a king, and the flush draw was live. But something about the situation still felt wrong, even though he couldn't quite put his finger on it. When he looked up from his cards, he saw Hank Bowers nod almost imperceptibly in the direction of one of the other tables, and a player there immediately went all-in.

At the exact same moment, Ty Carter emerged from the crowd to pause near the bar entrance, where he began speaking with two men Caleb had never seen before. One was tall with salt-and-pepper hair and wore an expensive suit that seemed slightly too large for his frame. The other was shorter and much darker, maybe Hispanic or Native American, with rectangular glasses and a stiff, almost military bearing. Neither of the two strangers looked like typical casino patrons.

As Caleb watched, Ty murmured something to the taller man, who bent close to whisper something in return. The short one nodded, looking satisfied.

Just what the hell was going on here?

"Your call," the dealer said, pulling Caleb's attention back to the game.

The pattern fell into place with a click he almost felt. Eight tables. Thirty-two players. But the energy wasn't flowing randomly—it was circulating in a specific configuration, like a circuit board or a ritual diagram. The players weren't just competing, he realized with a chill.

No, they were part of something larger.

"I'll call," Caleb said as he pushed his chips forward. When his fingers touched the felt, a pulse of supernatural energy seemed to flow through the table, connecting to the others like nodes in a network.

The river card was the king of spades.

Ken's expression remained impassive, but there it was again—that strange little twitch in his left hand. Across the tournament floor, Caleb could now see at least five other players making identical gestures, almost like they were puppets controlled by the same master.

"All in," Ken announced.

Lou folded immediately, his earlier aggression vanishing. In fact, he looked almost confused, as if he wasn't sure what he'd really meant to do.

Caleb studied his cards, the board, and then the larger pattern unfolding around him. Now he realized that the tournament wasn't just a poker competition—it was a supernatural energy collection system of some kind. Each hand, each bet, each elimination appeared to be generating and directing power.

And Hank Bowers was somehow orchestrating it all.

"I fold," Caleb said, deciding that making a

strategic retreat was probably the best option here. Much better to observe what was happening than to become part of whatever ritual was being conducted here.

Ken collected the pot without comment, his gaze briefly meeting Hank's across the room.

As the play continued, Caleb focused less on the cards and more on mapping the pattern he'd begun to sense earlier. The energy seemed to flow the strongest when big pots were decided, especially all-in confrontations. When a player was eliminated, a pulse of something—emotion? life force?—was transferred throughout the tables, following some kind of predetermined pattern.

Caleb glanced over at the spectator area, where he spotted Delia, who seemed to be doing her best to follow the play. When their eyes met, he gave a small, deliberate nod toward Hank Bowers. She followed his gaze, her brow furrowing as she observed the tournament organizer methodically making his way around the perimeter.

In his peripheral vision, Caleb saw Ty Carter and his two associates separating, taking positions at different observation points around the tournament area, almost like sentries.

Or maybe counterweights.

But he couldn't allow himself to get too distracted by possibilities, not when he needed to remain focused on the game.

The next significant hand formed a turning point. Daniel, who'd been playing conservatively, suddenly went all-in pre-flop. Lou called instantly, as if he'd been expecting the maneuver.

"Pocket aces," Daniel announced, turning over his cards.

"Kings," Lou responded as he revealed his hand.

The board ran out: seven of clubs, three of hearts, jack of diamonds, four of spades, and—predictably—the ace of clubs.

While Daniel raked in his chips, Caleb suddenly experienced a surge of energy different from the others—purer somehow, less artificial. Looking up, he saw Ty Carter watching the exchange with something like satisfaction on his even, handsome features. Whatever ritual Hank was conducting, Ty seemed to be doing his best to counter it.

Two supernatural forces, using the tournament as their battlefield.

When Lou stood to leave after getting knocked out of the game, Caleb noticed something odd—a small sigil visible for just a moment on the man's wrist as his sleeve rode up. Then it was gone, either hidden again or maybe just fading away.

Across the room, another player was elimi-nated, and Hank Bowers immediately appeared at that table, offering seemingly casual congratulations to the winner while placing a hand briefly on the departing player's shoulder. The touch looked innocent enough, but Caleb sensed energy being harvested, collected.

The pattern was becoming clearer with each elimination. Players weren't just losing; they were being drained. And, judging by the methodical way Hank moved through the tournament area, this had been his plan all along.

Caleb should have guessed no one would be that friendly without having some sort of ulterior motive.

Ty Carter, meanwhile, seemed to be intervening selectively from his spot on the sidelines, allowing some eliminations while subtly influencing others. When Ken made his move against another player, Ty's attention sharpened, and a counter-current of energy surged, disrupting whatever gambit Ken had been attempting.

"Play to continue for thirty more minutes," the tournament director announced over the PA system.

As another hand began, Caleb weighed his options. He could continue observing, gathering information, or he could make his move—to try to break the pattern by advancing to the semifinals while disrupting whatever ritual was building.

When he looked over at the place where Delia stood, he noticed her watching Ty Carter's associates, her cool blue-gray gaze intent on their movements. The taller man had positioned himself near an emergency exit, while the military-looking one had taken up a spot directly behind Ken Steele's chair.

Their gazes met briefly, and in that moment, Caleb realized she sensed it somehow as well—the supernatural currents flowing through the tournament, the building tension between opposing forces.

He turned his attention back to his cards. Whatever game was being played here went far beyond Texas Hold 'Em.

And he'd have to figure out how best to survive it.

Although Delia hadn't been able to see everything that was happening at the poker tables, she hadn't missed the way Caleb had inclined his head toward the burly middle-aged man who seemed to be in charge of the tournament, or at least had a position of some importance in the organization. Whoever the guy was, it seemed Caleb wanted to make sure she kept tabs on him.

She didn't see anything too out of the ordinary —he made the rounds of the tables, gave several players encouraging pats on the shoulder when they were eliminated, and generally seemed to be acting as both an observer and a support system—but despite all those outward appearances of innocence, she could tell something weird was going on here. Exactly what, she wasn't sure, but the atmosphere in the room had a strange edge to it, the sort of thing that made the hair want to stand up on the back of her neck.

And then she spotted Ty Carter. He was standing near the bar, but he wasn't alone. No, two men who looked strangely official lingered nearby, and they exchanged a few words.

She couldn't hear what they were saying, though, not from this distance, and not with the constantly shifting and murmuring crowds making it difficult to remain focused on anything for longer than a few seconds. The only thing she was able to tell for certain was that the two strangers remained next to Ty for a couple of minutes before they began to weave their way through the crowd, taking up positions at right angles to him, as if they were separate pieces of a tripod or something.

Weirder and weirder.

Ty Carter didn't seem to be doing much of anything. Whatever the other men had said to him, it didn't appear to have had much of an effect, because now Ty stood there with his arms crossed, his gaze still fixed on the play taking place at the various tables a few yards away as if it was the most important thing in the world.

Maybe it was.

Would it be completely awkward if she went over and talked to him? Wasn't that what you were supposed to do if you bumped into an acquaintance in a public place?

The way he reacted to her friendly overture might tell her a whole lot. She didn't know what was going on at the tournament, and any additional data points could only be helpful.

That seemed to decide things. Since Ty was still standing near the bar, she could make it look as if she'd approached simply to get a drink. And because the tournament organizer had continued to make his rounds of the gaming area, it wasn't as if she would have to work too hard to keep an eye on him.

Not that she knew why Caleb had wanted her to do such a thing in the first place. Yes, the vibe in here wasn't anything she'd expected, crackling with weird energy like the atmosphere before a thunderstorm, but that could have just been her nerves talking. She certainly hadn't seen anything physical that she could actually put a finger on.

It was harder to push her way through the crowd than she'd thought it would be. Eventually, though, she made it to the bar and ordered a white wine spritzer. Something wimpy like that wouldn't hurt her powers of observation, but it provided a good alibi for why she was over there at all.

When she turned around, drink in hand, she saw Ty Carter watching her with something that almost looked like amusement.

"Hello, Delia," he said. "Did you come to cheer Caleb on?"

"I did," she replied. "It looks like he's holding his own, but I'd be the first to admit that the rules of Texas Hold 'Em are pretty much Greek to me."

"Oh, Caleb will make it to the next round," Ty told her. He spoke the words simply, as if they were such an incontrovertible fact that there wasn't any point in discussing them in depth. "He's become quite good at all this."

She supposed he had, or he wouldn't have even gotten this far. "What brings you here?" she inquired, hoping she sounded as if she was merely indulging some mild curiosity. "Picking up tips for the next time you enter a tournament?"

Ty's gaze shifted from the gaming tables and focused on her instead. Although the lighting in here was dim enough that she shouldn't have been able to clearly see their color, they still felt far too bright, piercing and blue as the zircons that were her mother's birthstone.

"Oh, I don't think there's any reason for me to enter another tournament," he said. "That first round was just to give me a sense of how these things worked. My real task is something very different." If possible, his stare grew even sharper. "But I think you already knew that."

Right then, Delia wasn't quite sure what she knew, except that if it hadn't been for Caleb playing a few yards away from where she stood, she would have found an excuse to get the hell out of there as quickly as she could.

"So...something weird *is* going on here."

Ty didn't even blink. "You're perceptive," he said. "I thought you would be able to sense the undercurrents in this room, especially now."

Delia thought she knew exactly what he was referring to. "Something I might not have been able to do a few days ago. But now that part of my mind is awake, isn't it?"

"It is," Ty replied. "And it will continue to awaken further...if you let it."

"Why did you do that to me?" she asked, even as she realized her tone sounded way too plaintive. "What if I don't want it?"

He smiled. "Your gifts would have come to the forefront even without my intervention. It just would have taken a while longer."

What was that supposed to mean? That Caleb had been right, and exposure to his demonic nature would have eventually jolted her psychic abilities out of hibernation, even without Ty Carter's meddling?"

"Are you...?" Delia let the words trail off, then told herself she needed to grow a spine and ask the damn question now that the man was standing in front of her. "Are you an angel?"

His smile didn't waver for a single second. "It's perhaps a bit more complicated than that."

Applause erupted from the people watching the competition, and Delia shifted to see what they were clapping about.

A group of people stood in the center of the gaming area, all of them smiling.

One of them was Caleb.

"I told you he would advance to the next round," Ty said.

"Yes, you did," Delia replied. But even as she opened her mouth to ask how exactly he'd known that, he disappeared.

No, he hadn't turned away from her and walked into the crowd. He'd just vanished into thin air...and no one standing near them seemed to have noticed a damn thing.

Nice trick.

So, did that mean Ty Carter really was an angel...or another demon? They all seemed able to teleport. However, since Delia had never seen Caleb do that sort of thing when anyone else was around, she didn't know whether he had the ability to make anyone nearby completely ignore the way he was bending all the rules of physics.

There are more things in Heaven and Earth, Horatio.

A shake of her head, and then she sipped her white wine spritzer and waited for Caleb to be done with his official business so he could come over and meet her.

They definitely had a whole lot they needed to talk about.

Chapter Seventeen

—·‹‹‹·☾·›››·—

"THEY WERE SUCKING THE ENERGY OUT OF the players?" Delia asked, expression aghast.

"That's what it sure looked like," Caleb said.

They'd gone back to his house, mostly because, while a celebratory meal felt in order, they both knew they had way too many things to talk about that they didn't dare have overheard by any regular bystanders. The casino was slightly closer to his place than it was to Delia's, which was why they'd ended up there.

Also, he liked the Chinese restaurant just a few blocks away better than the one near her house.

Now they were drinking pinot noir and passing around various plates of noshables, and some of the jangliness from the tournament was beginning to recede. Not completely, because Caleb didn't think he'd ever be able to forget the way Hank had put his hand on the other players' shoulders or how it had felt like energy was being sucked out of them as if through a straw, but it still was much better to be home.

"So...the whole tournament was a setup to rob people of their life force or something?" Delia asked.

"I don't know," he replied, which was only the truth. "Maybe the energy-stealing is just a handy side benefit, and their real motives are even more sinister."

Her brows drew together, and she set down the egg roll she'd been holding so she could reach for her glass of wine. "I'm not sure if you can get much more sinister than taking away someone's life force."

Caleb, however, had spent several years in Hell...and had been raised by a half demon...so he knew there was a whole world of sinister out there that she should never have to explore.

"What worries me is that it sure feels as if Hank has known all along that I was part demon," he said.

If possible, Delia appeared even more troubled by that additional wrinkle in the situation. "Is he a demon, too?"

Probably better to ignore the whole "too" thing. Caleb could tell she hadn't meant it in a derogatory way, only that it was easier to lump all demons together rather than trying to put a fine point on her comment.

Anyway, he didn't think he could answer her question with any degree of certainty.

"I don't know," he said. "He doesn't feel that way to me, but not all demons do. It's possible that part of his game was to let me know I wasn't hiding my identity quite as well as I thought I was."

"To put you off balance?" she asked.

"That could have been part of it," Caleb replied. "The problem is, since I don't know what their overarching plan is, it's hard for me to say anything about their motivations."

Honestly, the only thing he knew for certain right now was that he'd somehow made it into the semifinals...even if his appetite for playing in the competition seemed to diminish with every passing moment.

"I wonder what they'd do if I walked away," he commented next, and Delia's eyes widened slightly.

"You mean...just bail out of the tournament?"

"Yep," he said as he reached for the container of chicken fried rice and spooned some more onto his plate. "I mean, what's it even getting me at this point? I've made it to the semifinals, so it's pretty clear that I can hold my own at a poker table without using my powers. And with this whole thing with Hank Bowers...."

Not much point in going on, since Delia already knew the whole sordid story.

Rather than appear sympathetic, though, her chin lifted slightly, and her blue-gray eyes seemed positively steely.

"Isn't that letting them win?"

"Maybe it is," he responded, even as he thought they'd gone way beyond worrying about who was winning and who was losing. "I guess I just don't see the point in putting myself in harm's way when I don't have to."

"But Hank already knows what you are," she pointed out.

All right, that much was true. However, it didn't seem as if Hank Bowers—or whatever it was that was hiding inside him—intended to do much with the information. By walking away, Caleb hoped he would send a signal that he wasn't going to interfere...and that he expected the same courtesy from Bowers in return.

The coward's way out, possibly, but he thought he'd much rather live to fight another day.

"Maybe so, but I get the feeling he'd leave me alone if I bailed on the whole thing."

More a hope than a gut feeling, and yet the more he thought about it, the more Caleb liked the idea of bowing out of the tournament. It wouldn't be such a big deal, after all. They'd just call in one of the people who were eliminated from the quarterfinals and put them in his place. No harm, no foul.

Delia, on the other hand, looked anything but thrilled with him for even toying with the idea of backing out. "What about Ty Carter?"

"What about him?" Caleb asked.

Her eyes narrowed again. "Don't be disingenuous."

He didn't bother to argue with that assessment, not when he knew that was exactly what he'd been doing with his response. "Okay, I think he was doing his best to intervene...him and those two other guys who were with him. I'm still trying to figure out whether Bowers noticed, though."

"I don't think he did," Delia said at once. "I was trying to keep an eye on him the whole time, and I have to believe that if he'd sensed what Ty and his two buddies were doing, he would have shown some sign of it and might have done what he could to stop them. And if they were trying to keep things from getting completely out of hand, then that means we're not in this entirely alone."

Possibly, she had a point there. "But what's their endgame?"

She only shook her head, then broke the end off one of her egg rolls and put the morsel in her mouth. After she was done chewing, she said, "If they're really angels or part angels or whatever, maybe they don't have an endgame beyond doing their best to ensure that people don't get hurt."

As much as Caleb would have liked to tell her she was being hopelessly naïve, he was forced to admit he didn't know all that much about angels or their motivations. Maybe they were involved solely to reduce whatever damage Hank Bowers and whoever else was in his cabal might be inflicting on innocent bystanders.

The sigil he'd seen on Lou Bishop's wrist. That one brief glimpse hadn't been enough for Caleb to tell exactly what it was. Some way of controlling the man? Did that mean he wasn't a demon, but only someone who'd been in the wrong place at the wrong time, a useful tool for Hank to discard when he didn't need him anymore?

He didn't know. Sure, he was a quarter demon, but this still felt way above his pay grade.

"Did Ty say anything to you?"

One corner of Delia's mouth quirked. "He said he knew you'd go on to the next round."

Caleb supposed he should be glad for such faith in his poker-playing abilities, but that wasn't really what he'd been asking about. "Anything else?"

Her expression abruptly sobered. "He basically admitted that he woke up these weird psychic powers of mine...not that they were of much help today. But he also said they would have come to the forefront eventually even without his intervention. He just sort of helped them along."

One mystery cleared up. That didn't mean a whole lot more of them weren't still unsolved.

"I guess that's something," Caleb said, then poured some more wine for both of them, since their glasses were almost empty. "But I'm not sure it's enough to convince me to stay in the tournament."

She'd picked up her glass after he'd refilled it and now settled against the back of her chair, expression earnest. "I have to believe you were there for a reason. Otherwise, you would've gotten knocked out early in the competition."

He couldn't help shaking his head at that comment. "Thanks for the vote of confidence."

Maybe she didn't quite roll her eyes, but he could tell she wasn't going to let it go, either. "This isn't about my confidence in your abilities. It's about believing there has to be some purpose to all this beyond you just figuring out whether you could hold your own at Texas Hold 'Em without any help from your powers."

Well, that was how it had all started. Idle curiosity...along with a desire to show that he could do just fine at acting like a regular mortal.

But the whole thing had grown far beyond that, turning into some monstrous bloom straight out of *Little Shop of Horrors.* Backing away now might not even be an option.

Even if he still wanted to argue his side of the situation.

"Sometimes things don't have any real meaning," he said. "They just are."

"Are all demons nihilists?"

"I'm not a nihilist," he returned calmly. "Just realistic."

Both her eyebrows lifted, but she didn't reply at once, and instead scooped up some lo mein with her chopsticks and put it in her mouth. A moment while she chewed, her expression still thoughtful, and then she spoke again.

"I think we both have to acknowledge that our 'real' might be a little different from that of the rest of the population. Not when you're part demon, and I have these psychic powers appearing from nowhere, and we're dealing with a guy who might be an angel or at least angel-adjacent. In that kind of world, it's very possible that things *do* happen for a reason. And if that's the truth, then you need to acknowledge there may be a real purpose to you playing in that tournament, even if it's just to protect the other players from getting hurt."

Caleb wanted to argue that no one had been hurt. Sure, he'd gotten the sense of people's life force being drained by whatever infernal spell or enchantment Hank Bowers had been trying to cast, but it wasn't as if the losing players hadn't walked away from the table under their own power or anything close to it.

Then again, he supposed that having people carried off in stretchers might have been bad for business...or at least would have attracted far too much notice.

Maybe they would have gotten hurt, though, if it hadn't been for whatever kind of interference Ty Carter and his two companions had been running.

And since Caleb knew he was hip to Hank Bowers' game, that meant he would be extra vigilant in the next round.

"Okay, fine," he said, knowing he wasn't being exactly gracious in defeat, not with that annoyed note in his voice. "I won't bail on the competition. But if Bowers or any of the other players turn into big, scaly demons and go on the attack, I'm outta there."

"Oh, come on," Delia replied. She was smiling now, a sure sign that she knew she'd come out on top in this particular debate. "You know I always carry holy water with me. No matter what kind of tricks they try to pull, we'll be ready for them."

Not for the first time, Caleb thought it was a very good thing that he had someone like Delia Dunne to watch his back. After spending most of his life thinking he was utterly on his own when crunch time came around, he had to admit her support was a welcome change of pace.

"True," he allowed. "Or at least, we'll be as ready as we can be. But if there's one thing I know about demons, it's that they don't like to do anything that outs them for what they are. They much prefer to work in the shadows."

"I wouldn't exactly call running a poker tournament 'working in the shadows.'"

Caleb shrugged, then popped a piece of cashew chicken in his mouth. "It is when no one else knows demons are involved. See, the thing is, if people are forced to admit that demons are real, then they also have to allow for the existence of Hell. And if Hell exists, then Heaven does, too, and that's not anything the folks downstairs want to become a common belief."

Delia didn't look all that convinced by his argument. "Lots of people already believe in Heaven," she pointed out.

"They do in a sort of lip service sort of way. But that's not the same thing as knowing it deep in your gut, of acknowledging it like you would that the sky is blue or the sun sets in the west every evening. Right now, it's not anything a person can see with their own two eyes."

Because she didn't respond right away, Caleb could tell she was pondering what he'd just said, doing her best to square it with her personal experience.

"Okay," she said at length. "I suppose I can see your point on that one. So I also can understand why demons wouldn't want anyone to know they really exist. I suppose that's why they're so into disguising themselves and doing their best to conceal what they are."

"Exactly," Caleb replied. "Also, coming up here is kind of like a vacation for them. Sure, they get up to all sorts of mischief when they're topside because that's what they do, but they're also doing their best to enjoy themselves."

Delia gave a disgusted shake of her head and reached for her wine. Just as her lips parted to respond, however, Caleb's phone buzzed in his pocket.

Under normal circumstances, he would have ignored it and let the call go to voicemail. However, since there were only two people he could think of who might be calling him at this hour, and one of them was currently sitting across the table from him, he figured he'd better pick up.

"Hi, Jim," he said after a quick glance at the screen. "What's up?"

Delia straightened, her face now bright with interest. Like Caleb himself, she'd probably realized that the private detective wouldn't be calling in the middle of dinner unless he had a damn good reason.

"I found something sort of strange," Jim said. "You know how it seemed as if Paul Reeves' carpet cleaning business was some sort of front?"

"Yes."

"Well, it turns out he actually has been servicing some properties. I did some digging, and it turns out they're all owned by the same company."

For some reason, tension knotted in Caleb's stomach.

When Jim spoke again, his words weren't entirely unexpected.

"Those properties all belong to an outfit named Aegis Holdings."

Chapter Eighteen

—·《《·☽·》》·—

DELIA DIDN'T KNOW WHY SHE WAS surprised that Aegis Holdings was involved in all this. Even though she hadn't been able to fully figure out the pattern yet, she still knew the company was rotten.

But that private detective Caleb had hired was damn good. Not only had he unearthed that little factoid about Aegis being Paul Reeves' sole client, but he'd also emailed a list of Aegis's properties to Caleb later that evening just after she left to drive home.

Now they were tailing Paul Reeves' work van as it headed into a neighborhood where she'd sold a property only the week before. It was a nice area of homes built about fifteen years earlier, just old enough that a lot of them still had wall-to-wall carpet, unlike newer houses that almost universally had either tile or wood or luxury vinyl plank floors.

Delia was driving her Kona, just because she and Caleb had both agreed that it was less conspicuous than his new Mercedes, especially after she removed the door magnets advertising the Dunne & Dunne real estate agency. And once Paul had pulled into the tract, she purposely hung back and let him disappear around a corner, figuring it wouldn't be too hard to find out where he'd stopped, not with that van parked at the curb or in the driveway of the house he was working on.

Sure enough, she spotted the van after they turned down a street located in the middle of the housing tract. And since it was pulled into the driveway rather than sitting on the street, there was absolutely no question as to which house he was inside.

"Hang on a sec," she said after she parked her SUV a couple of houses down, then undid her seatbelt and pulled out her phone.

"Need to make a call?" Caleb asked, only half-joking. After all, she'd hastily canceled her morning appointments so they could play amateur detective, so he probably thought she needed to handle something before they went in to confront Paul Reeves.

But that wasn't why she'd gotten out her phone.

"No," she said. "I want to Google the address

of the house Paul Reeves is working on. If it's owned by Aegis, then it's probably just a vacation rental, but in case it's a long-term property, I want to make sure it's unoccupied. You don't want us to go busting in there if there are any renters around, do you?"

"Probably not," he admitted.

It didn't take very long to discover that the house was currently up for rent—a standard year lease, and not just for a week here or there. Most likely, the HOA in this neighborhood had banned short-term rentals.

Which kind of begged the question as to why Aegis had bought the property in the first place, since they seemed to be focused on vacation homes.

Then again, the condo Aaron Sanchez was renting definitely wasn't an Airbnb.

Delia wasn't going to get bogged down in the whys and wherefores, however. No, the important thing was that the house was currently unoccupied. Maybe Paul had come here to get it ready for some new tenants, since the first of April wasn't too far off.

"Okay, looks like the coast is clear," she said as she returned the phone to her purse.

"Good," Caleb replied, his gaze moving toward the front door of the home. It was shaded by a small portico and had tall, slim windows on either side, probably to allow at least a little light into that section of the house. "So...what's the plan?"

Honestly, that part of this whole endeavor was still a little fuzzy. "I guess we go in and see what he's up to. If he's really cleaning carpets, he's probably going to be preoccupied and not even notice us right away."

In fact, a large hose snaked out of the van's cargo area and into the home's front door, leaving it slightly ajar. It would be easy enough to get inside.

Caleb had obviously come to that same conclusion, since he said, "Okay. Let's see what we can find out."

He also unfastened his seatbelt, and they both got out of the little SUV. Even though she knew he could handle himself in a confrontation—and even though she had a half-dozen vials of holy water weighing down her purse—she could still sense the way her heartbeat sped up as they approached the entrance of the house.

Through the partially open door, she heard the faint whir of machinery. Maybe Paul Reeves' carpet-cleaning business was mostly a front, but it sure sounded to her as if he was working now.

Maybe his lords and masters at Aegis wanted him to make sure their properties looked good, even if he didn't have any other clients he needed to impress.

Caleb pushed the door open just wide enough so they could both slip into the house. The hum of the steam cleaner continued without even a hiccup, which told Delia that Paul Reeves didn't seem to have noted that two interlopers were now inside the property.

And it also helped that he was working in the back, most likely in the family room off the kitchen, since that was how a lot of these houses were laid out. They might vary slightly from floor plan to floor plan, but the basic architecture didn't change very much.

Sure enough, there was Paul Reeves, moving the brush head back and forth over an expanse of beige carpet that already looked as if it was in pretty decent shape. Clearly, though, the people at Aegis wanted to make sure the place was immaculate before the new tenants moved in.

The less people had to complain about, she figured, the lower the chances that anyone would look at the company too closely.

"Hi, Paul," Caleb said, casual as if they'd just bumped into one another at a blackjack table.

At once, Paul Reeves raised his balding head from his inspection of the carpet and glared at the intruders. He still wore the same thick glasses he'd had on at the tournament, and he was flushed and perspiring...and looked royally pissed off.

"What the hell are you doing here?" he demanded.

A fair enough question, Delia supposed, but Caleb still looked as if he didn't have a care in the world.

"I've got some carpets I want cleaned, and I thought your Google reviews looked pretty good."

Scowling, Paul turned off the steam extraction unit and set the nozzle down on the floor. "Then call my office."

"No one was answering."

The man crossed his arms. On the back of one wrist was an odd little tattoo, something that reminded Delia vaguely of the symbol the artist formerly known as Prince had used once upon a time, although this one was more angular and not nearly as friendly-looking.

Caleb must have noticed it, too, because he shot a knowing glance in her direction and gave a very small nod.

"That's because I'm a one-man operation," Reeves said.

"I suppose that works out okay...considering how your only client seems to be Aegis Holdings."

Paul Reeves was already flushed from exertion, but his face turned an even uglier red, his skin almost the shade of those awful canned beets Delia's Aunt Rosie had always tried to feed them when her family went visiting in Chicago.

But even though the man's anger was obvious to her—and, she supposed, to Caleb as well—that didn't stop him from trying to stonewall them.

Voice flat, he said, "I don't know what you're talking about."

"Sure you do," Caleb replied. He'd been doing all the speaking so far, which was just fine by her. Delia knew she'd never been all that good at confrontations, while Caleb seemed to positively revel in them.

Or at least, he didn't back away when it came time to get in someone's face.

"I've got the receipts," he continued. "So there's no point in pretending. I suppose I'm just trying to figure out what's in it for you. Or is it more that you don't have any say in the matter, thanks to that sigil on your wrist?"

At once, Paul clapped a hand on his arm, his chubby fingers hiding the mark that had been inked into the skin there.

"I think you'd better leave," he growled. "You're trespassing on private property."

"Maybe we are," Caleb replied. "Then again, the door was open. We might be operating in a sort of gray area here." He glanced over at Delia. "I think the H_2O might come in handy right about now."

For a second, she just looked at him blankly. Then she realized what he was trying to say.

A splash of the holy water she carried might be enough to break the hold the sigil had over Paul Reeve, if only temporarily. And that might buy them enough time to get some useful information out of the guy.

She didn't reply out loud, only gave a small tilt of her head in Caleb's direction so he'd know she understood what he was trying to say.

"There's nothing 'gray' about it," Paul Reeves retorted. "And if you two don't get out of here now, I'm going to call the cops."

While he was speaking, he'd been focused on Caleb, apparently dismissing her because she'd been silent this whole time and didn't appear to be much of a threat.

Boy, was he wrong about that.

Her hand was already inside her purse. One of the little vials of holy water touched her fingertips, and she popped the cap and pulled it out, then rushed at Paul Reeves and splashed at least half the vial's contents on his arm.

"What the fuck are you doing, you bitch?" he snarled.

"Whatever I have to," she said sweetly as she backed out of the way.

In that same moment, though, the expression on Paul Reeves' meaty features turned almost puzzled, as if he couldn't quite figure out what he was supposed to do next.

"Who are you?" he asked, eyes blank, confused.

"A couple of friends," Caleb said casually. "And we'll get out of your hair just as soon as you answer a couple of questions."

"I don't know anything," Paul Reeves responded, but again, he looked more perplexed than anything else.

"Well, I guess we can find out for sure soon enough." Caleb paused there—not, Delia guessed, because he didn't know which questions to ask, but more because he wanted to make sure she didn't have anything she needed to interject.

Because she was more than happy to continue to let him do the talking, she shook her head very slightly.

"It's pretty simple," he said, his gaze fixed firmly on the other man, whose eyes looked blurry and muddy behind his thick-lensed glasses. "What's Aegis's stake in all this? What are they really up to?"

Paul Reeves' features twisted then, and Delia wondered if she needed to splash some more holy water on that sigil, just to make sure it was effectively blocked. But then his face went almost blank, and he said, "Some kind of ritual. I don't know much about it."

Somehow, Delia guessed that whatever "ritual" Aegis was cooking up didn't involve anything benign like making sure they had a nice, wet spring or raising enough funds to sponsor a food bank or something.

And since Caleb's jaw had tightened upon hearing Paul Reeves' words, she guessed he'd been thinking just about the same thing.

"Well, tell me what you do know."

More perspiration dripped down the man's forehead. His nostrils flared, but then he responded, "They plan to use the tournament's final round to activate a network of supernatural energy collection points. I don't know how, and I don't know where any of those points are. I was just in the tournament to see if there was anyone playing who might cause some trouble."

"Like me?" Caleb inquired, expression amused.

"Yeah, like you. They don't know for sure what to do about you, so the word came down to watch what you were doing but not interfere."

Well, Delia supposed that was encouraging. It also explained why they hadn't worked harder to make sure Caleb was knocked out in the first round.

He crossed his arms. "Do you know who broke into my house?"

Paul Reeves frowned. "What house?"

Undeterred, Caleb pressed, "What about the brakes on my Porsche?"

The older man's brow furrowed. "I don't know about any Porsche."

Of course he didn't. As far as Delia could tell, the man didn't seem to know much about anything.

However, even though he'd been shot down twice, Caleb didn't appear ready to give up. "What do they plan to do with all the energy they're collecting?"

"I don't know." Sweat had begun to drip off the man's face and onto his already blotched T-shirt. In that moment, Delia almost felt sorry for him. She had no idea how he'd gotten tangled up with Aegis or why they'd targeted him, but it sure seemed as if he was an unwitting pawn more than anything else.

Caleb appeared to have come to the same conclusion, because he shook his head, saying, "Then I guess we'll let you get back to work."

Once again, he looked over at her, and she got the signal right away.

Time to get out of there.

They both turned and walked away. Even as they exited the house, Delia couldn't help tensing a little as she wondered if Paul Reeves was going to do something to stop them.

But either the holy water was exerting enough influence that the thought hadn't even crossed his mind, or he'd decided getting into a physical alter-cation wasn't a very good idea, not when Caleb was at least ten or fifteen years younger than he and in much better shape.

And the man might also have been wondering exactly how many vials of the blessed liquid Delia still had stashed in her purse.

Whatever his reasons for not going after them, she could only be glad that he'd decided discretion was the better part of valor.

"Now what?" she asked after Caleb had fastened his seatbelt and she'd begun to pull away from the curb.

He glanced over at the clock on the dashboard, then grinned.

"Now I've got a semifinal to win."

Caleb knew his outward nonchalance about the tournament was all show. As Delia pulled into the casino's parking lot, his mind was already racing through everything they'd just learned. Aegis Holdings had its fingers in way more pies than he'd initially thought, and if Paul Reeves had been telling the truth—which he suspected was the case, thanks to the holy water temporarily breaking the sigil's hold—the plan somehow involved the poker tournament itself.

"You sure you want to go through with this?"

Delia asked as she guided her little white Kona into a spot someone had just vacated. "If those Aegis creeps are watching you...."

"That's exactly why I need to be there," Caleb replied, his tone firm, then glanced at the dashboard clock again. "The semifinal starts in thirty minutes. If what Paul told us is true, then the final round is when they're really planning something big. I need to make it to the finals to see what they're up to."

Delia didn't look convinced by this argument. "And put yourself right in the middle of whatever supernatural energy collection scheme they're running? That seems risky."

"I've always been a gambling man," he said with a grin. "Besides, I'm not exactly what you can call your run-of-the-mill poker player. Maybe that's why they're not sure what to do about me."

Thanks to the way she didn't respond right away to that comment, Caleb was pretty sure he'd scored a point.

They got out of her SUV, and as they were walking toward the casino entrance, Delia's phone buzzed.

"I'd better get it, just in case it's a client," she said. But when she pulled out her iPhone and stared down at the screen, her expression grew troubled. "It's Pru."

"Then put it on speaker so we can both hear," Caleb said at once. He had a feeling that Prudence wouldn't be calling if she didn't have something important to share.

"Go ahead," Delia said as they paused by a couple of palm trees just outside the casino entrance. No one was hanging around there, making the spot private enough.

Hopefully.

"I've got you on speaker," she added. "I'm here with Caleb."

That clarification didn't seem to bother Pru very much, since she immediately launched into the reason for her call. "I've found something weird," she said. "Those Aegis properties? It looks like they're all sitting on some kind of grid, but I can't figure out what it is. The pattern doesn't line up with anything I recognize."

"There's no rhyme or reason to it at all?" Caleb asked.

"Not that I can tell," Pru replied. "That doesn't mean I'm not going to keep hacking at it, trying to figure out what it means."

"But it's not random," Delia said.

"Definitely not. But whatever's going on with it, I did notice that a bunch of pieces of the grid seem to converge here in Las Vegas. And guess what's at the very center?"

"The casino where the tournament is being

held," Delia said, which was exactly what Caleb had been thinking as well.

"Exactly." A small pause, and then Pru added, "Be careful. I still don't know what we're dealing with here, but it sure feels as if this was all planned well in advance of the competition."

Most likely. And even though none of them had a very clear idea of what they were facing, Caleb doubted any of it would be good.

After Delia promised Pru they'd take every possible precaution and then ended the call, the two of them entered the casino and headed toward the tournament area. Caleb spotted Ty Carter near the entrance, looking tense and not at all Zen the way he usually did. The part angel...or whatever he was...obviously noticed him and Delia approaching, because he immediately made his way over to intercept them.

"I've been looking for you," Ty said in a low voice, then sent a glance around their immediate area as if to make sure no one was listening. "Something feels especially off today. Multiple supernatural signatures are converging on this casino—more than I've ever felt in one place before."

Well, that wasn't good, even if his warning echoed what Pru had just told them. And while Caleb still wasn't sure whether he could trust the guy, he also knew that Ty Carter was probably the closest thing to an ally that he and Delia had at the moment.

"Any idea what we're dealing with?" he asked.

Ty shook his head. "Different kinds of energies. Some demonic, some...I'm not sure yet. The one thing I do know is that they're all focused here, on this building. You'll need to watch yourself in there." He glanced toward the VIP viewing area, an accommodation that hadn't existed during the earlier rounds of the competition, and then over at Delia, addressing her directly as he added, "Including your friend Aaron Sanchez in the spectator section."

Delia frowned, her gaze tracking to the spot where Aaron sat among the high-roller spectators. He wore a black dress shirt and was chatting with the man sitting next to him, an individual with an impressively bald head and a large diamond stud in one ear. "What about him?" she asked. Although she looked calm enough, a certain edge to her voice told Caleb she wasn't thrilled to see the guy making a return visit to the competition today.

Ty's mouth tightened. "There's something off about him. He feels like an entirely different person."

Again, not the sort of news Caleb had really wanted to hear, although he supposed he should count himself lucky that Sanchez was only a spectator and not a fellow competitor.

"Anyone else I should keep an eye out for?"

Ty was silent for a moment. Although he didn't move, Caleb got the impression that he was using his own special abilities...whatever they might be...to scan the crowd and see if he detected any anomalies.

Then he shook his head. "Hard to say. The energies in here are chaotic enough that I can't get a clear impression from anyone else. But you obviously need to watch yourself."

Something Caleb had already been planning on doing, so he wasn't sure how helpful any of this had been.

Except, of course, to put him even more on edge.

"Well, thanks for the heads-up." He looked over at Delia. "We should probably get moving."

She gave a reluctant nod but didn't protest, and Ty, seeming to sense he'd done what he could, melted away into the crowd.

When Caleb entered the tournament area, he sensed it almost immediately—a subtle vibration in the air, like static electricity but somehow more alive. To most people, the vibe would have been imperceptible, but, thanks to his particular talents, Caleb didn't have a problem detecting the energy as it seemed to build all around them.

"I need to get to my seat," he told Delia. "Find a spot where you can watch without being too conspicuous. And keep that holy water handy."

She gave him an uncertain smile...and surprised him by reaching out to give his hand a quick squeeze before she, too, disappeared into the crowd.

He hoped Ty would keep an eye on her, wherever he was.

His table during this semifinal bout included three players he'd observed during the previous round: Steve Wilson, who was somewhere in his forties, with cool gray eyes and the sort of craggy features that looked as if they never smiled; a former World Series of Poker champion named Jackson Palmer; and the sole woman of the group, Michelle Keegan, who sported a dyed black bob and who'd had an impressive run so far. As they took their seats, Caleb studied each of them carefully.

Steve looked different today—his normally tanned complexion seemed pale, and dark circles shadowed his eyes as if he hadn't slept. From his position at the table, Caleb was just barely able to make out Aaron Sanchez observing the competitors as he sat in the VIP section. Maybe he was only imagining things, thanks to the warnings Ty had given him a few moments earlier, but Caleb thought there did seem to be something off about the way Aaron watched the people at the table—too still, too focused.

As play began, Caleb did his best to split his attention between the cards and the odd energy patterns in the room. Every time chips moved across the table, he could see faint traces of energy following them, spiraling toward collection points he hadn't noticed before—small, unobtrusive objects set strategically around the tournament area, disguised as everyday items...an ice bucket, a fake palm placed up against the velvet rope, one of the stanchions that held up the aforementioned rope.

After three hours of grueling play, both Michelle and Jackson were eliminated, leaving just Caleb and Steve at the table.

And that was when Caleb noticed the pattern forming. The energy wasn't random—it was being channeled into a specific configuration that reminded him of the ritual diagrams he'd seen in occult books. Although in general he'd tried to ignore that side of himself as much as possible, back when he was in high school, he'd gone through a phase when he'd tried to learn a few things about demonology and the supernatural, and although he'd never practiced any of those rituals, some of those patterns remained engraved in his brain.

Whatever was going on, Steve was clearly part

of it. Every time he won a hand, Caleb could see energy draining from the chips and flowing into a sigil that was partially visible under his watchband —similar to the one he'd seen on Paul Reeves but more complex.

When they took a short break, Caleb found Delia waiting for him near the restrooms, her gaze expectant.

"They're channeling energy through the game itself," he said in an undertone. "Every bet, every win or loss—it's all feeding something. And I think I figured out Steve's secret."

"What is it?"

"He's been drawing power from his opponents. That's why everyone who's played against him has made unusual mistakes. He's literally been draining their focus and decision-making abilities."

Alarm flared in Delia's blue-gray eyes. "Can he do that to you?"

Caleb smiled grimly. "He can try."

She didn't seem too reassured, but because they were already being called back to their seats, there wasn't much he could do except flash her a smile and hope she understood that he had this.

At least, he hoped he did.

As play resumed, Caleb decided he should probably adjust his strategy. Instead of fighting Steve's energy drain head-on, he created a circular energy flow within himself—a technique he'd learned years ago when he was messing around with his demonic gifts and figuring out what they could and couldn't do. The energy shift was so subtle that Steve shouldn't immediately notice... but effective enough to neutralize his advantage.

The final hour of play became a psychological battle as much as a card game, with Caleb manipulating his personal energy as needed to prevent his opponent from gaining an advantage. Throughout, Steve grew visibly frustrated, his usual tactics continuing to fail as they encountered the defenses Caleb had put in place.

The decisive hand came when Steve overcommitted on a flush draw that didn't materialize. Caleb called his bluff, and Steve's last chips slid across the table.

"Good game," Caleb said, extending his hand.

Steve stared at him for a moment before reaching out and grudgingly giving one brief pump. As their hands touched, a jolt shocked its way through Caleb's body—Steve trying one last desperate energy pull.

Nice try, buddy, Caleb thought, and allowed a flicker of red to show in his eyes as he held Steve's gaze.

The other man's eyes widened. "What the hell are you?"

"Just another player," Caleb replied, holding back a grin. "For now."

As the tournament officials announced Caleb's advancement to the final round, he noticed Aaron Sanchez approaching from the spectator area. The other man extended his hand, even as he wore a smile that didn't quite fit his face, almost as if he was unfamiliar with using that particular set of muscles.

"Congratulations, Mr. Lowe. That was quite impressive."

As they shook hands, Caleb caught a glimpse of Sanchez's eyes—and for a split-second, so fast that Caleb wasn't sure he hadn't imagined it, they flashed completely black.

Shit. The guy wasn't just influenced by one the way Paul Reeves had been, but fully possessed.

"We're looking forward to an exciting final tomorrow," not-quite-Aaron continued, his grip a fraction too tight. "Aegis Holdings has high expectations for this competition."

Caleb wouldn't allow a single muscle in his face to twitch. "I'm surprised the tournament sponsors are taking such a personal interest in me."

"Oh, they take a *very* personal interest in you, Mr. Lowe," Aaron said, still wearing a smile that wasn't much more than a baring of teeth. "More than you know."

Before Caleb could respond, Aaron had turned and walked away, moving with an unnatural smoothness that sent chills down Caleb's spine.

He doubted the real man had ever walked like that.

Delia approached him as the crowd began dispersing, her lovely face glowing with pride. "You did it," she said. "That was amazing."

"Yeah," Caleb replied as he continued to watch Aaron's retreating form. "But we've got bigger problems now. Aaron Sanchez has been possessed —completely taken over. And whatever Aegis is planning, it's happening tomorrow during the final round."

The cheerful flush in her cheeks abruptly disappeared. "What are we going to do?"

Caleb had already gathered his chips, and he waited now as a tournament official came to count them. With the man standing right there, he couldn't answer Delia's question but had to wait until they were alone again. Once the chips were counted and the official had moved on to the next table, Caleb said in an undertone, "We're going to need more holy water. A *lot* more. And I need to talk to Ty again."

"About what?"

"About disrupting ritual energy patterns," Caleb said grimly. "I'm still not entirely sure of Aegis's end game, but no matter what, we have to be ready to stop it—without getting ourselves killed in the process."

Although she still looked pale, Delia managed to quip, "Oh, is that all?"

He grinned. "So far."

As they headed outside, Caleb could still sense the energy in the casino building, throbbing like a heartbeat, preparing for something momentous. Tomorrow would bring either triumph or disaster —and he wasn't sure which one he was betting on yet.

Chapter Nineteen

—·«((·☾·))»·—

IT HAD BECOME SOMETHING OF A RITUAL for them—to go out to eat after the competition, to do something so relentlessly normal that they could forget at least a little about what had transpired earlier in the day.

Unfortunately, Delia didn't think she'd ever be able to forget any of it.

Aaron Sanchez possessed by a demon. The tournament as a cover for some sort of massive supernatural ritual, one whose true purpose still wasn't entirely clear.

About the only good thing that had happened today was Caleb advancing to the finals.

If you could even call that part of the whole mess "good."

Maybe more like necessary, at least according to Ty Carter.

Caleb had already drunk more than half the bottle of cabernet they'd ordered to go with their steaks. True, she'd seen firsthand how the demon blood he carried within him gave him a tolerance for alcohol that would have made a frat boy green with envy, but Delia still wasn't sure whether attempting to tie one on the night before the finals was that great an idea.

However, she didn't say anything. He was an adult, and since she was driving, it wasn't as if she needed to worry about him getting behind the wheel while impaired...not that she thought he'd ever actually do something so reckless. No, he'd call a cab and leave his car behind, and then come back to get it in the morning.

Or maybe just disappear into the men's room and teleport home from there.

Actually, scratch that. Even drunk—if he could get drunk—Caleb wouldn't do anything so careless. He knew better than to attract that kind of attention to himself.

And because they were in a public place, they couldn't dissect what Pru had told them, or what had actually happened during the tournament. Delia had suggested to Caleb that they get takeout, but he'd shot down that idea pretty quickly. No, he'd wanted to go to a real restaurant and order a bottle of wine and have someone bring the food to them.

"Also," he'd added, "I want a steak, and that's not the kind of meal that improves with delivery."

Probably not.

So instead, they talked about the competition on strictly mundane terms, with Caleb giving his thoughts on the three other players who'd made it to the finals.

"I've heard of all of them, so whatever's going on, it's not like Aegis has put its own ringers in there," he said.

Even a small mention of that diabolical organization made Delia think maybe he was skirting too close to dangerous ground, but she only nodded. "It seems like they can take control of people pretty easily, though."

Caleb's expression grew shadowed...or maybe that was only the flickering light from the small candle in the glass holder that sat on the table. Quite a few restaurants had switched over to battery-operated tea lights just because there was a lot less mess involved, but they still did things old school at Domenico's.

"It does," he agreed. "Not me, however. So I suppose I'm the monkey in the wrench."

Possibly. Once again, Delia wondered why the tournament organizers—who clearly were either members of Aegis or at least mind-controlled by them—hadn't worked harder to make sure Caleb hadn't advanced to the final round. Surely they were worried that he'd do something to disrupt the competition, and therefore whatever ritual they were planning.

But...maybe they couldn't stop him, not really. After all, he might have been mostly human, but he still had a pretty formidable complement of powers at his disposal. It was possible there wasn't much they could do.

She hoped.

Even so, she thought leaving him alone at his house seemed like a very bad idea. The mere notion was enough to send a trickle of cold shivering its way down her spine, like she'd just walked through a particularly nasty draft.

"I think you should crash at my place tonight," she said, and Caleb stared at her as if she'd just suggested that they go base-jumping off the tower at the Stratosphere.

"What?"

"Safety in numbers," she told him.

For a moment, he didn't say anything. Then one dark brow lifted ever so slightly. "A premonition?"

A very good question. Was she now able to get vague hints from the future, or were her current heebie-jeebies nothing more than her imagination getting to her?

Whatever was going on, she'd learned to trust her instincts over the years.

"I don't know," she said honestly. "But it kind of makes sense that if they were going to make a last-ditch attempt to knock you out of the competition, they'd do it when you were home by yourself."

Once again, Caleb went silent. Delia could almost see the thoughts darting around in his brain as he weighed what would be the best course of action. True, he'd probably get a better night's sleep and would be sharper at the tournament if he spent the night in his own bed, but on the other hand, getting attacked while you were sleeping generally didn't contribute to a sense of well-being and relaxation.

"All right," he said at length. "We'll need to swing by my place first so I can pick up a couple of things, though."

"That's fine," she replied, almost giddy as relief rushed through her. "Whatever you need."

A lopsided grin tugged at his mouth. "I hope you're right about this."

Delia found herself smiling in response. "I know I am."

Although he would have preferred to sleep in his own bed, Caleb had to admit that the guest room at Delia's house was pretty comfortable...and not entirely unfamiliar, since he'd crashed there before after getting attacked by a gang of demons at his old house.

He'd slept for a solid eight hours and only awoke around seven-thirty because his nose detected the rich scent of coffee slipping under the door. After a luxurious stretch, he got out of bed and went to the overnight bag he'd packed the evening before, and pulled out a T-shirt and a pair of sweats. If his relationship with Delia had been a different sort, he might have wandered into the kitchen while wearing only his boxer briefs, but he had a feeling she probably wouldn't respond too well to that kind of display.

Maybe someday that would all change, but he knew today wasn't that day.

She was standing in the kitchen, long red hair pulled back in a scrunchie, slim legs covered in yoga pants. No need for her to rush around this morning, since it was a Saturday and she didn't have to go into the office. If it had been a normal weekend day, she might have still had a few showings with clients or an open house, but he knew she'd cleared her schedule for him.

Yet another reason for him to be utterly grateful to the universe or whatever other force had steered her into his life.

As soon as he approached, she said, "Coffee?"

"God, yes."

She flashed him a smile—no makeup this morning except maybe a little tinted lip balm, but she was gorgeous nonetheless—and then got a mug down from the cupboard and poured some Italian roast into it.

"How'd you sleep?"

"Pretty well," he replied. "And it seemed like everything was quiet."

"Very quiet," she said. "I'm not sure if that's a good thing or not. Like my friends with kids say, if they're too quiet, then you know they're getting into some kind of trouble."

Caleb wondered how many people in her circle had families. Certainly Pru appeared to be relentlessly single. But since he'd heard pretty much the same thing from the people he'd known back in Greencastle who'd started having kids early, it seemed that was one truth he couldn't deny.

"Well, even if they're plotting something, they left us alone last night, and I'm grateful for that." He sipped some of his coffee, which was almost too hot to drink but not quite. Good thing, too, because he knew he didn't want to wait to get any of that sweet caffeine in his bloodstream.

A hint of a smile flickered around Delia's mouth. "Me too. Do you think we should do any more investigating today, since you don't have to be at the casino until three?"

Caleb had already thought about that, so he

had a ready answer. "Probably not. For one thing, they know we're hip to Paul Reeves' game, so it's not like we can follow him again and get any other answers. And while I have a feeling Pru could probably get Hank Bowers' address for us, I don't see the point in confronting him beforehand. He might be playing a key role in all this, but I have to believe whoever's really pulling the strings would have some kind of backup for him, someone who could step in and take over if necessary if he got sidelined for some reason."

"Makes sense." Delia sipped some of her coffee, and then her brows pulled together. "And I'm happy to stay as far away from Aaron Sanchez as possible."

Words that Caleb was only too happy to hear, although he knew she'd only said that because her one-time date was now possessed by a demon, rather than because she'd had such a horrible time with him that she never wanted to see him again.

"Probably for the best," Caleb agreed. "I'm still not sure why a demon decided to possess him at all. It's not like he's been competing."

Another frown, and Delia said, "Maybe they're trying to use him to get closer to me. It's possible he sensed something the night of our date, something that signaled my powers were expanding, and they thought they could slip a demon into him and have it do whatever was necessary to keep me away from you."

Caleb hadn't considered that angle, but he thought it made some sense. According to what Ty Carter had told them, Aaron had only been recently possessed and should have been wholly himself the night he went out with Delia. But it was very possible that whoever in Aegis Holdings was controlling all this had been surveilling her and had decided that her erstwhile date and fellow real estate agent was the perfect person to take over.

"Whatever their game was, it didn't work," he said. "And now that Ty's warned us about Aaron, it should be easy enough for you to stay away from him."

"Far, far away," Delia replied. "Luckily, the casino will be extra crowded today because of everyone coming to watch the finals, so it should be easy enough to give him the slip."

Caleb hoped her confidence wasn't misplaced. But he guessed that Ty Carter would be there to keep an eye on things, and would probably intervene if he saw Aaron going after Delia.

And that didn't even take into account Ty's two fellow angels, or whoever those guys had been. Caleb hadn't seen them again, but he'd been so absorbed in staying in the game during the last round that he probably wouldn't have noticed them unless they'd come up and kicked him in the nuts.

"Let's hope so," he said.

Because right now, hope was pretty much all they had.

After coffee and a quick breakfast of bacon and toast, they both showered and got ready to face the day. Delia's phone had been very quiet all morning, which she thought a little surprising. Usually by now, she should have gotten at least one call importuning her to show a house or reassure someone that their escrow was going as smoothly as possible, but everything had been dead silent.

Just luck, or were the Aegis people somehow messing with her phone?

She really didn't want to consider that possibility, mostly because it would indicate that their network was much bigger and more powerful than she and Caleb had ever imagined.

As she headed out into the living room, she wondered if she should suggest a mindless activity that would use up a few hours, like maybe going to an outlet mall or seeing if there were any open houses nearby. She kind of doubted he was very focused on finding a new flip, but it would still be something to do.

But the doorbell rang just as Caleb emerged from the guest suite, and he sent her a worried look.

"You expecting anyone?"

"No," she replied at once. "It's not like I have company all that much anyway, but I would never have invited someone over today with everything that's been going on."

He frowned, even as she went to the door and peered out through the peephole.

Standing on the front step was Ty Carter.

At once, she opened the door. "Ty?"

"I need to speak with you," he said.

A nice way to open a conversation, not even a "hi" or a "good morning." Then again, she supposed if you had a long view the way an angel did, then those sorts of pleasantries might feel like a waste of time.

If he was even an angel at all.

"Come on in," she told him, stepping aside so he could enter the house.

He took a few steps in, then paused as he spotted Caleb standing over by the fireplace. "You stayed here?"

"I did," Caleb said imperturbably.

Delia noticed how he hadn't added that he'd stayed in the guest room, but she decided not to say anything. Let Ty Carter think what he wanted.

"Good," Ty said. "You were probably safer here."

Which had been the whole point of the exercise, of course, but she supposed it was good to get outside confirmation that she hadn't been jumping at shadows.

"Can I get you anything?" she asked politely. "A glass of water or some iced tea? I can make coffee, but—"

Ty held up a hand. "I'm fine. This isn't a social call."

Which was already what she'd figured, but she'd still thought it best to follow the forms.

"Then what's it about?" Caleb asked.

"The tournament, of course," Ty said without hesitation. "We've been working on this all night, and—"

"Which 'we'?" Caleb cut in. "Those two guys I saw you with the other day?"

"Who it was isn't the important thing," Ty replied. "What's important is that we've been tracking the convergence of energy at the competition. It's very clear that the people coordinating all this plan to activate a sort of supernatural circuit powered by the energy they're channeling through the tournament. Once the circuit is opened, they'll be able to use that power to cause all kinds of havoc."

Caleb crossed his arms, one brow cocked at an ironic angle. "Can you narrow 'havoc' down a bit?"

"No," Ty said without missing a beat. "It is sometimes very difficult to understand the motivations of beings such as these. What I do know is that people—regular people, innocent bystanders —will most likely get hurt, possibly worse. So we have to do everything we can to keep the people at Aegis from completing the circuit."

"How are we supposed to do that?" Delia asked. While she probably didn't want to hear the answer, she also knew that they'd started down this road, and now the only thing they could do was finish what they'd begun...and hope like hell they safely emerged on the other side.

"It all comes down to the final game," Ty replied. His gaze flickered over to Caleb and then back to her, keen and cool, blue as the sky she'd seen out her bedroom window earlier that morning. "Hank Bowers has been coordinating the whole thing to make sure one of his minions is in the last round."

"None of the people I'm playing against is new to this," Caleb argued. "I saw their names pop up all over the place when I was studying the local poker scene."

Ty didn't even blink. "Yes, they're well known around here. But that doesn't make any difference.

One of them will either be possessed, as they've done to Aaron Sanchez, or they will at the very least be subjugated by a sigil of control, the way Paul Reeves and several of the other players have been."

So that's what that strange little mark was. Delia wondered who had put it on Paul Reeves' arm. Hank Bowers, or someone higher up the food chain?

It probably didn't matter. What mattered was that someone in the final four was under either demonic possession or compulsion...and the only person standing in the way was Caleb Lockwood.

His jaw had set, signaling that he understood the assignment. "So I have to win, or the circuit will be complete and all hell will break loose."

Ty gave a satisfied nod. "That's exactly it. But we all have confidence in you—you've acquitted yourself very well so far."

Yes, he had. Still, this was a lot of pressure on someone who'd never even competed in a poker tournament before...let alone been tasked with destroying a supernatural circuit.

"There's no other way?" Delia asked.

"Unfortunately, no," Ty responded. "Caleb must be the one to interrupt the energy and ensure the circuit isn't completed."

"No pressure, huh?" he quipped, but Ty didn't even smile.

"It's a great deal of pressure, and we understand that. But it falls on you to thwart them. Best of luck to you."

Before either Caleb or Delia could respond, he winked out of existence, leaving them standing alone in the living room.

She set her hands on her hips. "Why even bother to knock on the front door if he's going to come and go like that anyway?"

"Because suddenly appearing in your house wouldn't have been very polite." Now Caleb did crack a grin, looking much more like himself. "I suppose that's something angels would care about."

He had a point there. "Now what?" Delia asked.

His smile didn't flicker for a second. "We have lunch. And after that?" A pause, and then he added,

"Well, I suppose I have a tournament to win."

Chapter Twenty

—·《《·☾·》》·—

From her vantage point near the back of the tournament area, Delia could feel the wrongness in the air. The energy pulsed and swirled, making her skin prickle as though she'd just walked through an electrical field. She'd experienced similar sensations before when cleansing haunted houses, but this was different—stronger, more purposeful.

And growing by the minute.

Her phone buzzed, and she hastily dug it out of her purse. Prudence.

"Tell me you haven't started the final round yet," she said.

"They're still getting set up, but I think things will be starting in a few minutes." Delia paused there and let her gaze sweep the crowd. A chill worked its way down her spine as she spied Aaron

Sanchez's familiar form lurking near one of the support pillars on the other side of the gaming space. It didn't look as if he was even trying to blend in anymore, his normally friendly expression now cold and predatory. She glanced away quickly, praying that he hadn't noticed her looking at him. "What did you find?"

"A whole bunch, and none of it's good." Keyboard clicks rattled through the phone, telling Delia that her friend probably had her own cell phone pressed against her ear while she continued to type away on her big iMac. "I mapped all the Aegis Holdings properties in Las Vegas and started to realize they weren't purchased at random. At first, I couldn't really figure out what I was looking at, but then when I started researching grid patterns, something I found online explained what was going on." She paused there, then added, "Every place they've bought sits on a ley line."

Delia frowned. "What the hell is a ley line?"

"They're patterns of energy that supposedly crisscross the Earth's surface," Pru replied. "A property positioned on one of those lines would have access to those powers. If you have enough properties like that, then you can tap into a whole lot of energy."

A few months ago, Delia would have said this was all hocus pocus. With what she knew now, though, she understood they were in a whole lot of trouble. And it seemed Prudence did as well, because normally, she was about the least woo-woo person Delia had ever met. "Okay," she said, knowing how terse she sounded. "Anything else?"

"Just that all this confirms what I found yesterday, even though then I wasn't all that sure what I was looking at. The casino is the convergence point of all the local ley lines."

Even though she'd known that already, Delia's stomach still felt as if it had dropped to the gaudily patterned carpet beneath her feet.

"Which of course is why they had to hold the tournament here," Delia said.

"Exactly," Pru replied.

The whole tournament was some kind of activation mechanism, Delia realized. Once the circuit was made at the poker table, it would be like throwing a switch that connected all those various properties simultaneously, creating a river of unholy energy flowing right through the heart of town.

Movement out of the corner of her eye made her glance up from her phone. Aaron Sanchez was walking swiftly toward her, his movements smooth, purposeful.

Deadly.

She told Prudence, "Gotta go," and shoved the phone back in her purse as she prepared to flee.

But it was too late. Aaron's hand shot out,

grabbing her wrist with inhuman strength. His skin felt wrong—cold and somehow slick, like a snake's scales, even though it looked normal enough to the naked eye.

"You should have stayed away," he said in a hissing undertone. "This was never your fight."

"Let go of me." She tried to yank her arm out of his hand, but his grip only tightened, feeling like a band of iron around her bicep.

A reddish light flickered in his coal-black eyes. "I'm afraid I can't do that."

His other hand reached for her throat, and Delia recoiled. No one nearby seemed to be paying any attention to them, and she wondered if he was using some sort of demonic power to make sure their gaze was focused elsewhere, to ensure no one would intervene to prevent him from choking her to death then and there.

If that was the case, then there wasn't much point in screaming.

But then he was catapulted backward, his grip on her arm releasing with shocking suddenness as he was thrown to the ground like a rag doll by some invisible force. Ty Carter materialized in the space between them, the shock of his presence sending ripples through the supernatural energy field.

"Run," he told her. "Stay close to Caleb, no matter what."

Caleb could feel it all around him, a sensation impossible to ignore...even if he really wished he could.

The heavy, pulsing energy hung thick in the air as he took his seat at the final table. Most of the spectators crowded behind the velvet rope or over in the VIP section probably couldn't sense what seemed to surround him like a miasma of choking smog, but he still saw a few people rubbing their arms or looking around in confusion, as if they could tell something wasn't quite right even if they would never have been able to explain the sensation.

A man named Ted Miller sat directly across from him. On the surface, the other man seemed to be exactly who everyone expected him to be—a previous World Series of Poker contender, someone known almost as well for his endless parade of loud Hawaiian shirts as he was for his cool, deliberate play at the gaming tables.

But Caleb could see past the façade now. The man's eyes were too bright, almost feverish, and his hands moved with an unsettling precision as he fiddled with his chips.

The other two players had already been eliminated far too quickly, as if the powers controlling Ted had decided there was no point in stringing this out, not when it was obvious how the tournament was supposed to end. Just as Ty predicted, it had come down to this—Caleb against whatever Ted Miller really was.

The dealer began spreading cards, and Caleb felt the energy concentrated inside the casino spike like a seismograph during an earthquake. The overhead lights flickered, drawing nervous murmurs from the crowd, although no one seemed inclined to leave the casino for the safer open-air spaces outside. Off to one side, Hank Bowers watched the proceedings, a look of supreme satisfaction on his face.

He probably thought he had Caleb right where he wanted him.

Focus, Caleb told himself. *Just play the game.*

But it wasn't simply a game anymore. Each hand felt charged with supernatural significance. Every chip pushed into the pot seemed to amplify the power building inside the casino. Caleb's demon blood throbbed in his veins, responding to the energy that crackled through the room, even as he did his best to ignore the uncomfortable sensation.

You're mostly human, he thought fiercely. *So act like it.*

He looked up from his cards and caught Ted staring at him, a knowing smile playing at the corners of his thin-lipped mouth. The other man's fingers traced patterns on the felt of the table—patterns that made Caleb's eyes hurt if he looked at them too long.

That same knowing smile was echoed on Hank Bowers' features as the dealer announced the final hand.

The lights dimmed again, staying dark for much longer this time, and Caleb heard whispers of confusion from the watching crowd. But no one left. They couldn't. The energy was holding them there, weaving them into whatever ritual Hank and his accomplices had planned.

Caleb's cards seemed to burn in his hands. He knew without looking that Ted had been dealt the exact hand he wanted. This wasn't about skill anymore—it was about power, about who could control the forces building to a crescendo around them.

Movement caught his eye, and he realized it was Delia pushing through the crowd, Ty Carter only a pace behind her. Her face was pale, her jaw set with determination. She gave him a very small nod, and it was as if he could hear her voice in his head.

Time to end this.

The dealer spread the flop, and the energy surged again, making the air itself seem to vibrate. Sweat broke out on Caleb's forehead as he reached for his chips, even while he realized that every decision he made now carried a weight that went far beyond mere cash.

The tournament might be in its final phase, but the real game was just beginning.

———

Delia watched from behind the rope line as Caleb studied his hole cards. The energy in the room had grown so strong that it made her teeth ache, as if she'd just bitten into an over-large ice cube. Next to her, Ty Carter stood absolutely still, his otherworldly presence acting as some sort of buffer against the supernatural forces swirling through the casino.

"Can you stop it?" she whispered.

"Only Caleb can do that now." Ty's voice was grim. "But be ready. The demon controlling Ted Miller won't go down without a fight."

Ted Miller, the man Caleb was playing against. He didn't look dangerous, seemed to be just a pudgy guy in his forties wearing an obnoxious Hawaiian shirt with a bright coral background and a series of hula dancers printed on the fabric.

As if to emphasize Ty's point, the chandeliers overhead swayed, their crystals tinkling against each other like wind chimes in a storm. A few more people in the crowd looked up nervously, but most remained mesmerized by the final hand playing out before them.

Ted Miller pushed a stack of chips into the middle of the table. "All in."

The words seemed to reverberate through the room, carried on waves of dark energy. Delia's breath caught as she watched Caleb consider his options. He had to know this wasn't just about winning anymore—this was about stopping whatever horrific plan Hank Bowers and his demonic allies had set in motion.

The man stood a few feet away from the dealer, his eyes gleaming with triumph. No doubt he probably thought he had them all exactly where he wanted them.

"Call," Caleb said.

That single word, delivered in cool tones that belied the tense set of his jaw, cut through the charged atmosphere like a knife. Ted Miller's expression flickered, something inhuman...scaly and dark and hideous...showing through his carefully maintained mask.

The dealer flipped over the turn card, and the supernatural energy swirling in the casino spiked so violently that several spectators staggered. Delia grabbed the velvet rope to steady herself, her knuckles white against the blood-red material. The dealer's hands shook slightly as he prepared to reveal the river card, and Delia guessed the man must have sensed something terribly wrong about the atmosphere in the room as well, even if he had no idea exactly what it was.

Then Hank stepped forward, his blunt fingers moving in a complex pattern too intricate for any human mind to comprehend. The air grew thick, heavy with malevolent power. Out of the corner of her eye, Delia saw Aaron pushing through the crowd again, his black, sharklike gaze moving from side to side, searching for his prey.

Searching for her.

"The circuit's almost complete," Ty murmured. "Whatever you're going to do, Caleb, you need to do it now."

Caleb's hand shot out, catching the dealer's wrist before he could turn over the final card. "Wait."

A simple word, but one charged with power. The supernatural energy seemed to pause, suspended like a held breath.

"This ends now." Caleb's voice sounded different, deeper, carrying echoes of something dark, something powerful.

His demon blood responding to the forces around them? In that moment, Delia realized this was a side of him she'd never seen before. Sure, she'd witnessed him exhibit enough powers to understand he wasn't fully human, but most of the time, he seemed like not much more than a laid-back guy who was surprisingly fun to hang out with.

All the same, it clearly wasn't a good idea to underestimate him.

Ted's plump face contorted, his features shifting between those of a nondescript human being and something reptilian, alien...hideous in a way her brain didn't quite want to comprehend. "You can't stop what's already begun," he growled.

"Watch me."

Caleb's other hand slammed down on the table. The impact sent a shockwave through the room, disrupting the carefully constructed patterns of energy. Chips scattered across the felt as the light fixtures overhead exploded in a shower of sparks.

Ted lunged across the table, his form rippling and changing, becoming the stuff of nightmares, even worse than the demon Calach, whom she and Caleb had banished just a few short months earlier. As Delia watched, horrified, Aaron broke through the last line of spectators, claws extending from his fingertips, blotches of black scales appearing on his neck. Next to her, Ty moved fast as lightning, one leg snaking out to catch the possessed man right behind the knee, sending him to the floor like a stack of bricks, where he lay unmoving.

Hank Bowers shouted something in a language that made Delia's ears ring, the words harsh and guttural, like something she might have heard an orc say in one of the *Lord of the Rings* movies.

But Caleb was already moving. Hands raised, he met Ted's attack with a blast of flames that burst forth from his palms and sent the possessed poker player flying backward. The demon that had possessed him screamed in rage as it was forcibly ejected from Ted's body, its true form visible for a brief, horrifying moment before it dissolved into smoke.

The disruption created some kind of cascade effect, like a row of dominoes pushed over by a careless finger. Whatever ritual Hank had been orchestrating collapsed in on itself, the carefully aligned energies from the ley lines scattering in all directions. The air crackled with discharged power as people finally broke free of their supernatural stupor and began running for the exits.

Delia held her ground, though. No way would she leave Caleb behind, not after everything they'd been through together.

Hank's voice boomed through the emptying room like a cannon. "Do you have any idea what you've done, you stupid boy?"

"Stopped you," Caleb said simply. He looked completely calm despite the chaos erupting around them, arms now at his sides, his face blank, almost neutral. "Game over."

Hank's hands rose, and dark energy gathered

around both men, surrounding them like black smoke, billowing and pulsing. Delia swallowed and took a step forward, even though she had no idea what she could do to prevent him from lashing out at the man who'd just destroyed all his careful plans. Would holy water even work against something like him?

But before Bowers could strike, Ty Carter appeared behind him, placing a hand on his shoulder.

"Enough," he said quietly. "It is done."

The man's face went slack, his eyes rolling back in his head as he collapsed to the floor like a marionette with its strings cut. Whatever power he'd been channeling dissipated harmlessly into the air.

It was over.

Delia rushed forward as Caleb sagged against the poker table, clearly drained from the supernatural exertion. "Are you okay?"

He managed a weak smile. "I think I prefer regular poker tournaments. Less drama."

"The authorities will be here soon," Ty said, still standing over Hank's unconscious form. "You should go. I'll make sure this is handled...appropriately."

Delia didn't want to think too hard about what that meant. A different kind of mind control, something to make the police believe that what had happened here was perfectly ordinary and nothing that merited any further investigation?

Luckily, it didn't appear to be her problem.

She offered an arm to Caleb, supporting him as they made their way through the now-empty tournament area. He moved slowly, feet dragging like he'd just run a marathon.

In a way, she supposed he had.

"You know," she said when they reached the exit, "I think you might want to try a different hobby."

Caleb's laugh was tired but genuine. "I think you might be right."

Chapter Twenty-One

— ·(((· ☾ ·)))· —

Obviously, there wasn't any talk about going out to eat afterward. No, Delia drove Caleb straight home, and he was gladder than ever that she'd offered to be the chauffeur today.

Right now, he was feeling like a wrung-out washcloth and didn't know whether he could have even mustered the mental and motor capacity to pilot his Mercedes back to the house.

All this time, he'd only played with his demonic talents...teleporting here, influencing a throw of the dice there...sending his consciousness into the body of a dead woman so he could be safely transported away from the Victorian mansion where a madwoman had opened a hell-mouth to summon Belial, her erstwhile lover.

But today Caleb had been forced to reach down into the core of his being, to awaken powers he hadn't even realized he possessed to defeat the demon who'd taken control of a poker champion's body—and to make sure the circuit Hank Bowers and his minions had tried to create was broken forever.

In a word, he was fucking tired.

Because of the way the demons had rushed the tournament, doing their best to make sure the ritual happened on their own time, it was barely six o'clock when Delia pulled into Caleb's driveway. Normally, he would never have eaten this early, but now he knew his body was ravenous, needing fuel to replace all the energy he'd used to stop the creatures' unholy plans.

"Pizza," he said briefly as Delia guided him up the front steps and into the house.

A smile hovered around the edges of her mouth, but he could still see the worry in her clear gray-blue eyes. "I can manage that."

Her arm remained steady beneath his until he sort of collapsed on the sofa. While it felt good to sit down, Caleb wished he could have kept holding on to her. Nothing romantic in that touch, sure, but it had still been good to have her so near, so strong.

So reassuringly human.

She got out her phone. "Vito's?" she asked, naming the restaurant they usually ordered from when they were at his house.

"Perfect."

A brief detour into the kitchen to get him a glass of water—he would have preferred something a little stronger, but knew he needed to hydrate before he put any alcohol in his system—and then she made the call, placing an order for an extra-large pepperoni with extra cheese.

How had she known the exact kind of pizza he needed?

Because she was Delia, of course.

Call completed, she set the phone down on the coffee table rather than returning it to her purse. "It'll be here in about twenty minutes." She paused there and sent him a searching look. "How're you doing?"

"I feel like shit," he said frankly. "But it'll pass."

She sat down on the couch next to him. "That was really something. Want to tell me exactly what you did?"

Caleb summoned a weak smile. "As soon as I figure it out, I'll let you know."

Delia chuckled. "You just...played it by ear?"

"More or less." He shifted so he could look at her directly and saw nothing but concern in her face. No fear or awe, nothing to signal that what she'd witnessed earlier had changed her opinion of him.

Then again, he supposed that once you

accepted someone was a quarter demon, you kind of had to roll with the punches going forward.

"What do you think Ty told the cops?" he asked.

Before she could reply, the man himself...whatever he was...appeared a few feet away, standing next to the floor-to-ceiling fireplace with its impressive slabs of white-veined black soapstone.

"I told them that Aaron Sanchez collapsed, and it seems Hank Bowers had a heart attack from the excitement."

Under other circumstances, Caleb might have given Ty some grief for appearing out of nowhere like that, especially when he'd been polite enough to knock when he came over to Delia's place.

Now, though, he figured he should just let it slide.

"What about the tremors and all the people fleeing the casino?"

Ty looked imperturbable as ever. "The entire valley experienced a small earthquake," he replied. "Nothing large, only a 4.0, but since people here aren't used to that sort of thing, it makes sense that the spectators would panic and run outside."

Delia spoke up then, her expression puzzled. "And no one was recording the event or streaming it?"

"Funny thing about that," Ty replied. "All the footage appears to have been erased. Some kind of weird magnetic resonance that interfered with the area in and around the casino."

Magnetic resonance, his ass. Caleb was pretty sure that wasn't anything close to what had actually happened, but he wasn't going to worry about it.

The important thing was that it seemed as if all the bases had been covered, which of course they had been. That was the whole point of Ty staying behind and acting as a sort of supernatural "cleaner."

Caleb glanced over at Delia, and her shoulders lifted almost imperceptibly.

"Oh," Ty went on, "because of the general confusion, there wasn't an awards ceremony. However, you can expect the casino to reach out to you in the next couple of days to give you your winnings."

Right. Caleb had been so wrapped up in making sure the supernatural circuit was destroyed that he'd completely forgotten that the winner of the competition would get a cool fifty thousand bucks. Sure, he had a pretty decent war chest right now, but he wasn't about to turn down a hefty chunk of cash.

He figured he'd earned it.

"And we really beat them?" Delia asked then, voicing a worry that Caleb hadn't been able to entirely ignore. "They're not going to come back and try this again?"

"Doubtful," Ty said. "I'd keep a watch on all those Aegis properties—I have a feeling they're going to be sold off very soon. Turns out most of their vacation rentals were operating illegally in neighborhoods where the HOAs don't allow them."

Caleb wasn't surprised that the demons running things at Aegis hadn't cared much about breaking the rules. However, with all the horror stories he'd heard about HOAs over the years, he was a little surprised no one had ratted them out before now.

Most likely, a good number of palms on various association boards had been greased well to make sure no one complained too loudly.

Or maybe some of them had been placed under demonic compulsion to ensure they stayed quiet. Either way, it sounded as if Aegis's Vegas holdings were about to collapse.

"That's good news," he said. "Maybe some of those houses will be good candidates for flips."

"Possibly," Ty allowed. "That's not my area of concern. We only wanted to make sure the demons' plan failed and that the entire episode could be written off as a series of unfortunate events."

Put together, they probably would have seemed downright crazy to anyone paying attention. But

Caleb knew all too well that regular people didn't like to allow even the slightest notion that something supernatural might have gone down in their immediate vicinity, so he guessed no one was going to ask too many questions or examine this afternoon's events too closely.

But it seemed Delia had a few questions of her own.

"And who is 'we,' exactly?" she inquired. "Are you part of some angelic A-Team or something?"

Ty actually smiled. "Nothing that showy. We go where we're needed, that's all. But if you want to assign us a label, I suppose you could call us the Guardians."

Guardian angels. Very funny.

Delia didn't smile, though. No, she looked thoughtful, absorbing what Ty had just told her.

"I suppose that makes sense," she said. "And thank you for intervening today. I don't know what would have happened if you hadn't been there."

Caleb wanted to protest that he'd been the one doing most of the heavy lifting. However, since he'd been absorbed in holding his own at the poker table, he hadn't been able to protect Delia from Aaron Sanchez. It rankled a little that Ty had been the one to come to her rescue, although he understood that the most important thing was her safety, not who had been the person to run interference with the possessed man.

The doorbell rang then, and she startled a little.

"Pizza," she said briefly, and got up from the sofa.

"I'll leave you to your meal," Ty said as she headed toward the door. "I just wanted to let you know that Aegis is no more, and the local authorities don't suspect any kind of foul play."

"You don't want to stay for pizza?" Caleb asked, more out of courtesy than because he really wanted Ty Carter hanging around.

"Thank you, but no. I have other matters to attend to."

And then he disappeared just as Delia opened the front door.

If nothing else, angels seemed to have pretty good timing.

It seemed she'd heard enough of the exchange that she didn't ask where Ty had gone. Instead, she set the oversized pizza box down on the coffee table, which wouldn't suffer any damage from the hot cardboard because the tabletop was glass.

Sounding deliberately cheerful, she said, "Well, I don't know about you, but I'm starving."

"Me too," Caleb responded. "But I wouldn't mind having some of that chianti I've got in the wine rack to drink with this pizza."

She surveyed him for a moment, expression

openly skeptical. "Are you sure that's such a good idea?"

"I'll be fine," he assured her. "That water I just drank perked me right up."

"Like a wilting flower," she said, and he laughed.

"Sure."

"Then I'll go get it."

Because she'd been to the house multiple times, she knew where he stored the corkscrew. After pausing to grab the bottle of chianti in question, she returned to the living room, then went back for a couple of glasses.

Somewhat clumsily, she opened the bottle and poured a measure of chianti into each glass.

"Want to toast to anything?" she asked as Caleb lifted his.

He didn't even have to stop and think about it.

"To beating the bad guys."

They clinked glasses and took a sip.

"You really think they're gone?"

He'd been in the middle of opening the pizza box and depositing a slice on the plate she'd brought along with the glasses, so he waited until he was done before he answered her question.

"I think we won the battle. The war?"

He shrugged and ate a bite of pizza.

Delia had also helped herself to a slice but didn't look as if she planned to eat it any time soon.

Expression troubled, she replied, "So...this is a war?"

"It's starting to feel that way," he replied. Probably not what she'd wanted to hear, but he wasn't about to start sugarcoating the situation. "I suppose we'll have to wait and see how everything shakes out, though. According to what Ty just said, it sounds like we should have some peace and quiet for a while."

Maybe that was wishful thinking. But Caleb knew now wasn't the time to start worrying about where all those demons had disappeared to and what they might do when they decided they'd licked their wounds for long enough, or to puzzle out why they'd wanted his old house and possibly broken into it. Did it also sit on a ley line? If that was the case, why hadn't they bought it right away?

He supposed it was possible they thought they already had sufficient properties, and his would have been more for insurance than because it was truly needed.

And who had put the whammy on his brakes? Hank Bowers, or one of his lackeys?

Impossible to say, although, considering how things had shaken out in the end, Caleb could see why they would have wanted him sidelined.

And he also wasn't going to allow himself to worry about whether Aegis was really dead or merely down for the count.

No, right now he was just going to enjoy having Delia on the couch next to him and let himself savor his victory.

Even though he wasn't sure how long it would last.

She'd only drunk a glass and a half of chianti, not enough to make her even a little worried about driving home from Caleb's house. They'd eaten pizza and talked, and had both agreed to scour the MLS tomorrow and see if any of the Aegis properties had started popping up as being listed for sale or auction. Delia didn't know who would be handling all that if the demons really had decamped, but she supposed they must have had some sort of contingency in place to dispose of all the houses and condos they'd acquired.

And midway through their pizza, she'd gotten a text from Marcy saying her clients had finally decided they wanted to put an offer on Caleb's former house, and yes, she knew tomorrow was Sunday, but would Delia be in the office to get it and respond?

Of course, she'd answered right away and said that would be fine. No way was she going to delay any of this, not when the local housing market might soon be facing a glut thanks to all those

Aegis properties being listed for sale. True, Caleb's old house was updated and ready to go and didn't need any work, which would always be a bonus for a lot of people, but she still couldn't help feeling a certain sense of urgency to get the place sold.

Maybe that was why she couldn't seem to settle down once she got home, and found herself wandering around the place, checking all the windows and doors, making sure nothing had been disturbed in her absence.

None of it had, obviously. Why would the demons have bothered to mess with her house when they'd already known she was right there at the tournament?

She made herself head into the main suite and get ready for bed. It was quite possible that she'd lie awake for a while, since she was still feeling jangly and a little off balance despite the wine and pizza, but she knew she needed to settle back into a regular routine. Tomorrow she'd deal with the offer from Marcy's buyers and maybe do a little more paperwork to get caught up on the stuff she should have been handling these past couple of days.

Not that she regretted giving up that time to be there for Caleb at the poker competition. Some people might have argued that she didn't actually do all that much, and yet she knew he'd wanted her there.

That was what friends did for each other, right?

She couldn't seem to keep herself from thinking about the way he'd clung to her arm as they'd left the casino, the way he'd shuffled along like a man fifty years his senior. He might have tried to act nonchalant about the whole thing, but the confrontation had taken a lot out of him, and she had a feeling it would have been much worse if she hadn't been there to offer moral support.

The days were getting warmer, but the nights were still cool, so Delia pulled the covers all the way up to her chin. Not for the first time, she found herself thinking it would be much better if she had a dog, a companion who could curl up on the bed with her and make her feel not quite so alone.

But she didn't have a dog, mainly because she knew that someone who worked her kind of hours shouldn't have a pet that needed such a high level of attention. She'd dutifully fed the fish when she got home and they seemed just fine, and yet she knew it wasn't the same thing.

Sleep came quickly, most likely because she was just bone-tired. No dreams at first, just a warm, comfortable darkness.

In that darkness, she saw a man approaching, shadows swirling around him like ebony mist. Because the lighting was so dim, she couldn't make out much of his appearance, except to note that he was tall and had dark hair.

No, it was his eyes that seemed to catch her and hold her in place, piercing and cold as aquamarine laser beams, utterly ruthless.

Utterly cruel.

She found herself sitting up in bed, her breath coming in short pants. Nothing about the dream should have frightened her so much, and yet cold sweat dripped down her back.

Everything about her room looked completely normal, totally prosaic, and her heartbeat began to slow down as she gulped in some air.

Just a reaction to everything that happened today, she told herself, even though the man in her dream looked nothing like Hank Bowers, or Aaron Sanchez, or any of the others she'd encountered who'd been possessed or influenced by demons.

No, she realized as she settled herself back down in bed.

Whoever the man was...he was worse than any of them.

Much, much worse.

Vegas Slayers continues with The Devil Went Down to Laughlin.

Also by Christine Pope
(Series With Asterisks Are Complete)

LEGENDARY

(Urban Fantasy/Paranormal Romance)

Silver Linings

Lion's Share (October 2025)

Trial by Fire (February 2026)

Here Be Dragons (June 2026)

———

VEGAS SLAYERS

(Urban Fantasy/Paranormal Romance)

Speak of the Devil

Devil in the Details

The Devil Went Down to Laughlin

Devil May Care (January 2026)

———

THE WITCHES OF MINGUS MOUNTAIN

(Paranormal Romance)

Stolen Time

Borrowed Time

Killing Time

Wind Called

Demon Loved

Christmas Past (December 2025)

PROJECT DEMON HUNTERS*

(Paranormal Romance)

Unquiet Souls

Unbound Spirits

Unholy Ground

Unseen Voices

Unmarked Graves

Unbroken Vows

Unholy Night

THE DJINN WARS*

(Paranormal Romance)

Chosen

Taken

Fallen

Broken

Forsaken

Forbidden

Awoken

Illuminated

Stolen

Forgotten

Driven

Unspoken

Hidden

Written

Given

Mistaken

FAMILIAR SPIRITS*

(Cozy Mystery/Paranormal Romance)

Spells and Spaniels

Cauldrons and Cats

Hexes and Hedgehogs

Charms and Chihuahuas

Runes and Ravens

LATTES AND LEVITATION*

(Cozy Mystery/Paranormal Romance)

Caffeine Before Curses

Muffins After Magic

Pastries and Prophecies

Eclairs and Ectoplasm

Sugar Skulls and Specters

Wedding Cakes and Wishes

HEDGEWITCH FOR HIRE*

(Cozy Mystery/Paranormal Romance)

Grave Mistake

Social Medium

Household Demons

Perpetual Potion

Jingle Spells

Wandering Monsters

Uninvited Ghosts

Prophet Motive

Ballroom Bits

Spell Check

Brew Confessions

Charm School (July 2024)

UNEXPECTED MAGIC*

(Urban Fantasy/Paranormal Romance)

Found Objects

Finders, Keepers

Lost and Found

Finding Destiny

THE WITCHES OF WHEELER PARK*

(Paranormal Romance)

Storm Born

Thunder Road

Winds of Change

Mind Games

A Wheeler Park Christmas

Blood Ties

Healing Hands

Wishful Thinking

Smoke and Mirrors

MISS PRIMM'S ACADEMY FOR WAYWARD
WITCHES*

(Fantasy/Academy Romance)

Misspelled

Dispelled

Expelled

———

THE DEVIL YOU KNOW*

(Paranormal Romance)

Sympathy for the Devil

Charmed, I'm Sure

A Wing and a Prayer

Wish Upon a Star

———

THE WITCHES OF CANYON ROAD*

(Paranormal Romance)

Hidden Gifts

Darker Paths

Mysterious Ways

A Canyon Road Christmas

Demon Born

An Ill Wind

Higher Ground

Haunted Hearts

THE WITCHES OF CLEOPATRA HILL*

(Paranormal Romance)

Darkangel

Darknight

Darkmoon

Sympathetic Magic

Protector

Spellbound

A Cleopatra Hill Christmas

Impractical Magic

Strange Magic

The Arrangement

Defender

Bad Blood

Deep Magic

Darktide

Star Bright

THE WATCHERS TRILOGY*

(Paranormal Romance)

Falling Dark

Dead of Night

Rising Dawn

———

THE SEDONA FILES*

(Paranormal/Science Fiction Romance)

Bad Vibrations

Desert Hearts

Angel Fire

Star Crossed

Falling Angels

Enemy Mine

———

TALES OF THE LATTER KINGDOMS*

(Fantasy Romance)

All Fall Down

Dragon Rose

Binding Spell

Ashes of Roses

One Thousand Nights

Threads of Gold

The Wolf of Harrow Hall

Moon Dance

The Song of the Thrush

THE GAIAN CONSORTIUM SERIES*

(Science Fiction Romance)

Beast (free prequel novella)

Blood Will Tell

Breath of Life

The Gaia Gambit

The Mandala Maneuver

The Titan Trap

The Zhore Deception

The Refugee Ruse

STANDALONE TITLES

Hearts on Fire (Paranormal Romance)

Taking Dictation (Contemporary Romance)

Golden Heart (Gaslamp Fantasy Romance)

Night Music: A Modern Reimagining of The Phantom of the Opera (Contemporary Romance)

Ghost Dance: A Sequel to Gaston Leroux's The Phantom of the Opera (Historical Mystery/Romance)

Flight Before Christmas (Fantasy Romance)

* Indicates a completed series

About the Author

USA Today bestselling author Christine Pope has been writing stories ever since she commandeered her family's Smith-Corona typewriter back in grade school. Her work includes paranormal romance, paranormal cozy mystery, fantasy romance, and science fiction/space opera romance. She makes her home in Arizona.

Christine Pope on the Web:
www.christinepope.com

 facebook.com/ChristinePopeAuthor
youtube.com/@ChristinePopeAuthor